ASPHALT

Asphalt

Carl Hancock Rux

WASHINGTON SQUARE PRESS

New York   London   Toronto   Sydney

Washington Square Press
1230 Avenue of the Americas
New York, NY 10020

"There Are No Honest Poems About Dead Women" from *The Collected Poems
of Audre Lorde* (by Audre Lorde, © 1997 by the Audre Lorde Estate, published
by W. W. Norton & Company, 2000).

"Midnight" from *Faust/Part Two* by Johann Wolfgang von Goethe (translated
by Phillip Wayne, © 1959 by Phillip Wayne, first published by Penguin Books,
1959).

"Betancourt" from *Transbluesency: The Selected Poems of Amiri Baraka/Leroi
Jones* (by Leroi Jones, edited by Paul Vangelisti for Marsilio Publishers Corp.).

"The Renegade" from *Exile and the Kingdom* (by Albert Camus, translated by
Justin O'Brien, Vintage Books, 1957).

Tropic of Cancer (by Henry Miller, Grove Press Inc., © 1961).

Copyright © 2004 by Carl Hancock Rux

ISBN: 978-0-7434-7401-6
     0-7434-7401-5

First Washington Square Press trade paperback edition May 2005

10 9 8 7 6 5 4 3 2 1

WASHINGTON SQUARE PRESS and colophon are
registered trademarks of Simon & Schuster, Inc.

For information regarding special discounts for bulk purchases,
please contact Simon & Schuster Special Sales at 1-800-456-6798
or business@simonandschuster.com

Manufactured in the United States of America

For
Ralph Lewis Hancock
1952–1989

What we thought is not confirmed,
and what we thought not God contrives.
—EURIPIDES

I b i d

Nothing remarkable here, no splendid courts,
no spacious stairways . . . there is only
rubble . . . traces of the Dorian burning, and
the open graves . . . the menace is all the greater
because it is never completely expressed.
We are haunted by a presence which
never completely reveals itself . . .

—ROBERT PAYNE, *The Splendor of Greece*

He was coming from, I was walking toward. I was walking toward something, having arrived at nothing. He was crossing the avenue, my brother—the remains of a boy crossing pernicious pavement channels. An easy task—straight and steady steps of celerity—aiming himself somewhere with an equestrian swagger that defied the shame of his body; hair matted, face distorted—head cracked open dry, clothes drenched in water, a dark countenance masking a fragile frame.

I'd flown through a turbulent sky—landed safely on even ground, a dazed survivor. Pushing back pavement with sturdy strides, people passing me, I wanted to continue roving and tending to the business of cohabitation with myself. Pockets filled with intentions—tried to reacquaint myself with myself. Tried not to provoke the quake of dreams or trigger the eruption of things that have been sewn tightly into the lining of my stomach . . . an almanac of wars and cracked concrete shifting. But a litany began in the words rolled up in my fists—gray pages printed in tones of black crunched between fingers, its calamities emblazoned onto my thumbs. The catastrophe of years resounded in sweat and ink: NEW SKYSCRAPER'S LATTICE TOPPLES DOWN, CRUSHES SKULL OF PASSERBY; GASH RUNS UP NECK OF SIDE STREET, CIVILIZATIONS BURIED BENEATH THE RUBBLE; CAVERNOUS PIT SWALLOWS PEDESTRIAN CAUGHT IN GEYSER; VESTIGIAL SHRAPNEL REDISCOVERED; WRECKING BALL CRASHES THROUGH CENTENNIAL HOTEL; FISCAL PROMISES; MENDED FLAGS.

The city was falling in the year of its reconstruction. The year of city renewal and city planning; of renaming streets and changing demographics, renovating buildings and erecting irrelevant statues, of sweeping fetid bodies beneath the gratings. Old graves were deconsecrated and cemented over with neon animation. New graves were dug for those who could not survive the metamorphosis of terrified urbanity. New buildings had been propped up, bronze and cast-iron plaques tacked onto their edifice, an eternal reminder of the dead in their absence—but the dead were not absent—the dead were everywhere monuments had been erected to mark their demise.

In the aftermath of war, dead men and dead women and dead children awakened to an attempted restoration. They walked among us, and where they walked they walked freely, through the tumbling of urbanity, through newly erected structures that had not been there before; they made pathways where pathways used to be, forged turns down avenues and up concourses, lost their step in search of familiar landmarks. The dead put their ears close to the ground, their hands to the walls, consulted with tenements, asked old buildings to tell them a story, old sidewalks to give testimony, to recall for them where they had once been shielded from the sun by the tall lean-back of an art-deco building's northern wall—there, where the gate of merchants and buyers made music with the click of a heel and the stomp of a sole. The endless noise of limp arches lured to storefront windows. Hand-cut stones glinting behind glass on heavy velvet. They looked for their belongings in the aggregation of paper cups and napkins littering curbs, cigarette butts, a single gold earring waiting for its match, the sparkling silver of small change displaced among fast-food leftovers . . . all of it—now swept up from sidewalks, washed clean.

The dead asked too that the streets recall for them the jeeps and the towing of artillery down sunken lanes; infantry and tanks and sleep deprivation; city dwellers ensconced in tight holes crowded with ammunition, water bottles, and prayers whispered in a thousand languages, the polyglot of bargaining with God. Evidence. The dead relied on the memory this city has been built upon, footprints and forgotten gestures layered in rock. The dead trusted the tenements to remember for us all: how we talked with our tongues, what we said through our lips, what we meant in our voicelessness.

My body was tightly girded, weighted down, silent—an unrecorded history belted itself around my neck, pressured into my lower back, vertebrae by vertebrae, twisting each disk out of place, muscles becoming the consistency of granite. A sculpture of trash heaped upon trash (the journey back is an arduous one), but I was blending into a body of walkers who had also arrived at the end of their cortege, restrained walkers waiting for an indication of light to resume our hurried dance of the reprobate. All of us negotiating our way through, traversing cities across oceans, cold stone corridors, airports, and vacant lots landscaped in oblivion, coming back—returning to the city of our youth. Alone, we were broken. Together we were intact; one body, one canvas of negatives and exposures, one state of immobility moving through a vast terrain, one unit intermittently balancing itself on a curb, waiting for safety.

He was moving on one side, I was on the other—train tracks suspended above us shielding all glimpses of sky. A rapturous wind wrestled with him only, the rest of us strangled in dense petrified air, a staggering heat, our shirts melting into our chests, eyes losing sight with the sting of tiny acidic beads prickling optics. His fertile flesh wrapped itself around a skeletal frame, changing colors from sand to soil, and he stepped off the curb—without invitation, into a perilous swirl of movement. We stood still as he charged forward, dove into the chariot of headlights, his shirttails fanning the rush of steel, his voice screaming above the roar of locomotion.

Comin' in?

With an open wound on his forehead staring down at a yellow line beneath his feet, he stood there—eyes following its distance. His body, broken into a composition of liberty, asked questions of the line and waited for its kind reply. He waited . . . for the ground to open up into a chasm on the axis of the earth and give something back to him—waited for a cinder to fall down from the cornerstone of a landmark and grind him into the gravel, for fire to begin again without provocation, consuming the vanity of kept secrets. He waited for the city to speak of the atrocities that have occurred in its corridors, to bear witness and lay blame—out loud. To justify what he's known all along. I stood on the other side of questions, blending into a body of walkers—the sun slipped through the train tracks above us, and shimmers of heat drizzling through rails illuminated the sparkle of burning rubber scraping against concrete and bitumen. Cars shunting around him, he laughed through a cracked skull—asked me a question from our divider.

Where this line go—you know?

It maps the course of men who have crossed over miles of black flecked with glass fragments, men carrying paragraphs of questions, selective memory and swollen ego. It maps the frail flat feet of self-invention.

The Alibi

*Perhaps all music, even the newest, is not so
much something discovered as something that
re-emerges from where it lay buried in the memory,
inaudible as a melody cut in a disc of flesh . . .
a song that has always been shut up silent.*

—JEAN GENET, *Prisoner of Love*

The building recessed from the street, the street pulled back from the water, the water separated the city from a townscape—isolated. In the shadow of a massive magnolia, two horse heads met at the gate of a thick cast-iron fence guarding a flagstone path that led to tall Greek columns supporting a front porch of stone entwined in ivy. Above its gabled roof, three candles—red, yellow, white—peeking out from behind a bay window through branches of pink foliage flaking down onto an otherwise colorless yard. The house breathed traces of nineteenth-century respectability; an ancient city in ruins, its monument to antiquity conquered, occupied too many times over—irrelevant.

I stood outside, with a newspaper under my arm, music on my back, across the street from a house set alone in the middle of a degraded landscape—cojoined nineteenth-century terra-cotta facades carved from rock and soil without respect for the mainland, winded and sinking into depletion, plotted out for pedestrians who once traveled short distances through even rows. Intimacy.

You comin' inside?

He was sitting on the stoop, projecting his voice my way—light coming from the windows and door behind him.

Comin' in?
What?
You comin' inside?
. . . Nah.
Where you from?
. . .

I said where—
Not from—to.
?

Clouds of curly black floated above a soft olive oval, big black
wheels for eyes—long lashes, satin robe flung over purple T-shirt,
orange sarong sashed around tight hips in faded jeans. Bare feet.

I mean where you comin' from?
Nowhere. Here. There.
How long you been *there?*

He took out a little tin box from his robe, sprinkled whatever was
inside it onto some rolling paper, licked the edges—rolled it—
looked up at me again with half a grin and cocked eyebrow.

So . . . you don't say much, do you?

He had some kind of a weird accent, slight, not thick—melodic.
Dropped consonants. Sang upward. I threw my voice back at him, dry.

Where *you* from?
Here.

I didn't know if he was saying he was from inside the house or this
vacant neighborhood or from somewhere in Brooklyn. He lit the
square, held it out.

You smoke?

I leaned up from off the wall where I was standing in the dark,
looked up and down the empty street . . . crossed over—toward the
windows with light and the magnolia with a white X painted onto it,
front doors of cracked beveled glass and the olive oval sitting on the
steps behind the heavy horse-head gate. A plastic cup (of something
and ice) sweated behind his hip.

*   *   *

Things look different to you?

Different from what?

Way it was—before.

Over our heads, electrical wires extended from the building's roofline to the streetlamp on the sidewalk in front, taped inconspicuously down its side and fixed to its base.

Rigged that shit myself. Don't know how long we'll get away with this shit. M-16s haven't said anything yet. You always wear military shit?

Nah.

I thought *you* was M-16—your hair's too long for that, they all got the same hair. Buzz cut. You ain't never gonna see no M-16 with hair, long like yours, in a ponytail. You Dominican?

The black wheels sparked, lit up, smiled from behind the smoke— tried to get a good pull from his square, held it out to me again. A bullet of air grazed the back of my neck, swept around, killed the fire—headed for some other destination. He struck another match, cupped it with black nails. I declined.

Why you was standin' over there?

. . . Why not?

Can't be standin' outside—at night like that around here, M-16s be patrolin', don't ask no questions—just be your ass.

. . .

What's alla that on your back, luggage?

. . .

You was away or somethin'?

Or somethin'.

You from around here?

Not really.

Came from Manhattan?

Yeah.

The Geneva?
Yeah.
They gave you a interborough pass?
Yeah.
Had to pay for it?
Yeah.
You got money like that?
Like what?
. . .
. . .
What was it like over there in Europe?
Who said I was in Europe?
. . .
. . .
Freaky, ain't it?
What?
The bridge—stickin' straight out like that, over the water . . . halfa arm stickin' out the water like that.
Yeah.
They tryin' to fix it.
I read that.
Said they gonna reconnect it to the other side.
Guess that would be fixin' it.
A billion trillion dollars or some shit. Gonna be a big party to raise the money. Another trillion dollars. Got that shit blocked up so nobody walk across it to where it stops—in the middle.
Who'd want to?
Me.
. . .
What's it like over there now?
Where, Europe?
Nah, across the water.
Manhattan?
Yeah.
It's . . . whatever.
Everything new and shiny, right?

Sort of.

I'm gonna see it for myself. Gotta get me a pass first. I already put in my papers.

. . .

. . .

It ain't over.

What ain't over?

War.

?

Ain't over.

That's not what I read.

Fuck what you read. Everybody comin' back . . . you comin' back after the fact—like everything's all resolved. It ain't.

It ain't?

Resolve self—resolve war.

. . . ?

He stood up, walked off the porch, through the gate, past the white X, crossed the street over to where I had been standing, leaned against the wall where I had been leaning in a shallow puddle of water (like that thin wet sheet covering granite in the square of the Place de Terreaux). I listened to him—sitting on the porch holding his square behind a veil of smoke—speaking to me from across the street with a new voice, not his own, as he tilted his head up toward the bay windows.

Hand-sculpted exterior. Terra-cotta ornamentation. Capitals. Friezes. Exterior openings framed by plain surrounds. When this house was built—wasn't the only one like it . . . there were others—mansions on single plots of land . . . set behind trees . . . limestone carriage houses. They built their houses . . . from the ground up . . . built houses to outlive generations . . . used marble from Italian quarries . . . sculptors from Paris to carve gargoyles into clay . . . masons from Sicily . . . master carpenters who whittled staircases from African mahogany. During the Depression, in the 1930s, they started turning these mansions into rooming houses. Crowded them—divided them—tore them down. Where you got off the ferry,

on the other side of the park down by the water—nothing but mansions like this one. Acres of them—all of them, torn down to make
room for war—and poor people . . . generations of poor people hidden behind the park, down by the water . . . always at war—but this
house . . . this house survived—this tethering post, these scrolled
foliate patterns . . . survived.

The new voice—concentrated, articulate, teary—stepped out
from under the shadows, crossed back over toward the gate, touched
the X on the magnolia's stomach and lifted his sarong above the
shiny wet flagstone, dwelled on the facade of the house from there—
one arm leaning flat against the bark, the other extended toward
cracked double doors.

This tree is older than this house. This house is older than the ones
surrounding it—rests on a raised foundation of brick. These doors are
the original doors. They had panels of stained glass once, and heavy
brass knobs. A gabled dormer rises from the roofline. These
columns—Ionic with egg-and-dart moldings on each capital—draped
in ivy. Those vines on the roof of the porch—wisteria—sprout lavender racemes . . . they come every spring. You can depend on them,
every spring—clusters of lavender dangling from the stalks. Every
spring, there they are.

He was still talking as he walked up onto the porch, took another
drag from the square, and opened the double-leaf doors, but his
voice muted into the old wood creaking beneath calibrated steps,
and the house spoke for itself: Minton-tiled floors and splintered
white marble vestibule, a second set of doors separating the vestibule
from the interior hall—ash and oak woodwork—mahogany chair
rails, handrails, banister, molded ceiling cornices. A massive parlor
opening—doors half painted blue, caked with polyurethane, propped
open by a yellow velvet chair ripped to its springs. Telephone lines
and extension cords forged holes through heavily ridged moldings
and dangled into the parlor room—a grand Victorian room turned
into some kind of semiprivate social club. Between two big ceiling-

to-floor windows dressed in black velvet—a DJ setup on a makeshift table of plywood sat unplugged. An old jukebox in the corner was dark and quiet—three or four guys in hooded sweatshirts, sharing a square, sat around it trading rhymes and insults.

The olive oval's hand brushed against one of their faces as he stepped over a dark line etched across the floor.

Used to be a wall here dividing the room, and pocket doors.

A cluster of girls, lying on top of each other on the floor in the back of the room, flicked matches in the air, held them up and giggled— moved slightly out of the way as a blond Rasta stepped over their huddle and knelt down onto a pool table centered beneath the glow of a cracked rectangular stained-glass lamp swinging from a tin-and-dirt-tiled ceiling. An old man in a Greek sailor's cap and some young guys playing chess on a couch upholstered in decrepitude— shifted their weight and leaned against black and silver graffiti as the Rasta angled himself around them to get to the other side of the table. He pushed his pelvis against the table's edge, lowered his blond locks and black-and-gray beard onto the green felt—took aim. The crack of the balls slamming into each other shattered through the acoustics of the cavernous space. The old man's face— folded beneath his chin, one cheek snagged up under a limp fist cushioning his head—made a quick glance my way, then back to the chessboard. His black horn-rimmed glasses sparkled in the glow of red and blue Christmas lights hanging from the back bar opposite the chess game—plastic cups, bags of ice, bottles of beer, Absolut, Hennessy, Johnnie Walker Red, (the same liquid in each; a translucent brownish green like dirty fish tank water).

Something bulbous crouched beside a steel door smoking something with a thick, pungent, sweet odor. Its arms and legs, wet wrought iron, fanned smoke out into what was left of an enclosed patio or deck; verdigris copper framing more broken glass, hosed in urine, yielding a fresh crop of cups and condoms.

The sarong made a sharp left into an alcove behind the bar—waved at me to follow through. I stepped over the constellation of girls,

clumped in seven, to get to a slight opening that let down into the dark
swallowing a narrow staircase—held on to the rough plaster walls and
tripped over another extension cord until the bulb hanging on a hook
in the lower level's entranceway hastened a sudden shrill of fluorescent
light upward. A deflated tire buttressed religious statues of bleeding
porcelain saints in the presence of rattraps and their dead, and a flue
connected to a cast-iron wood-burning stove protruded from a
fieplace with birds carved into it.

See that grating on the wall?
Yeah.
That's where the heat used to come through—forced-air heating
came up through the vents from the old furnace.

He held the bulb over his head like a torch, tucked the sarong into
the waist of his jeans, hooked me aside from the wallboard beneath
my feet, and kicked it away. Pressing a firm grip into my shoulder, he
knelt us down into the cool dank air climbing out of the hole that
burned straight through to the basement.

Old coal chute . . . and see over there, that's the old gas
burner. They haven't gotten around to restoring the gas lines over
this way.
What happens in winter?
We make fires. Me and this other kid, Chulo—we cleaned out the
chimneys, so everything is kinda okay for building fires, but more
buildings burned down in this neighborhood last year than in the last
hundred years—a fire every night. Only firehouse in this neighborhood been closed for years, the rest are across the water or way up in
the old rich neighborhoods—they're trying to save those buildings for
when the rich people come back, but they don't come around here
with no sirens and water. Not to put out no fire.
Look like this house already been through its share of fires.
Still beautiful, ain't it?
I'm not really into—*houses* and architecture.
Shape without reason doesn't mean anything to me either, like

those skyscraper's they're building across the water. Meaningless diagrams. You can't *read* those buildings. They're flat. Spirit has to justify form.

We were trying to stand when he accidentally dropped the light into the hole and the bulb went out. He pulled the cord up, pushed the wallboard back over the hole.

    Should've left it open.
    Why?
    Sound travels through holes—conversations from forever ago—everything a house ever said.
    ?
    Houses are people too.

Two turntables, a mixer, sampler, pitch—speed control, two CD players, a Pioneer DJ M-500 with built-in effects from the outboard; a G4 with Pro Tools. He was over at the bar, I was checking out the equipment on the makeshift table—unwrapped in boxes, except for the mixer, which was in a big plastic garbage bag with little shards of glass. He came over with two plastic cups of something and ice, a bag of chips clenched between his teeth, little cuts on his hands and ankles that I hadn't noticed before.

You spin?
Yeah.
You know how to set it up?
. . . guess.
So . . . ?

Running through the room—more wires—connected to even more wires running out back into the garden, over to a small two-story building behind the main house; an old carriage house converted into a garage that housed an old blue Chrysler poking its nose through rotting doors—gutted. I was close to having everything working, he got all excited—said they haven't been listening to music because the jukebox hasn't worked for forever, and somebody stole their old DJ setup, then he ran upstairs and came back down with a box of vinyl.

Some of my favorite records. What you got in that duffel bag?
Sound.
Like what—beats?
Sound . . .
Hip-hop?

Sound. Just sound . . .
?
. . .
Well . . . bring it, then.

Hands on the vinyl, ears to the bass—eyes on the room. Rakim, Memphis Bleek, Arvo Part, Common's *Resurrection;* what they want to hear—not as they know it . . . not in the same body, or speaking the same language as before. Sound layered over intonation— something familiar constructed from scratched vowels and stretched notes . . . a simple change in rhythm creating ducts of conversation. DJs are architects too—build rooms for people to walk around in, rooms inside of rooms—walls colliding into walls.

Stetsasonic—Fruitkwan, Prince Paul—ocean crashing against coral—pushing heavy across the floor, vibrating up through toes, angling melody and memory between thighs. Heads start slapping hands and bopping back reminiscing on memory bliss—classic post–Run-DMC/South Bronx five percenter/back to the Latin Quarter music—when fades turned into starter dreadlocks laden with beeswax and mohair Kangols nodded to suede Pumas. Grand Puba (*never in a scandal and I'm never caught schemin'*). Reverb, echo— in-port, out-port—midi—touch pad—bend, sampling, then skip to Meth and Mary. Hardcore harmonies rolling out of Mary's mouth, everybody trying to sing along, jump-starting arms upward, yelling out, floating above blue smoke, the sweet stench of Dutch and dime bags netting over the dance floor. Rhythmic vamping jolts a head out of a temporary nap on a corner couch and plastic cups of Hennessy are crushed beneath the stampede.

The beat comes down. The bass line up. Me, the grand wizard plotting and scheming a method of madness, fidgeting knobs and tweaking. Hi-Tek, Premier, Afrika Bambaata. *Lord have mercy* and *Holy Ghost revival*—Coltrane. Not just *blue* Trane, not just Monk, not just Miles but a million musicians playing over our heads, a band of angels responding to the percussion of stomps and hollers. Heads don't know what's happening to them, they just know *something* is happening. I'm the anointed one, turning them over to an urban space, a vacant lot near tenement dwellings reaping abandoned Bibles and oversized chairs, fire escapes leading to lovers or Jesus— a light box for laughter and a recipe for withstanding. Big Boi and Dre on some Sly Stone shit—*so fresh and so clean clean.*

Before this, before now—we *were* fresh and clean, pulled together, unfettered. Fooling ourselves into believing something about ourselves. Lil' Kim and P. Diddy wannabes—platinum and diamond dreamers in green and silver wigs—arguing about how Ras Kass could out rhyme Jay-Z any goddamned day (like it was political, like Fab, Nate Dogg, the Neptunes, and Lil' Mo were commissioners of hooks). Before now we stared down the barrel of 50 Cent's gun, sucked his nipple, and asked him to lull us to sleep. We were on some *everything is everything* shit. But now—everything is nothing and what little of nothing remains is all an illusion.

Shyne testified of bullets through the speakers; a martyr for the inevitable destiny of heads who've purchased the dream with spit and blood. Flip it, sample Billie—*them that's got shall get*—flip it, pre–P. Diddy down with B.I.G.—*all about the Benjamins*—back to Billie then back to Shyne, then metal scraping against metal (something someone said once on a dirt road paved over)—then back to Billie, cut to Depeche Mode's "Barrel of a Gun," then back to B.I.G. and Shyne's bullets and now somebody screams cause he gets it, what I'm talking about—the bullets in Billie's cracked alto; .40-caliber shells paid for with Biggie's murked corpse; Shyne and the brand-new body of his gangsta. The beats are traveling up the block and around the corner finding new sinners, day and night sinners on bare Brooklyn streets, loitering vacant sidewalks, sitting on lonely park benches, sipping beer, hollowing out Dutches—dull housing-project sinners with sad square brick faces. The beat finds us where we are, comes to sinners with evaporating faces and coarse hands, slurs the pitch of our voices from inaudible prayers to insurgent demands in deafening volumes, invites us in to dance in strange configurations between derelict walls. The bullets and the beats are saying *we're all sinners here, this is a house of sinners, and sinners have no choice in the way of their souls.* Bodies need bodies right now.

*   *   *

People straggle in—first in small groups, in droves, then the whole place fills with smoke and music. Bottles of beer, plastic cups, and short blunts, sucked in by the smoked flesh of puckered lips, huddle in a mass of delirium—waiting for the reply of a new rhythm. Hours spin by. A six-foot dagger with a mustache in a blue sharkskin suit comes out of nowhere, pushing people out of her way—this redhead kid with freckles and septum ring (so drunk he didn't even notice that his bottom lip was bleeding after he got pushed into the wall when the dagger in blue stormed by) starts bitching that nobody is behind the bar to serve him a goddamned drink. The blue mustache bopped back through the room with a gangsta lean—one hand holding her crotch, the other stroking the fuzzy goatee on her chin—politely tapped the redhead on his shoulder and motioned him to follow her to the back porch and down into the garden. She came back, he didn't.

The robed kid disappeared for a while too and the big woman in blue was collecting money at the door. He came back later, eyes blazing—she cursed him out in Spanish, he slouched onto the floor near me and the turntables, cocked an ear, pulled a little bag out of his jeans, got up and yelled something in my ear about *Poulenc, Auric,* and *Erik Satie,* made his way to the pool table, started doing lines— tongued some Korean chick with red bangs in a corner (I thought he was gay), did a few more lines—argued with this Puerto Rican kid about Jung *and the inborn disposition to produce parallel images or identical psychic structures common to all men.* The Puerto Rican kid said he didn't know what the hell the robe was talking about.

This kid in a Marley T-shirt, sitting with a girl dressed like Betty Page, argued Euclid with a foppish old man with breasts, screamed that there was *no such thing as parallel buildings.* The old man got down on his hands and knees, caressed the slanting floor, shot back *I understand nonparallel. I was talking about being honest!* The kid snatched two pool sticks, handed one to his girlfriend, snarled *Being honest is almost as harmful as being in denial.* Betty Page threw the stick to the wall, kicked off her high heels, got down on her hands and knees with the old man, asked him if he knew anything about *Noveau Realism and the archeological excavations of everyday life.* *Yes,* he said, *That's what I'm talking about.*

Our souls warped over Paul Van Dyk, Massive Attack, Nirvana pushed beyond its limits—Air, then a sweet-ass Jackie Mittoo solo scaled its way back to Babatunde. The girls on the floor struck their matches, nodding their heads beneath a halo.

The sun was almost up—almost everybody was gone except for the old man and his game of chess, some people moaning softly from the dark of the garden apartment stairwell, the constellations wrapped around each other and the thing crouched down by the back door. The kid had calmed down a little. He made us two more drinks (vodka and cranberry, he said, but I'm not sure about either) and invited me out to the garden—lit another Dutch—got to breaking everything down about the building and its owner, named Holy Mother Santa Lucinda. She sees things. Marks time. Talks to people.

If she likes you or if she feels like you need to be here, you can stay. All the rooms have furniture and space heaters but there's no phone lines, hasn't been for a long time. They use the pay phone on the corner. The *Alibi* was my idea. We're not legal. No liquor license or nuthin', but a whole lotta bars opened up like this in this neighborhood, in abandoned buildings, people selling liquor, cigarettes . . . weed. Like an old speakeasy. M-16s come through sometimes just to take a piss, fling their dicks around but nobody's worried. Everybody loves my parties. I'm legendary. My name's Man. You never heard of me?

Nah.

Manny for short.

Nah.

Lucinda and Mawepi live on the floor above, my flat is on the floor above that. This girl lives upstairs . . . careful with that one—she's a mind fuck.

What about the top floor?

It's not a full floor, what's called a mansard roof—like an attic.

How you know alla that kinda stuff?

I was studying architecture at this university but I was more interested in the psychology of architecture . . .

?

The psychology of buildings—not construction or structure as form.

So who lives up there?

Nobody. Just a big hole in the ceiling. There was a fire a long time ago, burned down six of the rafters. This kid was killed.

Killed how?

I don't know. I go up there to relax sometimes . . . sit on the roof. You can see everything from up there . . . you can see the bridge too. See where it was torn in half and sinks into the water . . . everything.

. . .

M-16s be patrolin' around here, watchin' who comes and goes. I thought that's why you were standing outside, with your newspaper.

Nah.

So you just gettin' back too?

. . .

Where you comin' from?

France.

What was in France?

Friends . . . work.

What kinda work?

Spinnin'.

You spin good.

. . .

You made your own records?

Yeah, scored a movie.

Yeah? Listen, the girl I told you about who lives upstairs, she bartends here—she shakes her ass down by the Navy Yard. Makes decent money shakin' her ass down there but if you ask me, I think she's sellin' it. We're losin' money, and there's not much money to go around, you know what I mean?

Yeah.

So, if you want to, we could work somethin' out—

Those her candles downstairs?

Who?

The old lady—those her candles in the basement?

The garden floor. It used to be her *botánica.*

. . .

So anyway, I need a DJ to attract a crowd. Lucinda and I split the door sixty-forty, her favor. I split my share with the DJ seventy-thirty, my favor. The DJ splits his share with the bartender eighty-twenty, DJ's favor, and the bartender keeps her tips, get it?

Yeah.

You met Chulo?

Who?

He pointed inside through the back window at a short Puerto Rican asleep in the corner with a cigarette in his hand. Looked to be about sixteen.

He sells weed and cigarettes and shit. I get it free. Half price for anybody else who works for me.

. . .

You need a room?

. . . Nah.

The rooms are big.

. . . Yeah but—

Did I freak you out . . . about the kid and stuff?

Nah.

Come look at somethin'.

The hallway walls above the parlor floor were thick and bumpy, plaster walls painted pink, and where the pink peeled away, a dirty yellow wallpaper shone through. Some parts of the wall had remnants of bright green with raised flowers. On the floor above the parlor, two doors—one steel, one wood—lead to the Santera's apartment. On the next floor, two more doors. The room behind Manny's was used for storage. It had a window that looked out over the garden. Manny's room faced the front. He started apologizing for it as soon as he opened the door.

That ugly-ass radiator came later, all these skinny little pipes on the ceiling are supposed to be for a sprinkler system—I think rooming houses had to have sprinklers in the old days.

A little mattress draped in different kinds of fabrics (what appeared to be different pieces of clothing ripped and flattened out in layers; velvets, corduroys, silks—wool) was propped up on beer crates and pushed against the wall, with a mosquito net hanging from a halo of wire hangers above it. It looked like he'd painted things on the walls; tall rectangular shapes with splashes of red and orange at the top of them, numbers and measurements scrawled across the shapes like architectural drawings but the words didn't make any sense.

Crazy, right? Those scribbles were already there, under the wallpaper. You into Cy Twombly?

Who?

Scatological hieroglyph shit, oil and crayon. Scribbles. *Illium.* That mythological shit. I think maybe somebody who lived here, made all those scribbles on the wall. You never know. I heard Henry Miller lived here once.

Who?

Photographs from newspapers and magazines were posted on the murals; an old man without legs rolling down the middle of the street on a flat board pulled by an old dog; a group of guys standing on a corner holding a hand-painted sign that read LOOKING OF WORK; military men with rifles standing under a bodega awning. There were a few articles and photos of privileged prodigals who'd come back to the city after victory was declared. Some of the photos of the wounded were double-exposed over portraits of movie stars. A little antique vanity with some books replacing two of its claw-foot legs was covered with paintbrushes, tin cans, palettes, prescription pill bottles of different pigments, and jars of turpentine. In one corner—a bunch of copper pipes, old watches, more bottles, and on the floor in the center of the room, a dollhouse made of cardboard and tree branches, walls

papered with sheet music, torn pages from books, old photographs. He
bent down, rearranged the junk inside.

It's papier-mâché like we used to do in grade school. I dipped the
pages in water and flour and molded them into rooms, cut branches
from the magnolia. That's going to be where the grass goes. I want to
paste some dry flowers and make a nice courtyard. In the back I'm
gonna make an elaborate garden. It's a mock-up of this house.
That's why I have the hole on the top. I ask people to give me things
to contribute to the house. That little wooden cross is Lucinda's, the
sheet music came from—the girl upstairs, Mawepi gave me one of
her cigars, and I used the tobacco for the soil under the tree. . . .
You're gonna have to give me something. Don't worry, you have time
to think about it.

As we walked back downstairs, he paused at Lucinda's and Mawepi's
door. Mawepi was the big woman in the blue suit who lives with
Holy Mother, doubles as the bouncer, and collects the five dollars at
the door when he's not around.

She has a short temper.
Yeah, I noticed that.
She also never lets anybody come up to this floor if they don't live
here. That room behind mine could be yours if Mawepi lets you talk
to Lucinda. You want it or not?

Before I could answer, he had tapped out the seventh beat with his
knuckles. The big tall blue woman opened the door, that little black
mustache dusting at the corners of her mouth. She had a big face
the color of rose water, wore a black stocking cap on her head knotted at the top. Mawepi stepped out into the hallway with a toothpick
between her teeth, closing the door behind her. The dingy yellow
lightbulb that washed through the hallway turned her royal blue
sharkskin suit green, and the diamond stud in her left ear shim-
mered as she folded her tree-trunk arms across her heavy bosom.
Manny giggled, whispered something into her diamond stud—a

hot afternoon on still water. She looked me up and down, stepped back from the door so Manny could pass through. Past the door, I could see an old woman with heavy black eyeliner and morning white hair sitting in a chair in front of a bay window. Manny said Lucinda never sleeps in her bed, only in her chair near the window and she never leaves her room or comes downstairs into the club. She gives readings from her room—in Spanish—while Mawepi translates. Invitation only. She selects you, sees you coming down the street, he said, from her window where she'd perch with a pillow beneath her elbows—contemplating out over the streets, alert to wandering passersby. When she'd point, you'd come, from wherever you were, with whatever you had, and you'd stay.

Mawepi closed the door in my face. Behind the closed door somebody said something in Spanish and somebody laughed, then I couldn't hear anything else.

The thing—crouched down by the steel door—moved to one of the decrepit couches by the pool table, crossed its legs and shifted, ran flat palms down the leg of its black pants, pushed its red eyes outward, sucked its sharp teeth my way, yelled something from the back of the room in a percussive baritone, vanquishing the dance floor. The remnant congregation dissipated into dark corners with plastic bags of this and that. Heads stepped out onto the patio and rolled *trees*, breathed in the lingering odor of decaying bodies thousands of miles away, turned their eyes away from the searchlights of helicopters flying low. The guys who had been keeping company with the old man moved toward the front of the room and then out onto the front stoop to find the backroom girls who had run out of cloves.

The thing's shaven head swung circles in the air—dark muscles flexing old scars—it tossed the chessboard over and yawned. The old man in the Greek fisherman's cap and cardigan sweater removed himself from his seat without protest and whispered a look my way: *You are walking beyond Troezen's gates in the pathway of a tameless bull, you have stirred to wake the ocean that held captive the beast, and soon the waters will pull themselves back to make way for its scales.* The thing held a flame up to its face. I played something to strain the ear. The beast barked open its eyes, spewed flames, advanced beyond the pool table toward me, smashed a beer bottle against an old sideboard, I turned the bass line up (my chariot of horses), pulled the treble out (my javelin) until all anybody could hear was a constant dogma of negative space toppling over the subwoofer—charging forward. The thing rolled its head back from spine to chest, bent its knees to the floor—fell backward. Slept. The old man paced himself over . . .

looked at me over the rim of his glasses, as if to say—*This time, you have slain the beast in the graveyard where your ancestors lay.*

The beat comes again, someone hears it, sees by the light of it, follows it, someone else wanders back in—thinks to himself: *I could live here, in the sound of safety.*

Mawepi thudded downstairs yelling about the music blaring. I went to get my stuff before anything got started—Manny came down and pushed in front of her.

Your key to the kingdom.

Between our two rooms, a bathroom with a tiny sink, toilet, shower stall. Manny pinned two blankets together, stuffed it with some winter clothes and coats to make me a bed, rolled a Dutch and centered it on the sock-stuffed T-shirt pillow—for later.

I was lying there between cardboard boxes and old newspapers looking at the crown moldings, tinted in the shadows of rustling branches, needles darting through thick branches, glow of the emerging sun cracking the sky with light, leaking through dirty glass and onto the wide heart-pine floors . . . making its way toward my feet. A gust of wind rattled the glass in its frame. Seven taps on the door. Manny pushed his head through, laughing, blurred eyes again, hand over his mouth.

I'm meetin' some people over in the park. You wanna come?
For what?
You ever been to the park?
Nah.
You should go with me sometime.
For what?
The hills. The grass.
I'm not into parks at night.
It's morning.
A little too early in the morning.
I go every night and wait.

For what?
Something beautiful.
. . .
Or something dangerous.
So what happens?
Sometimes both—

He walks into the room, fluffs the makeshift pillow, checks to see if
I smoked the Dutch yet. Cuts it with a razor, leaves half on the pillow, takes half for himself. I'm lookin' at him. There's something
about him I don't get.

Can I ask you a question?
What?
What was you talkin' about before, downstairs?
You mean about gettin' you a room?
Nah. I mean when you was talkin' about *it ain't over.*

He walks over to the window. Turns his back to me.

They set their borders, see? Locked themselves in like they had
located the strain that caused the virus—had it all under control.
They think they're ready to rebuild bridges.
They who?
They declared a civil war against the war of imperialism, formed
paramilitary forces—set up troops for a personal insurrection.
?
There never was some anonymous third-world enemy tearing us
down. The body was destroying its own body. No God. No Devil. It
was us all along, see?
Nah.

He smiles with an arched eyebrow, steps over to the door, holds it
open.

*   *   *

Can I ask *you* a question?
What?
Your name. You never told me your name.
Racine.
Racine?
Yeah . . .
Hello, Racine—I know you.

I like it.

Her lips reached for the filtered end of a little brass cigarette-holder decorated in faux jasmine. The smoke curls, an obsidian serpent, coiling around her face, eyes squinting in heavy mascara. Serpents rise up all around us, gathering as teal fog in the ceiling's rafters, vanishing into rays beaming down onto bopping heads and bodies slumped over. Bottles in green, orange, cranberry, and blue hang from the ceiling, lining the shelves against the brick wall behind the bar. The votive's flames threaten to shatter the holders as each candle protests its wick's end. I put the tips of my thumbs to the edge of the vinyl—she surrenders to the pulsation of beats with her hands thrown up in the air, faux jasmine holder making circles around her bald head, a priestess dancing to old-school beats coming off the turntables.

I said I like it . . . what you spinnin' . . . was that Hector Lavoe you was just playin? . . . most people don't know nothin' bout no Hector Lavoe . . . that was nice . . . I used to listen to Latin a lot, so I know.
Yeah.
That's all your own equipment? Laptop and everything? You got your own mixer too? Dope . . .
Ain't mine. Manny's.
Manny? Never mind . . .

I catch the CDs spilling off the table, put some vinyl away before somebody steps on or walks off with them. She's running her hand along the edges of the equipment, kneeling down, looking at the knobs.

*　　*　　*

Look at this . . . pitch and speed control . . . yeah, that's nice . . .
I used to go out with this kid who was a DJ back in the day . . .

She blows her smoke on the album jackets, fingers through the pile
on the table beside me, tries to lift Lavoe off the turntable to read
the label but I move her hand away, balance the shiny black disc on
its edges between my palms, place it back in its cardboard sheath
wrapped in plastic. Sacred.

You seen Manny around? He's supposed to be here tonight, it's
his night. You seen him?
Nah.
The poetry thing is gonna start in a minute . . . Manny's idea—
he's not even here to suffer through this shit. So . . . you moved in
upstairs, right?
Yeah.
I live on the fourth floor.
I know.
Manny said you just come back from Paris . . . scored a movie.
Yeah.
I never been to Paris. Don't even dream of it. No faraway places
in my dreams. I been in Hong Kong before . . . you been there?
Nah.
I was doin' a show . . . I dance.

Tricky, "Dis Never (Dig Up We History)." Oasis, "Don't Look Back."
Nirvana, "Come As You Are," Aphex Twins—I'm lining up what to
play next when Mawepi taps me on the shoulder, points to a bunch
of people standing on a small stage by the window. I have to stop
spinning. They start screaming into a little cordless microphone
while everybody else searches for hydro—some e—a drink. The
pageantry of poetry began. Mawepi gives the girl a look, like *Ain't you
supposed to be workin' the bar?* except she doesn't have to say it, her
eyes are enough. The bald head shuffles over to the long wood
counter, waves her arm at somebody stressing her for a drink. A short
skinny white guy with blue eyes, paint on his shirt, and a South

African accent, introduces his poem as being inspired by Bretenbach, then he reads from a brown paper bag: *Bones and teeth, Mus-
lims and Jews, Kafirs and Sikhs . . . shaheed, shaheed, shaheed.* The
South African takes a bow, a few people clap. The South African's
got another poem on a piece of toilet paper but the heads, they go
ahead and shoot pool, somebody breaks and the balls whack against
each other rolling around on the green felt looking for a hole to duck
into. They're getting anxious for the music. They came for the
music. They came for the anonymity of dreams.

A Long Island girl in some recycled black Versace gear screams
into the mike *my pussy is bleeding! bleeding!* A guy slurs weak
pickup lines loudly over her, trying to score with a square-hipped girl
in platforms and spandex. A would-be rapper trying to pass his
improvisational hip-hop lyrics off as a finely crafted poem gets a
lower score than the bleeding girl from Long Island, who sulks at the
bar, gnawing at her fingernails. When his total score has reached a
record-breaking low, the rapper curses at the pickup and throws his
beer bottle at him, hitting the wall near the girl in spandex, splashing
beer and glass all over her. Mawepi and two other guys drag him out,
kicking and screaming. Miss Mascara with the cigarette holder
blows a new snake my way, this one reaching into my left eye.

My father used to own this house . . . Manny tell you?
Nah.
My father was a jazz musician . . . James Henry Scott.
Oh, yeah?
You know his music?
Nah—Yeah.
You either know it or you don't.
Yeah, I know it . . . enough.
You can never know music enough.

I liked it better when she was on the floor doing her shit. She's got
this way of twirling and swaying and sweating and ignoring everything in the world except the music—that's all the conversation I
need. That's the part that gets me the most. But when she's not

dancing, standing around holding her cigarette, posturing—talking mad shit, you know right away it's a script. She's written the words beforehand, adjusts the script according to who she's talking to, but it's the same script. Could fall for her, could *be* with her if she gave the right vibe.

Beats ain't music . . . you can't know the music if you just know the beats. What's your name?

Racine.

"Racine." Fourth tune on my father's *Remembrance of Things Past* album. You heard it before?

Nah.

Then I got music you need to hear. My name's Couchette. Means "bed" in French.

Nice to meet you.

How long was you in Paris?

Long enough.

Where was you livin' before you moved there?

Nowhere. Everywhere.

A homeless DJ. How very *ghetto riche* of you.

Whatever.

You don't talk much do you?

Nah.

Mawepi cuts us a look, we talkin' too much. Couchette glides back over to the bar. Heads keep a steady eye on her as she sails from one end of the bar to the other, pouring the brownish green liquid into plastic cups, pushing the plastic cup on a little square of paper napkin toward them with slender manicured fingers, never making eye contact. The bald head makes her way back to me from the wood countertop, drying her hands with a towel, flips through my albums again.

The way you spin your music it's like poetry . . . you know . . . I mean, the way you choose certain songs, pull out the bass, mix them together . . .

Just spinnin', no poetry, no dreams, just reality.

How do you know reality from the poetry of dreams?

She tried to make her point again—bring clarity to it, but the music recalled her *back to life—back to reality,* gulped her back to the dance floor, where windows hang on opposing angles dressed in shades against other eyes: a scrim for moving silhouettes on the other side. There's this cistern in which she dances, a hollowed space. I put up some Third World and I'm feeling how she's back out on the dance floor—not like the girls too cute to do more than shake their asses just a bit. She dances in a dream. That's where she is, in a dream, when she's dancing—comfortable with it. Validates it. It's hard to know with girls like that, though—you don't know what part she's written for herself and what part she's written for you in her play but that, by itself, is kind of fascinating too. She fights her way back to me.

You living in the poem or you living in the dream?

Neither. I'm living in the music. The music makes the dreams.

Well then, sugar, you may not be living in the dream but you're definitely living in the poem. Those of us who take our dreams literally are definitely living in the poem.

Mawepi disrupts her flow, calls her back over to the bar. Couchette waves her hand, stops by me first.

You want somethin' to drink?

Whatever.

She fills a cup to the rim with some rotgut, slides the plastic cup at me with the wet square napkin beneath it, the soaked napkin dissolves beneath the cup—doesn't survive the journey from her fingers to mine. She shovels out the last bits of ice from a bucket on the floor, drops the cubes into my cup before I lift it, walks the empty ice bucket over to Mawepi at the door, plops it down at her feet, sashays back to the bar, and makes herself a warm cup of (rum and Coke?). She sips her drink leaning her hips against the bar while the rest of the people who haven't been served yet get a little loud, but she doesn't say anything to any of them. Doesn't give a damn. Cuts herself a wedge of lemon and squeezes it into her drink, spraying some guy who came staggering over. He joins the complainants, and she makes an announcement: NO MORE ICE! Drunk guy says he *don't care 'bout nobody's gawd-damned ice* and everybody else waiting chimes in. Couchette makes her second announcement—*BREAK!*

Some young white boy brownnoses up to a used-to-be-famous writer from a thousand years ago, licked him up and down with praises, misquoting lines from three of the old man's books (published way before he went to jail for cocaine possession, Manny informs me later.) The used-to-be-famous writer from a thousand years ago vomits his beer into the lap of this fat woman sitting next to him, swivels back to the white boy, and thanks him for the compliments with a wet handshake. Mawepi takes a wet mop to the vomit with one hand, slaps the shit out of the writer with the other. He staggers out, Mawepi curses out loud in Spanish as she pulls a big key ring from her pocket, slams the front door shut and locks it so no one can enter without paying, stomps upstairs with the empty bucket. Couchette plants one of her cigarettes in her holder, leans over to me for a light, arches an eyebrow as I cup the flame, grabs my hand, walks me through the crowd outside to the garden.

On a concrete bench covered in moss on the patio, I'm trying to keep a lookout, peeking through the door to see if anybody's hanging around the equipment, but my eyes pull toward the trees out in the garden in front of us, some in front of the little limestone carriage house, the rest on either side and behind it. I didn't really notice them before, with Manny, all them trees standing in the dark.

You got pretty hair. You Indian or somethin'?
Nah.
I cut all mine off.
. . .
My daddy used to love my hair—I cut it off.
. . .
He died.

Who?

My father . . . died right here in this house . . . Manny tell you?

Nah.

We left after he died. He killed himself. He used to own this house.

You said that. I mean who left?

My mother and me. We was livin' all over, sleepin' on people's couches and shit, till I got old enough to do my own thing. She's over in Bali now . . . remarried.

. . .

My mother is a dancer too . . . *was* a dancer . . . she taught me to dance but she quit dancin' and she's over there in Bali . . . you ever been to Bali?

Nah.

Went there from Hong Kong. We hung out. She just had a baby for this man about four years ago . . . he built her a house in the middle of a rice paddy field in Bali.

Then why you here?

That's her man, not mine.

She flicks an ash over her shoulder, glances back inside to see if Mawepi's come back down with the ice yet.

I moved back here about three years ago . . . I had just got back to New York . . . I was livin' out in California for a while. You been to California?

Nah.

I went to school out there. So anyway, I tried to remember our old address in Brooklyn. Lucinda used to live here when I was kid . . . she rented a room from my father . . . I was glad she had bought the building. You met Holy Mother, right?

Not yet.

Thickets, spiny branches spreading themselves out over a little plot of land—acres and acres of land. Light brown smooth bark, tall stalks, night coming through branches with silver blue light.

*　　*　　*

Anyway, when we lived here, this house had been messed up for years . . . my father kinda fixed it up but then shot himself in the head and after that the building was closed up . . . we used to live on the garden floor and the parlor floor . . . it was like a duplex . . . I wanted to rent the garden floor . . . you know . . . reconnect . . . but Lucinda had already made it into a storage place for her oils and candles . . . so I moved in the apartment on the fourth floor . . . fifth floor ain't got no roof.

What's up with the dead kid and all that shit?

What?

Your boy said some kid got killed up there, on the roof?

Oh, yeah?

It ain't true?

You want it to be true?

?

Manny tell you about my mother?

Nah.

. . .

. . .

My mother thought I was crazy when I told her I moved up in here . . . said I should let all of this go . . . she came by once to visit . . . stood outside . . . wouldn't come inside. . . . 'cause my father died here. Everybody lives somewhere somebody died, unless you build your house yourself . . . up from the ground and shit, but even then . . .

. . .

Before she left for Bali . . . said she had to focus down. Whatever that means.

What does it mean?

Means she had to put self first—had to focus on herself and her husband and her new baby.

. . .

You speak French?

Nah.

You like your room?

It's all right.

This house used to be so damn beautiful.

She rests her elbow on her arm, folded across her stomach, legs stretched out in front of her, crossed at the ankles . . . takes a pause in breathing when she inhales—swallows, allows a bit of time before the smoke seeps from between her lips and out of her nose then launches back into the conversation with ease, keeps her voice kind of quiet and even . . . it's just for you. This is between us.

They talkin' about getting the government to expropriate sites of martyrdom in this neighborhood. Shit, half the buildings around here are sites of martyrdom. Before the war ever got started, before the bridge came down, only 'bout half the tenements around here were occupied anyway . . . and the ones that were burned down or whatever during the war need to be renovated for all the homeless people . . . but they don't care nothin' 'bout that. Fresh wounds, know what I'm sayin'?

Nah.

I'm just sayin' I'm not with all these memorials and commemorative marches and prayers and anniversaries to mark the death of this infantry and that precinct. Ain't nobody commemorating the death of these buildings. These buildings been dying for years.

Naked buds falling, ginkgo, maples, yellow poplar . . . *ginkgo is good for memory.*

What's so amazin' out there?

What?

You starin' out in the garden.

Lookin' at the trees.

Can't see the trees, fool. Too dark. Ain't nothin' down there no way but broken bottles and paper plates. You workin' somethin' out?

What?

You tryin' to work somethin' out . . . I can feel your energy. Can I bum a cigarette?

Yeah.

Everybody smokes Marlboro in Europe, don't they?

. . .

I'm tryin' to stop.

. . .

See these little pins in my ears? Pressure points. I'm supposed to push them in when I get an urge, but it's not really workin'. You gotta want it to work, you know what I mean?

Yeah.

This ain't no real tobacco no way. The stuff you get now down at the marketplace is worse than the stuff they used to sell in the stores. Chulo tries to keep it clean but you never know what you gettin'. So when I'm ready, I guess I'll quit . . . that shit creeps up on you . . . I think the American government is sharin' in the black market profits any damn way.

You got a whole lot of conspiracy theories, don't you?

I just know what I know.

You hate it here so much why you here?

My father's blood is here.

She puts her head down, then throws it back to catch the last swig of her drink, takes my pack and taps it a few times on her knee, pulls out another cigarette, and leans over to me for another light. The match glow shows how pretty her skin is: soft purple leaves of the black ash tree. Her eyes swell up, glassy, a drop of water splashes onto her thigh.

She healed herself.

Who?

My mother. She healed herself and she wrote me and apologized for all the shit she did to me but I had already let all of that shit go.

Yeah.

Said there is no place else in the world to be right now other than Bali but that's what she said before everything went down over there . . . wanted me to come to Bali . . . she begged me to come over there. Land holds memory . . . you gotta face shit head-on . . .

ain't safe nowhere. This is as safe a place as any. Everybody better find themselves a safe place that's what I told her . . . right now this is mine.

She stands up, puts her hands on her hips, toward the back, like country women do when they stand up for the first time in a long time to stretch their backs, offer you something cold to drink before they ease back down into their chairs, taking slow aim, pull their skirts up to their knees . . .

You want another drink?
Nah.

The trees are skeletons, mapping out the country of the body: lines interconnected, complicated patterns, joints and tissues, tendon. . . . somewhere, encased in the jagged bone, a heart. A center.

Your real name is Racine?
Yeah.
Couchette's not my real name. My father named me Saeta after that song Miles played—on the *Sketches of Spain* album—but I never thought that name fit me so when I started dancin' all the girls had made-up names so I decided to call myself Couchette because I know that means "bed" and our beds are where we make our dreams. My mother hates it. Said my father already gave me my real name, but he didn't use his real name either. I got to be what I got to be. Couchette. That's what I am . . . a place where dreams can be made.

The crash of a solid bag of ice thrown to the floor announces Mawepi's return. Couchette takes her last drag, flicks the cigarette over the rail into the dark, pauses in the doorway.

. . . I got music you should hear.

Beneath the lampshade, Jill Scott, and my eyes run up and down her back, pulling black panties down to frame her roundness. A woman's body offers itself, instructs me in how to know it, takes no offense in apprehension if this exchange is unbeknownst to my hands. No need to impress with awkward performances. Touch the surface. Yielding. Henna. Inhaling. The clean hint of lavender soap between her legs, at the core of it, plump fruit, tender in my mouth, the flesh of it—the wet soft side of mango, my thumbs pressed into each side—peeling moist flesh back from the center. My face pushing in reddish orange, deeper toward the glistening dark seed atop its soft tissue—ackee—entering slowly, head first toward a cave of warmth and welcoming, southern province, my cheek and nose brushing against walls of amber clay, into the darkness of a sanctuary, fruit of pomegranate, persimmon—the pleasure of sweetness at its core. Suck its sweetness. Wash in it. Swim the rockless quarry with finger, tongue, nose, body.

My body—my whole body belongs to God inside her. Her doors open to me, like the woman in the dream, offering a hiding place before I return to the open fields of furtive turns and threatening circumstances, the woman who touches me softly—takes in my tongue. Takes my tongue from my mouth and confounds my language . . . *speak* . . .

She is walking. Moving. The lilac bleeds into the dark painted around her shoulders. She is young. So young. A child. Young. Younger. Thick neck. Wide nose, thin lips, red. I can smell plants and herbs and water moving all around me. She is moving all around me. All around the bed, and then . . . she is not one woman . . . she is two . . . then one again . . . not the same . . . has changed with turns and moans . . . becomes another woman, in a white shirt and long skirt. And she is young. So young. Tall. Moving. All around the bed, the flowers of urgency . . . a hot smell . . . and my body is soaked in sweat—sweat or water, water coming from my flesh, sweat the smell of sea salt or ocean. She is two women moving, moving all around my bed, one is taller than the other. The smell of sea salt and blood coming . . . blood and sweat soaking into the sheets.

She visits my back and stomach with warm hands, presses into my shoulders, pushes me off her, and lays me down, gripping my waist between her legs, then visits me with tongue and lips, familiarizes herself with eyes, with fingertips, then lifts—then stops, discovers. Sees. Wants to ask. The pause is asking. Her finger traces along the scar—ignores it, returns me to her breasts, to touch, to kiss, to her caves. Takes my hand, places it along a thin line keyloiding beneath her navel. We return again to touch, to kiss—return again to God without questions.

In the aftermath of motion, when everything is calming, our bodies recede into recovery, hearts slowing their pace, lungs pushing air . . . and now, in the dark, we notice our eyes for the first time, notice our eyes and our smiles, our own and each other's. Notice how our flesh folds on the face of our smiles, creases our eyes, notice the shape and color of our teeth, the scent and consistency of combined sweat, and without words, we both acknowledge this moment, this room, as the place for discovering the something we have in common, something more than rhythm and unexpressed fear or mutual appreciation. Something more than nudity. This is the place we meet each other for the first time, introduce ourselves to each other without disguises.

I want to indulge in this corner refuge place. Take part in what might be. Own it until it escapes me. But it always does escape me— the spiral of pleasure. For now, we'll lie with each other in the privacy of unexplained scars.

Balding trees cover blue stone in sorrel, ochre, plum, cobalt. Brownstone buildings bathed in rain bleed into the gutters. Mornings—hazed in a wet gray fog—deliver a sun that coughs itself into awakening with dazed and blurry eyes barely opening by afternoon. Briefly the sun allows some light—not much—as if in its recovery, the sun has overextended itself doling out spoonfuls of diminished beams, and now has only strength enough to redress its wounds, wave its hand once or twice across a land dense with abandon, retire early before next shift.

If not for the absence of spirit, this city would almost seem like those ancient capitals of amphitheaters hewn from limestone quarries, carefully excavated temples and burial grounds long protected beneath consecrated earth—but the cool of these wet Brooklyn mornings and their buildings in decay (however beautiful their foliate carvings and spiked cast-iron rails) smells unwashed, begins with the stench of last night's human waste doused in ammonia and slopped into the sewers; fried pork, canned corn, a dream soaked in homemade whiskey. What is not digested, fear and deprecation, remains stuck to the insides, reeks from the pores, spoils in open air—the bones of its citizens ground to nothing.

This neighborhood of Victorian mansions sits isolated—cut off from the rest of the world with borders all around it, a segregated islet without a ruling sovereignty. Disconsolate edifices with sheets of plywood nailed across their mouths live in a corroding cake of layers that peels itself back. The buildings attempt to summon you curbside—to take notice of their proud cast-iron banisters and lanterns of sculpted copper. They nod to apathetic strangers who take for granted the final grief of nineteenth-century walls incarcerated behind chicken-wire fences, then they lean back into the shadows of tree branches towering above rusting carcasses of metal—gored, stripped, tireless corpses parked at their feet.

These buildings die patiently on the land of their birth with sharp ears inclined down toward the bridge—across the water—from which hammering and drilling draws near. The sound of reconstruction—of newer, corporate, more lucrative structures—inspires trust. Where skyscrapers rise up again, sidewalks are narrow—and in some places, they do not exist at all. New sidewalks are cut in slivers, restrict the endless possibilities of feet in motion. Vanquished from all visibility are those intimate clusters of men and women who used to talk to each other along their way. Maybe the architects forgot to design walkways in their utopian plans, or maybe they ignored them altogether so as not to accommodate walking. Walking may soon become an outmoded way of travel, but here—except for the infrequency of buses that clunk from river to border with the threat of death—walking is the only way to see these acres of buildings before their extinction.

These buildings convince themselves—soon, men with flashlights and plans for renovation will come back to small, insignificant neighborhoods like these. Men will come back, as they always have, reminded of the fading beauty of Italianate row houses on wide tree-lined boulevards. Men will rediscover the classic frames and elaborate details of their unified block fronts, gently touch the surface of sandstone, explore rusticated basements and mansard roofs, then remember that these betrayed houses of American industrialists and European financiers, on the land of long-gone indigenous hunters and Dutch farmers, have withstood the desertion of their builders, survived many conversations, sustained themselves for decades unclaimed, welcomed masses of new immigrants, may well outlive all of their occupants. Someone will come and tend to their decay. Soon. You can hear these buildings praying to themselves as you pass them by.

Couchette had a door that opened to long morning walks on autumn asphalt. The ground pulls us into each other's breathing, and our shoulders collide with the warmth of stirring blood. We move through the pulse of anxiety masked with casual confidence, pace ourselves slowly but we are moving quickly—toward each other. In our daily search for morning coffee, Couchette takes my arm, promises to know of a place—a better place than the one we found before—somewhere on the other side of the park, or up the hill, or in the marketplace down by the old power plant. On different days, she's different people, worships between temples of agony and optimism; dons long sweeping skirts, beads and bracelets, seven rings on her right hand, five on the other, a small gold hoop in her nose, five silver and garnet studs in one ear, one silver stud in the other, a shawl. Sometimes she wears a red dot on her forehead like the Hindu women on Atlantic Avenue, to call them out of their absence. I'm always in the same pair of fatigues and army boots, affecting a severe march with heavy thuds and stomps.

The succession of red Xs signifying properties to be preserved as official war zones, and facades of banks and municipal buildings fastened with commemorative plaques designating sites of disaster, list the names of involuntary martyrs—some of whose bodies remain layered beneath collapsed granite. Names are embossed on bronze squares, pasted over by old posters: BRING THEM HOME. We are comrades in danger, mad scientists researching the genesis of madness, anthropologists walking past empty buildings and burned-out factories with vestigial signs, TRIAGE—MORGUE, spray-painted onto their walls.

Preoccupied morning walkers flow by us and into their pointlessness, discerning no difference between pale of day and pitch of night. The streets are empty with people caught somewhere between now and later, in search of reparations. They are not us, visiting the disquiet of our imaginations. They *live* here, in a day snagged behind a curtain of sheer black nylon—flattening them out. Agrarian figures in a silver gelatin print of insoluble urbanity. If they are made self-conscious, become too aware of you, they'll either scatter like roaches shocked by light or they'll pull you into their realism. Keep you there. If you are early (or late) enough to cross the threshold into their shadowy circus of desperation, you'll catch a peek of extreme dancers, side-street bargainers, alleyway hunters, or you might just see one unoccupied soul leaning into the storefront window of a once-fine restaurant—gazing at handwritten menus set on dirty white linen—empty like so many maimed, desecrated churches filled with spirit, unaware they've been evacuated at all.

A skinny guy with a D.A. sits on the stoop of an abandoned building with an old boom box playing a cassette tape of Gloria Lynn. He's arguing with a middle-aged woman (who I've seen countless times now marching up and down the avenue, starting up long, slurred conversations with strangers about her royal Polish descent) pushing a baby carriage down the street. Standing patiently by her side, a young man slurping a brew. The skinny guy waves his arm, ducks the wad of gum she throws at his head. The woman reaches for the young man's beer, he swings it out of her reach, she backslaps him in the ear, he throws his can to the ground—retrieves it.

She's short with milky skin and red hair cropped recklessly. Her shoulders are brief under her bloated head, and her breasts are mashed flat against her belly. The young man is obese, one shade of dirt, eyes of a three-year-old serial killer. He rolls alongside her like a flat tire, occasionally taking over the chore of pushing the carriage. The woman with the flushed blue pug-dog eyes tilts the carriage back, pops a wheelie—sprints across the street on broken high heels. Couchette tugs my arm along, and once out of view, I laugh myself against a wall, buckling over with hysterics—dry like a hacking cough. Straighten up, lace her fingers into mine.

What?
It's just funny.

What's funny?
They just make me laugh.

She lifts her skirt to step over a woman in a turquoise slip, dead or asleep in a pool of paint by a fire hydrant. The paint is white, soaked into the matted black hair that pillows her face. Her stomach is big, her torso twisted away from her legs. Her legs curl around a mangy tan and black cat. She moves slightly, to drag her bruised knees up into her chest. The cat repositions itself, nestles in the crest of a bent arm. Behind them, a broken violin sticks up out of a trash can.

What about her? She's funny too?
I'm not even bothered by her, not this morning. I can even appreciate her beauty.

I play along, walk through a street covered with creamy seedpods fallen from a ginkgo tree, brush them off the soles of my shoes as if they don't smell like vomit at all. Couchette squeezes my hand to indicate a turn or a stop, like riding a clutch. This wet Brooklyn reminds me of Rue Soufflot when the afternoon sun of Paris is hidden behind thick clouds of ruddy paste, the 89 bus dropping me off at the Panthéon, its dome huge and its golden rustic majesty defying the dark, and the flowers in the Parc du Luxembourg neatly arranged and ordered in a frigid assembly of warm colors, opened without light. Her hand squeezing mine brings me to a room in Garches. The room of an aging woman in a red sweater, sitting across from a boy in fatigues. The woman is blond and aging, small white hands with little brown splashes and blue lines. She squeezes the hand of the boy, strokes the head of her cat. The cat stares at the boy. The woman and the boy sit in her gingerbread house in Garches, just outside of Paris. Claude Luter and Pavarotti play music from the woman's small record player near an arrangement of dried flowers and freshly picked vegetables. The boy flips through her coffee-table books, through big waxy pages of black-and-white photographs—jazz musicians: the glory days of Bud Powell, Milt Jackson, Don Byas playing at the Club St. Germain. The boy flips through the scuffle of their instruments, their steps tapping against dense cobblestone, grating against the electro-wash of rustling raincoats—cigarette smoke curling around felt brims, blistering mouths up against cold brass, forcing tight air through cylinders and metal chambers. A flat C harpsichords its way out of the photographs of women in black turtlenecks and tight tweed skirts. Their eyes, painted with wide black lines across the lids, like cats. The cat and the boy flip through the pages, listening to a composition of breakdown—an improvisational score. The woman sets the table with wine, sliced apples, garden salad, strawberries, cheese, all neatly assembled, perused by the cat. A transparent hospitality drizzles over them as they eat. The boy brushes crumbs from his fatigues, walks out into the vegetable garden, and thinks to himself, *I could live here if it weren't so transparent and fatigued.* Brooklyn is not Paris or Garches. The resemblance fades quickly.

A tall man comes toward us—an aging basketball player's body, toothless. He lassos his legs in front of each other, leaving one foot behind in another country, discovering new land with the other. Girlish gray braids skip around his shoulders as he swings a brown shopping bag from the crest of his arm, stops and invites us to peek inside the paper bag at perfectly white rolls of cotton.

Got socks for ya!

His fifty-something-year-old poor Black Detroit accent is all wrapped up in a Girl Scout's singsongy pitch.

Go 'head. Look in the bag! Look in! Whatcha need today pretty lady? Anything today, pretty lady?

Couchette isn't laughing. She's a little nervous. He startled her, jumping around the corner like that. Nobody else on the street except the woman asleep or dead under the fire hydrant. He holds the bag open by its handles, towers over us, legs astride.

*   *   *

See anything you want young man?
Nah. I'm all right.
Anything, pretty lady?

Couchette says no with a tenderness she thinks won't upset him. He smiles, toothless.

Awright pretty lady. You let me know what you want. You let me know what you need. I have it next time. I be sure to have it, all right pretty lady?

We turn to walk away; he bids us a good day from behind our backs, then screams, his bag swinging wildly.

FUCKIN' ASSHOLES!

I jolt around, knees bent, arms up—fists tight. He's wriggling around—legs akimbo, a monstrous wave foaming up, launches one foot in front of the other toward us, barely keeping a comfortable distance.

A FALSE VICTORY HAS BEEN DECLARED! THE ENEMY IS AMONG US!

Couchette pulls me—wants to keep walking. I straighten up. He follows behind, doesn't say anything else. I'm aware of him, but I won't act nervous. He walks past us, dropping a trail of rolled white socks in our path as he takes the lead, punches his invectives with perfect aim as he walks ahead, dropping balls of white in our way.

THE GOVERNMENT WILL NOT ERECT STATUES OF THOSE SOUTHEAST ASIANS, AFRICANS, MIDDLE-EASTERN PEOPLES INTERRED DURING WAR! THE GOVERNMENT WILL NOT COMMEMORATE OR ACKNOWLEDGE THOSE AMERICAN VICITIMS WHO DIED ON THESE STREETS AT THE HAND OF THEIR OWN FUCKIN' MILITARY! ONE MILLION SOUTHEAST-ASIAN AMERI-CANS, MIDDLE-EASTERN AMERICANS, AFRICAN AMERICANS HAVE NOT

RETURNED HOME FROM UNJUST POLITICAL IMPRISONMENT! THEY PLACED
ME UNDER ARREST FOR A BRUTAL MOUNTING RAGE!

His gruff tenor soars beyond its limitations, like a gospel preacher set
free to sing not of God but of himself. Neither of us says anything.
We curve around him, he lags behind. We pretend we can't hear him
shouting. Pretend his shouting has nothing to do with us. We don't
understand what he is talking about. It's not for us. We don't understand anything about being *placed under the arrest of a brutal,
mounting rage.* Couchette says we should pick up our pace, says it
with her gallop. I tell her not to worry, say it with a firm grip of her
hand. His gruff tenor follows us through the streets of empty buildings covered in ivy. I've pulled my hand from hers. A tension builds.
My hand is hot, wet. They sting. My knees are swelling.

THE RESISTANCE PARTY HAS BEEN ACCUSED OF TREASON! THE
RESISTANCE PARTY BRINGS HUNDREDS OF THOUSANDS OF DOLLARS TO
STARVING AMERICANS! AFGHANIS! PAKISTANIS! PALESTINIANS AND
OTHER VICTIMS OF WAR! MANY MORE MASSACRES TO COME! MANY
MORE MURDERS!

We cross the street. We are not in the chokehold of incompletion. We
have not succumbed to a flaccid state of being—we don't live in a
vacant room without current. Our dreams are not buried somewhere
in an arid region of dry caves all over. We have not inherited another
plague. The past isn't lingering too damn long now. Our remedies have
not expired; music touching words, words inside of music.

YOUR MOTHERFUCKIN' GOVERNMENT!

Couchette smiles at me, a soft polite smile. I smile back, but I'm
ready to do what I'm ready to do, what I have to do if he tries something. I keep making sure we're just a step away from a broken bottle.

YOUR MOTHERFUCKIN' GOVERNMENT WILL NOT ERECT STATUES OF
THOSE ONE MILLION SOUTHEAST-ASIAN AMERICANS, MIDDLE-

Eastern Americans, African Americans who have not
returned home from unjust political imprisonment!

The sock man is just a couple of blocks behind us, every syllable
clear. I'm looking at the ground in front of us, thinking about the
woman by the fire hydrant, sleeping curled around water, and a man
shouts at the back of our necks. We turn the corner without looking
back. Turn another corner, then we're back where we started, walking past the fire hydrant again.

Back at the woman—no face as far as I can see under the mass
of thick black hair matted into a comforter. White paint splatters up
burgundy sores and ripped turquoise—a subject of fragility, pregnant
with ambition. I'm trying to see the beauty in her stomach; maybe
she carries a fetus inside it, curls around her stomach to protect the
fetus, sleeps near the hydrant should it need drink. Maybe her fetus
will be born a man on the sidewalk, she'll breast-feed him, her
breasts seep syrup. Her hair is woven heavy and thick for protection
against cold winters. Maybe she'll teach him to finger paint, and the
cat will play him the violin with its tail—an aerial sonata. The cat
will teach the newborn to play the violin for his mother. His mother
and the cat will sleep together beneath the fire hydrant, listening to
her son construct original compositions for violin and his mother will
roll around on her mattress of white paint to make herself a clean
white gown, and the cat will do the same—make himself white and
clean. They'll dance waltzes in white on a sunny street corner covered with ginkgo seeds to a sonata for broken violin—but what happens when it rains? The ablution of Brooklyn streets will wash
white paint from faceless ruddy red, wash the white cat into a ball of
mange, send the violin crashing down into the gutters.

The brownstones have sucked the sock man into their mouths,
hold him beneath their tongues until his voice pauses at an intersec-
tion, drifts off into something we can forget, evaporates into nothing.
Couchette sits down on the stoop of a building, slips out of her shoes
and rubs her feet. I lean over and kiss her on the cheek, to ease her.
Her lips are trembling.

*   *   *

You got a Joe for me?
One left.
We'll share it.
You all right?
Fine. You?
Fine.

The chipped steps of the building cradles us for a moment; its neighboring sisters look down on us with half-curved smiles. These buildings are broken. They smell. Their eyes are dim, but they hold their arms out to us for respite, and when we get up, refreshed, to go on our way again, they must whisper among themselves: *There is no faceless terror that wreaks havoc on our membrane and muscle so much so that yesterday sits heavily on our spines or gouges tunnels through our walls, drags us through the years, dismembers us, sets our pieces down at our feet. Some of us know how to keep a straight face, stand decrepit beneath the spotlight, smile at yesterday, then push it back and away from us. Some of us have always been afraid of the air, way before the enemy crossed the bridge with contaminant spores. Some of us have always lived in terror, fought the dark, awoke to the somber wail of mourners marching behind catafalques transported to shallow graves, shielded ourselves from the downfall of fire in wide open spaces—some of us have always fought something invisible without the honor of bronze plaques commemorating the exodus of our joy or the time of our ruination. We can deal with these voices thrown at us from the corners of dirty streets strewn with clean white socks.*

A diner's just reopened with stale morning glory muffins and eggs—weak coffee—like the merchants and the few patrons hunched over Formica tables . . . weak, bitter, tasteless. We never have more than four cups between us, rarely order the food, sit for hours sharing rituals of cigarette smoking, chlorophyll drops in bottled water (her holistic preventive medicine for contaminated water), enjoy the music piped through little speakers, stare at the desolate through storefront windows; soldiers (barely beyond puberty) walking the avenue with their assault rifles, men wheeling up the streets in makeshift wheelchairs, tribes of expatriate suburbanites touring the blocks with tentative curiosity and prospects of coming back in dribs and drabs, the project kids with their beer . . . blue lips sucking in air . . . Couchette retreats into languid territories.

They met in a bar. He thought she was the most beautiful thing he'd ever seen. She's half Filipino . . . half Irish . . . big white teeth . . . bright eyes . . . she said he made her feel beautiful. . . . She had a book by Longfellow, and she had some Proust and a copy of *Faust,* and he asked her about her books and they walked through the city all night long talking about Longfellow and Proust and *Faust* . . . she knew poems, he knew about the Bible and music. She said she thought it was kinda strange that he would bring that up . . . Jesus and music . . . but she fell in love with him anyway . . . fell in love with that feeling . . . I was about sixteen . . . when she . . . met this man . . . he told her she was beautiful too . . . she needed to be beautiful . . . Nobody ever told me I was beautiful. If they did, I didn't hear it . . .

I wanted to raise my hand in the air like a kid in school and volunteer, but I lit a cigarette instead.

She packed her bags . . . moved in with him . . . her new

man . . . they went over to Bali . . . she had the baby . . . It's so beautiful in Bali . . . she lives in a grass hut, in the middle of a rice paddy
field . . . you have to walk a mile up a narrow path . . . she makes
jewelry in her grass hut . . . from beautiful stones . . . I took a bath in
an aqueduct . . . we're all right now . . . she'll always be my
mother . . . I'm proud of her . . . how she's taking care of herself . . .
healing herself in Bali.

She's got her cheek against the glass window, watching dull colors move through the neighborhood.

They made sure to build them projects on the other side of the
park . . . away from all the mansions . . . elevated train used to run
down Myrtle . . . always a dark and noisy street . . . used to be a
shantytown . . . people slept with their chickens and pigs . . . until
the middle-class people in Victorian mansions on the other side of
the park complained about the smell . . . had the shantytown leveled . . . which made me wonder about all the shantytown people . . .
Where did they go? Book didn't say . . . I turned the page—no shantytown, no shantytown people . . . last word . . . LEVELED . . . that's
the end of that.
          . . .
By the time my father bought his house, they were callin' this
neighborhood *Jungle town* . . . highest tuberculosis and infant mor-
tality rates in the country . . . worst housing conditions . . . crime
rate . . . city decided to try and fix it up . . . built a community center . . . a playground . . . used leftover war materials from bombs and
shit . . . bombs to build playgrounds . . . planted some grass and
stuck a sign in the ground . . . can't pave over everything.

Manny staggers in, dressed in moon dust and sequins. He and Mawepi get into a little argument about something, but he waves her off, laughs, nose all red, eyes wide open. He gets to the middle of the dance floor, shaking his purple glitter and robe around the room, pushes past people, stands in the corner, kneels down by the Christmas lights. Rose- and mint-colored lights fall off his shoulders. His tank top is ripped, one side slips below his chest. A trickle of blood creeps down from his hairline, soaks into an eyebrow. Somebody tries to say something, he can't hear because the music is too loud to hear voices, and Manny doesn't want to hear voices, he wants to hear music. He waves his arm at Couchette, Chulo and Mawepi try to pick him up from the floor, but he pushes them away, tumbles around until he can get his bearings, staggers over to the bar, takes a beer, twirls some more. Chulo whispers something to him, Couchette whispers something to him, he keeps jumping away, laughing, every time somebody gets close to him. Looks at them and laughs, then hops, then he looks at me with his bloody eyebrow, throws up his middle finger—*Hello, Racine . . . I know you.*

I transition from an old remix of Ja Rule's to some Aaliyah, because I know he likes the sweet breathiness of her death rattle. He hugs Chulo around the neck—hangs on—moving to some counterbeat in his head. Couchette slides another drink across the bar toward somebody with a little wet square of paper beneath the plastic cup. The paper does not survive the journey. Manny twirls. I spin. *You got another record for me, Racine? Play one just for me.*

The paper square dissolves on the downbeat—does not survive.

The sky is all copper striped with gold ore draping itself across the vacant bridge, streaming into her room—onto porcelain dolls on a blond wood vanity dresser, silver bracelets on salvaged cherry-wood end tables. Two marble fireplaces bricked up decades before divide twelve-foot walls, supporting a ceiling trimmed in elaborate moldings. An old chandelier with a few remaining pear-shaped crystals dripping from its tiers hangs from a plaster rosette painted gold. Her walls are papered with green-and-red velvet paisley, maps of the world, photographs of Billie Holiday, Coco Chanel, Thilly Weissenborn's nude Balinese virgin, James Henry Scott's *Remembrance of Things Past* album jacket, hanging above a worn peach-velvet fainting couch, its stuffing and springs spilling out beneath it. Books tangled up in her linen sheets: F. Scott Fitzgerald, Longfellow, *Faust*. Audre Lorde. Costume jewelry entwined in toothpaste and perfume.

Couchette stashes her tip money in a jewelry box covered with seashells, slips DJ Cam's *Gangsta Shit* into the CD player. Listens to thirty seconds of it, replaces it with Zappa's *Peaches en Regalia*, follows it with John Forté's *What a Difference* (just to hear Dinah Washington again, she says). Couchette stays quiet . . . doesn't say much. I don't either. No maps. She writes her mother a letter on perfumed stationery, I flip through her vinyl lined up on a shelf at the top of the wall, pull down Max Roach's *Freedom Now Suite*. Abbey Lincoln. Coleman Hawkins.

Be careful with it . . . don't scratch it.

A woman sings a field song to a tambourine, like an evangelist with a bullhorn—*better make your hammer ring . . . driver man will start to swing . . . ain't but two things on my mind . . . driver man and quittin' time*—then Coleman Hawkins soloing on tenor sax, flitting between rows of cotton. The curtains are pulled back waiting for sun to cough up pins of light, cold shadows breezing through the predawn chill. She keeps the windows open, lifted up high, Abbey's voice blares out the window, bounces off of the brownstone walls across the street. Couchette folds her letter in three sections, tucks it away in a drawer—no envelope, no stamp—flips through a pile of postcards, holds up one of her father, black-and-white close-up.

He's wearing a sweater, smoking a cigarette, leaning over a piano—lines carved into his face like valleys, gashing a weight of depression heavy around his mouth, sweat streaming down from his forehead, little drips of sweat hanging from his eyelashes like tears. Resting my head on the pillow at the base of the couch, I look for traces of Couchette in his face. She takes it from me. Now I see the resemblance, something unspoken. Roach is playing fast now, but he's not taking the lead, which is some other shit to me—cause it's *his* shit, but he's banging fast, hittin' *hi-hat* soft while the trumpet and the sax do their thing—then a little space is made and Roach makes his statement, nothing but drums talking, bad-ass beats, and Abbey singing some hook about *listen listen listen.*

Couchette tapes her postcard to the refrigerator door with a plastic magnet. Holds a picture of her mother up to the chandelier—pretty thin bronze woman with bright white teeth, hair long and wavy, sitting at a bar in a yellow dress, holding a cigarette from a faux jasmine holder.

Ain't nobody been more . . .

Abbey is *oooing* over Couchette's words as they trail off into nothing—and it's some haunting shit like, Max barely there, just tapping and brushing and Abbey *oooing,* completing Couchette's thoughts. How do you sample this? Couchette is frozen, supporting herself against the refrigerator door. She lowers her head, *ooos* with Abbey—pushes herself off the white lacquer surface—her body floats into the melody, feet making tiny tapping motions with Max Roach, nothing like how she danced the night I met her, but everything about the intensity is the same—she's inside this. Abbey starts screaming, just fuckin' screaming, and Couchette throws her hands up into the air, waves them around, swatting demons away, does some African shit, holding up her *lapa,* a few sacred steps, and Max is beating the shit out of Abbey and Abbey is screaming for Couchette who is waving her arms around, the record volume up high—sun trading places with shadows, light, dark, light, dark—sun and shadows painted onto the floors of densely wooded areas carpeted in pink lilacs near dammed up brooks, moving into white sands. Roach pounds fast.

I'm running up one mile into the hills, one mile up from the road to the Blackwater River, over pond holes, and river bluffs, my feet stomping into crispy beds of evergreen moss. How can you sample this, pounds, and screams, sun and shadows, light, dark, light, dark, sweat dripping from eyelashes—and running up toward Blackwater River, spying down into the quarry?

The record ends. No music. No pink lilacs screaming. I get up, wade through the record pile. She looks at me the way I had been looking at her, except I don't know what she sees when she is looking at me, am I different now? Did I do something while Abbey screamed? I don't know—it's like in church when you get the Holy Ghost and then you don't know what you did with your body when you got the Holy Ghost but next thing you know your body is somewhere else in the room and people are standing over you—scrutinizing. Or like when you were in school—playing, just playing, running in circles, all the kids yelling and laughing and screaming, and the sun is hot and you're just a kid running in a playground until your body can't run anymore, it contorts, and quakes you to dreams, like convulsions, and you are swimming in a creek but everybody is standing around you, watching your seizure—not sure what to do, teachers shoving a spoon in your mouth to hold down your tongue, school guard advising against the spoon, puts your head in his lap so it won't bang against the concrete, you don't feel any of it—eyes dilated, you are swimming in a creek, and then it's over and the kids say you were making crazy noises, like a bird or some shit, and your whole body is wet—soaked—Blackwater River water, and then they tell the lady with the black bangs who takes care of you that you had an epileptic seizure and then the doctor says it's not an epileptic seizure, says they don't know what it is, and all you know is you were swimming.

I find her copy of Scott's *Remembrance of Things Past*. It was the album her father was most proud of, she says, because it was the first album of his with him as a leader, not a sideman. It was the turning point in his career, but he never released another album. He'd been writing it all his life, she says—and that's how he was. He was thirty when he recorded it and it would have taken another thirty years to put that much lifeblood into the next album. Scott didn't survive.

Don't play that one, not yet . . . I wanna tell you something. Play Art Pepper.

Couchette lays her head back on the couch, I crawl over to where she is, put my head in her lap. She scratches through my scalp and pulls her fingers from root to tip of my hair, motions me up toward her lips, our tongues lacquered in tobacco, the pulse of our hearts and the tide of blood rushing through us warm. Between us, I can hear what she isn't saying; *Tell me something no one else knows but you.*

I can't make words come out of my mouth. Can't make sound. Let our tongues . . . let tongues and music speak for us.

That's Joe Mondragon on bass . . . you ever heard of him? Larry Bunker on drums . . . Scott and Pepper met after the war . . . Pepper used to hang out on Central Avenue trying to find some junk or some black jazz musicians to play with or both . . . the legend is that Scott and Pepper met in some alleyway off of Hollywood Boulevard and then they went to some club and sat in with a band . . . both of 'em high as shit . . . Scott still in his uniform. They were playin' with the same kind of intensity but slower than the rest . . . slowed the whole melody down . . . the drummer got mad and walked off the stage and so it was just Scott and Pepper draggin' the music out real slow and the audience loved it . . . they was best friends after that but Scott and Pepper fought a lot and Pepper replaced Scott with Russ Freeman or somebody then they stopped talkin' for a while when Pepper started playin' with Sonny Clark's trio and Scott hooked up with Sonny Stitt . . . but Scott always said Pepper and Lee Konitz and Paul Desmond were the only sax players not tryin' to sound like Charlie Parker . . . Scott said Pepper wasn't just good for a white boy he was better than that . . . Pepper could hold his own with Stitt and was better than Ricky Ford and Eddie Davis 'cause Pepper had suspense . . . took his time getting there you know what I mean? . . . it wasn't a quick nut with him and that's how Scott liked music to be played.

She lights her next cigarette with the last one to Scott's piano solo.

He had started experimenting with different sounds . . . less traditional shit—like what Coltrane and Miles were doing—most of the album was recorded on the parlor floor . . . back then, the neighborhood was already ghetto . . . and the building had been closed down for years . . . set up his piano and some recording equipment on the parlor floor . . . fixed the building up himself . . . when we lived here, all the fireplaces were white alabaster with birds and angels . . . somebody must've ripped some of them off when the house was closed up all those years after he died . . . they do that, you know . . . rape these houses when they're empty . . . floor above the parlor had a kitchen and a bathroom . . . and the floor you and Manny on, had already been divided into two studio apartments . . . with half baths from back in the days when most of the landlords in the neighborhood made extra money renting out rooms to people from the Navy Yard . . . Scott rented . . . to whores, jazz musicians, anybody he met on the street who needed a place to stay . . . rarely collected rent from anybody . . . he was a little bit . . . a little bit fucked up . . . like when he and my mother broke up and he had started in on himself again . . . gigs were harder to come by . . . I was four when he died . . . or five . . . I remember some of it . . . living in this apartment . . . and a couple of people lived in the rooms downstairs . . . he wasn't recording anymore . . . all he had to show for his life's work was . . . one album . . . this stupid-ass house . . . Pepper made three records at the Village Vanguard the year Scott killed himself . . . never even called Scott to come sit in with him . . . never even called my mother to say he was sorry to hear about what had happened . . . Scott rescued Pepper's ass all those times . . . got him out of jail . . . lent him money . . . shit like that . . . but Pepper crossed him when Scott had made this album . . . There was a radio interview with Pepper and Pepper dissed Scott . . . said his music didn't work . . . said it was a lot of contrived experimentation . . . that really hurt Scott . . . but then after Scott made his record . . . Pepper started experimenting too . . . gave the credit to Coltrane.

I take her down to my chest, kiss the crown of her head. The short hairs bristle against my lips and ashes from her cigarette sprinkle onto my stomach. She pulls herself back up from me, readjusts herself, and rests her head in my lap. As if she doesn't feel like kissing right now, as if she'd rather listen to what the music is saying now.

But she doesn't let the music speak—not for itself.

It's different when you abstract shit on the piano . . . make the piano the main thing . . . Scott loved Monk and Bud Powell even back when nobody paid them any attention . . . but he was never as technical as Powell . . . or as good at writing melody as Monk . . . played better than Waldron, who was Billie Holiday's last pianist. Scott and Waldron knew each other, but Daddy didn't care much for his playing . . . said Billie was already galaxies away from Waldron . . . too far ahead for Waldron to keep up let alone save her life . . . he liked some of the newer musicians like Ran Blake . . . another white boy . . . loved listening to Ran Blake and Jean Lee. She took her tone from Billie but she went somewhere else with it. Abstracted the shit.

Couchette tosses Pepper to the other side of the room before the last cut is finished, puts Scott on the turntable. Sets the needle down midway.

—Listen . . . hear that? . . . Listen to that . . . That's how he made music . . . by not being scared of it . . . he put this orchestra together of wind instruments and strings and there he is in the center with his piano composing songs from two or three notes . . . hammering them out like he was losing his mind . . . listen . . . see how he'd stop abruptly like that . . . hear that? . . . nothing . . . no music now . . . playing like he was crazy for four minutes straight like that . . . like he was a man running toward a cliff . . . a man who had come to the edge . . . and you're not sure if the man is gonna fall off the cliff or if he'll stop there and look down into it . . . and the music stops . . . you don't know what happened . . . can't tell . . . whatever happened . . . it ain't through happening yet . . . so you wait with him in the silence . . . I love silence . . . I respect it . . . Scott teaches you to respect the silence.

I'm wanting her to understand something about me now. I want her to know what *I'm* hearing . . . Her arm reaches back behind me, my fingers massage into her thigh.

That's the wind section coming in like that . . . beautiful . . . isn't it beautiful? . . . these sustained silences . . . then the winds and descending arpeggios . . . like he was sayin', *I didn't fall off the cliff . . . and I'm not standing on the edge of the cliff . . . the wind just came along and lifted me up off the ground.*

She dries her face with her skirt, pours us a drink. Outside, the clouds are fat—about to burst open and pour down rain. Somebody has parked their car across the street, speakers in the trunk with the hood open. The bass of Missy's "Get Ur Freak On" competes with Scott's tinkling keys on "I Thought About You." She closes the window to the bass line competing with Scott. Draws the curtains. Fuck the sun. Scott is the sun. It's always almost morning.

My mother wasn't home. I was in the room, playin' or somethin'. Heard this big bang. Lucinda came runnin' downstairs . . . picked me up . . . took me outside so I wouldn't have to see Scott splattered all over the floor . . . same night there was a fire in the building . . .

one of the tenants started it, I think . . . all these fire trucks and police and shit . . . somebody died . . . my mother and me . . . we moved into the projects for a while . . . tried not to ever walk past this house . . . then, like years later . . . there was another fire . . . it was still empty from the last one . . . nobody knows how it started . . . I think . . . they found some homeless man beneath the stairs.

Scott plays fire and stairs and black smoke bolting from walls. She picks up from somewhere she hasn't even been yet.

So you understand, Racine, when people talk about war, or these people on TV talk 'bout peacetime, I can't hear it . . . what is that, Racine? You got this little space in yourself sayin', When did it start? What happened? Who was there? Did I win? How do I know it's really over? Do you . . . you understand me, Racine?
Yeah.

It begins way before anybody declares it . . . starts with somebody in a room listening to music. It's . . . this long line . . . this deep historical thing . . . too hard to track, this complicated thing, unresolved . . . nobody knows exactly what or why. Nobody knows, They just . . . simplify it for you . . . like in comic books . . . here's the villain, here's the victim, here's the hero. The hero is you.

The piano and horn stop, Scott's startled us again, just when we thought he was hitting a groove, when we expected a chord change that made sense for the melody, he stopped playing.
Tell me a story, Racine.
I ain't got no veins to open up for you.
I just want to know somethin' about you. Anything.
Like what?
Like . . . about your family.
Ain't got none.
Never did?
I . . . I had a—
A what?

I had a brother . . .
Had?
Had.
What was his name?
Frederick.
And?
. . .
Yes?
He . . .
Yes?
He died . . .
How did he die?
My brother fell.
From what?
A cliff.
A cliff?
Yeah.
Where?
Zuni, Virginia.
How old was he?
I don't know.
You don't know how old he was.
I don't know.
You don't know?
No . . . I don't know.
What's wrong, Racine?

Something's out of order. It's hard for me to hold myself still in sudden space. Silence. No sound. Dead air. No music.

Racine . . . when you listen to music . . . what happens to you?
What?
Do you see things when you listen to music?
Nah.
It's in your face. You have this reaction on your face. I want to know what you see when you listen to music.

*   *   *

Wind instruments again. Air lifting Scott's body off the ground, again. I
see Couchette turn her face to the music, long neck swivels around.
The back of her head—perfectly round and clean shaven with a little
dent at the bottom of the cranium. She lights another cigarette, her
eyes, the lids keep dropping down and flipping up—slowly—evening
shades tricked by light. The smoke dissipates from the space between
her lips in a tuft of white sweeping behind her ears. Head tilted to one
side, she has become one of her photographs. She turns back to me,
wants me to return the favor of music and secrets, like the woman in
the South Bronx apartment, waiting for the boy to say something other
than yes or no, waiting for him to explain to her why one moment they
were sitting there, just sitting there in her living room, listening to
music, and the next moment he was writhing on the floor, yelling, body
jolting, shrieking like a bird. Waiting for an explanation. Like the Social
Worker who brought him to the lady with bangs, and the blue men with
shiny buttons who brought him to the Social Worker. Who did this to
you? Where is your mother? Where do you live? Do you know your
address? Do you know your name? Where are your clothes? But the
boy had no explanations, no real memories before the brown blanket . . . he couldn't explain who the people were that came to him when
he quickened himself to the ground, couldn't get it out . . . it was in
pieces, all of it . . . shattered glass . . . regrouping slowly . . . in music.

Close your eyes . . . tell me what you see, now.

Scott plays fast. Runs toward a cliff. Fast. Fire. Black with
splashes of red. Black smoke, bolting fire.

Racine?

I feel like I owe her something, and I don't want to feel like that. I
don't want to owe her a response. She's contemplative, ruminating
over something in her head, gazing at me from where she sits, poised
on the fainting couch. I see her even with my eyes closed. She
doesn't say anything. This is a violation, she's got binoculars to my

soul. A violation, the turning point of what was supposed to be unspoken. I don't have anything to say. Don't have anything I want to say. The words in my head are always more eloquent than the ones that come out of my mouth, and when they come out within ear's reach of someone I trust, there's always a betrayal. A withdrawal. A departure. A death.

Tell me what you hear.
Nothing.
Nothing?
Music, that's all.
Nothing else?
Nothing.
I'm looking at your face. I know that's a lie. Racine. I'm looking at you and your mouth is trembling. Tell me, Racine . . . what do you see?
. . . things.
Tell me.
Just things . . . that . . . uh—
That what?
Things . . .
Tell me.
I don't know—hands.
Yes?

Her hand arrives at my chest, softly, presses on the breastbone. Her palm pushes in to my heart, beating fast, she feels it. I'm afraid of how mangled words quake dreams into being. Her ear presses against my chest, and the tiny hairs on the top of her head prickle under my chin, gently . . .

Racine.

The record stops spinning. We lie there on the floor, leaning against the couch, without words . . . my eyes shut tight . . . one of her hands flat against my chest, the other wiping the moisture from my face. My eyes . . .

Racine, you can open your eyes now.

Even if I wanted to, I couldn't open them now . . .

Hear that music? Hear them beats and things? Hear them chord progressions?

Woman with shiny black bangs holds a glass in a South Bronx living room. Puts a record on a console. Avant-garde drums. Anarchy.

You don't know nothin' about this, do you, boy?

Black bangs plastered down to her forehead, legs crossed in satin robe, singing along to "In a Sentimental Mood." Stretching the words out from the roof of her mouth with Abbey Lincoln, unsteadily—a wolf howling gently at the moon—*moooood*.

Kids today don't know nothin' 'bout no music! You hear that? You hear that tempo? Arthur Blythe on alto, with John Hicks, Fred Hopkins, and Steve McCall!

Big shiny black records, big square cardboard jackets, blue-and-pink photographs of men blowing trumpets, women with thick black eyebrows painted in boomerangs, shiny black discs suspended between flat palms, long red nails pointed out, big black shiny disc fitted onto little metal pin, tiny silver needle positioned gently onto a twirling saucer. Bass lines, and trumpets, and shiny black bang foster lady in red-and-yellow satin robe moving her head real slow in circles. James Henry Scott. Cool reverberation of the drum, humming off-key loud. An inside joke laughed out loud on a green upholstered couch covered in plastic. The lights from Yankee Stadium shining through open blinds, gin and ice tinkling in her glass, breaking walls of inarticulation, little boy in her living room speaks only on occasion, to snap his fingers off-time and dance in a two-step. The little boy, fast-forward dreaming in a two-step, is fascinated with rituals of vinyl. Her rituals are crashing down the wall of inarticulation. *I'll be your family, boy. You be all right.* I'll be your family. Me and James Henry Scott.

Boy looks at the woman, shiny black bangs, a braid down her back, two gold teeth. Looks to the window with the light from Yankee Stadium shining through. Looks to the curtains, gold with green leaves, looks to the carpet, red wall-to-wall carpet, with cigarette burns. Looks to the walls, off-white walls . . . a nice off-white, the social worker said. Linen white, the woman said to the social worker. Linen white . . . matte. Nice off-white linen walls. Boy looks to the window again with the light shining through. Woman hums to the music, has an arm around him. They sit on a sectional uphol-stered in blue. Boy looks to the door, thinks to himself he should stand. He should stand and leave. Thinks to himself, he can't leave. . . . Where would he go? What's on the other side of the door if he should open it? Thinks to himself closed doors make safe rooms. Closed doors and closed windows trap safe air in. He looks to the door again. It has a lock at the top. It has a long metal pole braced up against it that fits through another metal lock. It has a chain. Thinks to himself locked doors make safe rooms. It's a safe door. It's a safe room. This woman with black bangs is safe.

Boy closes his eyes, looks around the room again; his old room. The window looks out to the black ash tree. Through the window the boy can see the road with the moon lighting up the path, Frederick in his T-shirt and jeans, walking up that road in his good blue-suede Pumas, smoking a cigarette, and the boy thinks to himself he'd bet-ter not say anything to anyone. Not to the shiny black bangs with music in her head, not to the blue man with the shiny brass buttons, not to anyone. It's good not to speak, good not to say anything. Fred-erick said, don't say anything. Frederick said, *don't say shit. You bet-ter not say shit. But where you goin'*? Boy wants to know. *Up the road a piece, maybe over to the quarry, mind ya' business, don't say shit,* Frederick said. *Don't tell nobody. Hold on to my mixed tapes for me. Don't let nobody hold my music. Don't let nobody take my music away from you. Don't say shit.*

Frederick climbs out the window that looks out onto the black ash tree. Frederick leaps out of the frame. The boy watches a T-shirt running up the hill toward the moon and the boy tries to turn his attention to his Bible study. Was not Esau Jacob's brother? saith the Lord: yet I loved Jacob and I hated Esau, and laid his mountains and his heritage waste for the dragons of the wilderness, and the boy cries, real tears. Real tears fall from his eyes, and the lady with the black bangs says, *Whatsa matter?* and the boy cries, sobs loudly, and black bangs says, *Whatsa matter whichoo?* and the boy thinks to himself that he does not want the Lord to love him and hate his brother, thinks to himself he does not want Frederick to leave, knows he cannot say anything because Frederick said, *You better not say shit,* and the woman with the black bangs says, *Why you cryin', baby?* and the boy thinks to himself, he does not want the dragons of the wilderness to devour his brother, and he does not want his brother to leave, and he turns his mind to his Bible study for peace and restitution and the Bible saith:

The Israelites left Rameses and camped at Succoth, they left Succoth and camped at Etham, on the edge of the desert, they left Etham, turned back to Pi Hahiroth, to the east of baal Zephon, and camped near Migdol. They left Pi Hahiroth and passed through the sea into the desert, and when they had traveled for three days, camped at Marah. They left Marah and went to Elim, where there were twelve springs and seventy palm trees, and they camped there. They left Elim and camped by the Red Sea and camped in the Desert of Sin. Boy does not want Frederick to camp in the Desert of Sin.

Boy remembers that the Bible said sometimes God has to destroy the body in order to save the soul, and he looks up, sees that T-shirt moving toward the moon outside the window, leaving Dophkah, Alush, Rephadim, where there was no water to drink. Leaving Zuni, Jesus, Mr. Eddie, and the Lord says cross the Jordan into Canaan and drive out all the inhabitants of the land, and destroy their temples and their idols, take possession of the land and settle in it, for I have given you the land to possess, and if you do not drive out the inhabitants of the land, those you allow to remain will give you trouble in the land where you live, and I will do to you what I plan to do to them. And the boy fastens his eyes to the door with the pole. The metal pole on the door slides, the chain collapses. The locked door cannot stop God.

And the boy looks to the window, looks to the tiny dot moving up the hill, wonders if Frederick knows he must possess the land he is going to inhabit, and if he does not possess the land, God will destroy him. Mr. Eddie opens the door—comes into the room with dragons. Mr. Eddie says the boy and his brother are cursed. Mr. Eddie rebukes Satan for the liar he is. Boy screams, afraid of the wrath of God, stepping into the living room. Woman with shiny black bangs panics and runs to the phone. Arthur Blythe is on alto, with John Hicks, Fred Hopkins, and Steve McCall, and Mr. Eddie says to the boy that he has to leave this house now. They both do.

Boy wants the lady to turn the music off, to hear what Mr. Eddie is saying, but she's left him in the room alone and she's yelling into the kitchen phone because boy falls to the floor, screaming like a bird, and Mr. Eddie says Lilly begat Emma and Eddie, and nobody begat Geneva. Geneva came from nobody. And Geneva begat Frederick and Racine, and Lilly went up in a whirlwind, and Emma died in the land God had given her, and Geneva was destroyed by fire, and Frederick left Zuni, left Ezion Geber and camped at Kadesh, and left Kadesh and camped at Mount Hor, and died on Mount Hor, and all the bloodline is cursed. The woman with black bangs screams into the phone, the boy lies trembling along the boundaries of an inheritance. Mr. Eddie mounts a Greyhound bus up north, Frederick moves—up a long line, toward the hill, the tree, the rock, the water . . . the boy escapes through the window, walks with Frederick, walks behind him, toward the trail through the dark, up the road, through cornstalks, and he wonders, what is safe about rooms with closed doors and locked windows?

You got some Peter Tosh? Play me some Peter Tosh.

Somebody's put a request in my ear, but I switch from slow to fast: 140 bpm coming up now, giving way to UK trance. Switch to Tupac's "Hail Mary," opening up into the Doors: "The End." Before Mawepi can waddle across the room with her ghetto bop, Couchette is already opening a beer for somebody. Mawepi doesn't break her stride, heads over to me and starts talking but I've already put my headphones back on. Mawepi waddles back to the door with her bop, a hand cupped between her thighs. The girl with the red bangs rotates a bracelet around her wrist at the bar. Her eyes are red, she's thin. The little beads on her bracelet are barely hanging on the string that connects them. She swigs down her last drink and by the time I look up again from the turntables, she's gone. After the four or five heads who'd dropped by for a minute or two, leave, Mawepi locks up early and runs upstairs to Lucinda.

Couchette gets edgy. Tense. Bitches about everything, out of nowhere. Paranoid. Mad because Manny's not around much, bitches about it. Nobody knows where he is or when he's coming back. He's gone for days sometimes, which makes things harder for her she said. She's upset because Lucinda is sick, and Mawepi locks up early and Couchette can't make any money from a possible late-night straggler or two. Some nights, Mawepi doesn't come out of the room at all because she's trying to nurse Lucinda, so Couchette has to collect money at the door and serve the drinks—which shouldn't be too difficult because fewer and fewer people are coming around lately. She gets bitchy, says the music is whack and that's why nobody's coming through. Says I'm chasing people away with this whack music I'm playing. *You're playing too loud. Why you playing so goddamned loud? Lucinda's not feeling well—so don't play the music so damned loud.*

The beats are pounding hard into the floor. The room is damn near empty. She loses herself in the music she hates so much, comes back and whispers non sequiturs.

She tried to kill him once.
Who?
My mother. She said she loved him, wanted to have more children with him. Tried to shoot him.
—

Do you think it's all right?
What?
To want to bring children into the world.
. . . I don't know.
I used to think it was wrong.
. . .
But I want them now.
. . .
I'm gonna have me a baby. A beautiful baby, right or wrong . . .

My eyes were open for hours without images, waiting for a dream. I was trying to force myself to sleep on the makeshift bed of blankets and clothes, but I couldn't sleep. The room was too cold, the world too quiet. Couchette had begun to pull away, danced down at the Ditty Bar almost every night, either came home with company or didn't come home at all. People didn't come to the Alibi much anymore, the party was dying down. Manny hadn't been around for weeks, not since Holy Mother came back from the hospital. She came back in a wheelchair. It was the first time I'd seen her. I don't know what I saw, but it wasn't a woman. They brought something back from the hospital in a wheelchair with gray flesh shrink-wrapped around sharp, brittle bone. Something with white hair braided down its back, with plastic tubes hooked up to a plastic bag with liquid. The thing smelled sour; Couchette's eyes filled up but none of us went to Lucinda's room . . . to bathe her . . . or hold her hand. None of us. We just withdrew to our rooms, closed our doors. Waited until everything was quiet again.

I lit a seven-day candle and looked up at the tin ceiling encrusted in paint, nothing going through my head except the shape of the tiles—how ugly they were, geometrical patterns swollen in layers of shiny beige paint. I kept looking up, into their grooves, the shadows candlelight made against them—kept looking up into moving shadows, looked down on a city of shapes from a window seat, flying over black velvet embroidered in stars. A thousand stars sewn in geometrics. I saw ground, touched it with my feet, waited for a yellow car to pull up in front of me—felt myself slide across black vinyl.

The driver asked, *Where do you want to go?* I leaned back and let the night streak by over the highways and the exit signs and tree-lined blocks until we'd come to the bright white bowl of Yankee Stadium sitting empty against velvet. I watched the Bronx slant up the straight back of an old mansion at the bottom of Woodycrest, flanked by the art-deco apartment buildings of Jerome—overdressed in pink-and-orange hand-carved ceramic tiles. The car climbed up Ogden; the old wood-framed houses had been replaced by prefabricated exterior brick walls. We drove up Shakespeare, past the Tudor-style apartment complexes of stone and the driver moved slowly because he was afraid of the upward climb but I wasn't. I goaded him. He kept climbing, and we were horizontal—circumspect to the moon.

I held on to my chest, felt it overheating—my heart pounding its way out of its cage. The driver pulled up to a plain six-story apartment building mounted at the top of the hill and asked me again, *Where do you want to go?* I had no idea.

We slid through a room with a woman and music. We slid through the noise of scratched vinyl, through the woman's heavily greased scalp, over her tobacco-stained tongue, down her throat, into her organs—dry and barely functioning. The backseat window was open, and the seasons had become each other; winter was a steam tunnel through which clusters of bodies slid alongside each other groping for a narrow exit; spring sculpted a cool glance of illusions from frosted glass and steel; summer sustained itself in polluted downpours—black ink leaking across the page, making a mess of our scripted intentions. But autumn was a reliable abstraction of intervals, vaguely referencing what you know it to be without inspiring trust. The car sped through this gallery of seasons, a seamless skein of conventions exchanging positions with the grace of a well-blocked ballet, and the citizens we drove past on the hill, the concourse, the edges of the park—citizens of internment—looked to be not so simplistic as to expect anything as clearly defined as a beginning or an ending. The unpredictability of weather plots out a daily realism more pointedly than their expectations enable them to. I lean back for a second, contented to be here in the backseat of something comfortable and disconcerting. We slid down Anderson Avenue, pass the old schoolhouse, all the way back to Jerome Avenue again, and I told my heart that I needed to see the Grand Concourse. I needed to know it was still there, and we swirled past the shiny white bowl sitting empty again, beyond the empty tennis courts loitered with men waiting for strangers. We drove beyond Mullally Park, under the Macomb's Dam Bridge, up to the Grand Concourse where all the buildings with their geometrical tiles and penthouses lived. We were speeding down River Avenue, by the loading docks of the meat-packing warehouses and the dark corners of women waiting for strangers, over the Third Avenue Bridge to the FDR, and my eyes reached out to touch the East River. My heart calmed itself—relieved to see Roosevelt Island was still there, and the haunted hospital still standing in the middle of the river, and the balconies of Sutton Place were still looming over the highway.

Then I looked out over the skyline of all the newly erected buildings, a noble attempt at an overstatement. I looked for the glimmer of their exaggeration, but confidence was just making its way toward pride before it settled down into conceit. The lines of these new buildings—standing up by themselves for the first time—were too new, too sharp, too intentional, too unsure of themselves to be unapologetic for their ostentation. The driver asked me again, *Where do you want to go?* Before I could answer, we were driving through Zuni, to Oaks and Elms, bougainvillea and frangipani, then the yellow car pulled over and I looked up and saw the remnants of a bridge, cut off in the middle. Against black velvet the Brooklyn Bridge was a man with his tongue stuck out, stretching halfway across the river.

A little red boat came toward the pier, docked itself at my feet. *The Geneva.* An old Black Hispanic man with white hair, no teeth, chewed on a cigar, invited me in and took me across the water to dry land, landing at the sloping docks of Brooklyn, manned by men in blue suits with shiny buttons, men in military fatigues carrying assault rifles and flashlights. They flashed their lights in my face, searched my body, allowed me to walk beyond the brick wall laced in razor and wire, into a city. I didn't understand anything about the cracking concrete I had stepped out onto on this side of the river, walking through row after row of quiet, stepping over cassette tapes, old vinyl records, a Bible, books—strewn throughout its neighborhoods. I no longer recognized anything about the embroidery of black velvet and its tiny lights sewn into the landscape so I walked into the recognizance of morning until afternoon became night again. Stood at the edge. Realized something.

On this side of the river all they had was the quiet of vacancy, and the faint kickback of metal in an uproar, sneaking up from the mainland. All they had here was the promise of that distant noise—that and vain expectations of rejoining the world someday.

The front door opens downstairs, slams shut. I sat up because I didn't know who the fuck it could be. I thought (only for a second) maybe it was Couchette—but I'd heard her when she came in about an hour earlier. She'd come upstairs with someone, took him (or her) to her room. The pipes clanged—she'd taken a shower. She was playing music now—Scott's "For Unmarried Girls Before They Wed." I hadn't heard anyone leave. I didn't open my door to look upstairs, not even out of curiosity.

The walking echoed underneath me, through the parlor floor. I heard glass against glass. Somebody was making themselves a drink. The pounding came upstairs to my floor, bypassed Manny's room, came right for mine, paused. The dingy yellow hallway light that shines under my door was shadowed by somebody's feet—then there was a knock—Manny. He kept tapping the door softly with his knuckles, whispered my name until I gave up and opened it.

He was stalled in the doorway with a drink in one hand and a CD in the other. He was laughing as soon as I opened the door—laughing with his eyes looking straight at me, like he saw me through the wood. He held the CD out to me, asked if we could listen to it—just one song. I kind of groaned, told him I was asleep. He shoves the CD at me—*Einstürzende Neubauten*—some abstract shit, this industrial music he had told me about. He said it was the best music he'd heard in forever, said the beats were kinda like Nine Inch Nails, but not. Said it would transcend me if I heard it. I stepped out of the way so he could walk in. Felt obliged. We had this understanding, I should keep his equipment in my room instead of downstairs because anybody could break through the parlor floor window or walk through the front door with the fucked-up lock in the middle of the night and steal the shit. He didn't want to keep it in his room either because he said he couldn't be responsible—left it at that.

You got papers?

Nah.

Manny took a bag of weed out of his sock.

Tzara was a drug addict, did you know that, Racine?

I don't even know who Tzara is.

I put the CD in the laptop, he took his coat off—searched it until he found a Dutch, then threw his coat to the side, sat on the floor under the window Indian style with his drink protected in the open space of his legs.

Manny, you know about Lucinda, right?

What?

She was in the hospital. Everybody was lookin' for you, Chulo, Mawepi, everybody. Mawepi said Holy Mother wanted you to give her a bath. Asked for you.

Where's she at now?

Downstairs in her room, I think. . . .

I'll check on her tomorrow.

You should check on her. She asked for you, man.

If he was upset with himself at all he didn't show it. I sat back down on the bed. There was this faint stink in the room that wasn't there before. I took another look at Manny. He had on a dirty tank top, jeans, Timbs. He didn't look good.

How's Couchette?

What?

Couchette.

Ask her, she's right upstairs.

You and Couchette gettin' on okay?

We all right.

He pulled a razor from his pocket and split the Dutch, emptied some of it, sprinkled the weed in, bopped his head up and down as the room transformed into a machine shop with the sounds of engines and chains rattling—the temperament of metal inflections. Metal was walking through tarp and wallboard tunnels, from plane to curbside to road to pier, through a city with a thousand kind apologies. He hummed a little bit to the sounds, and it dawned on me that I hadn't seen him since the leaves turned. Manny looked up at me, smiled, like he heard what I was about to ask him before I asked it.

Wondering where I've been?
Not really.

He pulled out another little plastic bag from his other sock, crushed little white rocks to dust between his fingers and sprinkled it into the mix of tobacco and weed. He licked the leaves of his Dutch, hand rolled it back together again, searched his pockets and coat for a light, came over to the bed, lit his woolie with the seven-day candle, filled the room with a nauseating sweat, then walked back over to the window, lifted the pane.

She ever tell you she wants to have kids?
Who?
Couchette.
Why?
She can't have any. She tell you that?
If she did or didn't, that's—
She tell you they had to cut her open and take it out?
Take what out?
The baby. It was growing in her ovary or something. They had to take it out. It didn't make it. She never told you that?

He keeps his back to me, holding the woolie between his thumb and pointer fingers, blowing smoke out of the window, but the smoke comes back in on the crest of a weighty breeze, sweeps through the room and makes its way to me. I think maybe I'm still asleep, maybe he didn't say what he just said.

You ever been down to the anchorage?
Only when I go down to the marketplace.
They're rebuilding it. The bridge.
Yeah, I know.
Think they should?
Why not?
Maybe some bridges should never be rebuilt.
?
You ever stand under it, Racine? You ever look up at all the wire ropes, steel cables? There was a tension between those cables, between two stone towers. Neo-Gothic. Only reason the tower on the Brooklyn side didn't fall down is because it's resting on bedrock. The Manhattan side is built on sand. You can't build on sand. Did you know it's got the bodies of the original builders trapped inside? Crazy when you think about it. Doesn't make sense that a bridge like that could just come tumbling down—only half of it sticking out over the river. Defies the laws of gravity, doesn't it? You'd think if a bridge is destroyed between two ends, if its tension is relieved—the basic foundation of everything that held it together would collapse completely. The weight of it would pull everything into the river. How can you rebuild it, if you can't trust the structure?

Manny stood up, leaned against the wall by the window. The laptop was turned toward him, his dark almond eyes caught the blue light and reflected it back in sparks—but something about the face wasn't the same.

They're going to open that club under it in the anchorage and have a big celebration. You going?
I don't know.

*   *   *

Manny sat back down on the edge of the sill—straddled it. His face wasn't a soft olive oval anymore; it was an upside-down triangle shellacked in sweat, dull with the rough edges of an unfinished statue chiseled from stone. The brow wept above the recession of the eyes. The eyes sat at the bottom of two graves gouged into his head; the flesh of his cheeks contracted into hollow space deep below the ridge of bone. His neck was a frail stem balancing a bowling ball. His head was too big for his body. He turned around and stared at me, frowned like he was trying to remember something he'd always meant to ask.

Racine, have you ever just wanted to . . .
Have I ever wanted to what?
Have you ever wanted to just burn everything down, ever just wanted to put an end to all the bullshit?

Before I can answer or even try to understand his question, we turn our attention to a sudden screech coming from the laptop. The room is filling with screeches and a cocktail of nauseating odors: the sweet stench of tobacco, white rocks burning into bitter weed, and now—the decomposition of liver, kidneys, heart—dying organs scattered inside him, waiting for burial.

As usual I don't know what you're talking about.
Yes you do, Racine. Yes you do.

Under the raucous sound of metal, a bass line said something. Metal crashed against metal in a steady pulse. Manny takes another hit, talks through the smoke.

Did you hear about what happened today?
What happened?
On the bus?
Nah.

He's still got that spark in his eye like a boy with a stolen secret, but he's visibly thinner than he was the last time I saw him. His stomach is swollen, protrudes out like a snake's after it's consumed prey larger than itself. He's getting a little too excited. Jittery. Paces back and forth in front of the window, keeps a look out for something . . . or someone.

This kid . . . this kid, he was waiting for the bus, with about two or three other people, downtown in front of the municipal building. The bus came, they got on. Next thing I know, the whole thing went up in flames, right there in the middle of the road.
  Really?
  Yeah. Yeah, I was there.

Metal wheels scrape against train tracks. High voltage over bass lines and drum beats, and in this bit of blue screen light I notice that his hand is bandaged with strips of dirty white cotton stained in blood. There are dark splashes on his Timbs, and he's got some dirt on his face. The sheepskin is smudged with dirt, and now I can smell something else in the room—smoke. Gasoline.

I didn't hear anything about that, Manny. It wasn't even in the papers.
  Like I said, Racine, it ain't over.
  What ain't over?

His tussled black hair is raging—a thousand spindles and dusty ringlets swaying with the backdrop of dry leaves rustling behind him. He hops around to the music, punches the air—rapturous, then suddenly he settles down to an inquisitive calm, leans on the window sill and crosses his ankles, holding the woolie elegantly between pointer and index finger.
  He leaned out the window, his head aiming toward the bridge. Metal clanged against metal. Chants and clanging.
  Manny doesn't say anything. Slides his back down against the wall until he's sitting under the window again. Holds his head in his hands. His eyes are unfocused. He takes another hit of the woolie, another sip of his drink, puts the woolie out in his cup and lights a cigarette. His eyes focus again. He stands up.

*   *   *

Anybody who could get the hell out did. We had to apply for a
pass to get from one borough to the next, had to carry identifica-
tion cards with us at all times—they did that for our security.
Everybody tried to act like everything was all right. I wish you had
been here to see it, Racine. You should have seen the fear. You had
to see it. You couldn't get down the street for all the fear in your
way. They didn't want to admit it, Racine. They just wanted to sit at
sidewalk cafés and sip their cosmopolitans at ease. But they
couldn't, because the M-16s were sixteen-year-old assholes from
trailer parks and housing slums who didn't know any more about
safety than they did about themselves. And they were angry,
Racine—the M-16s. They were so angry and they didn't know why.
Nobody ever told them why they were angry. They didn't know a
damn thing about what they were so angry about, they needed
someone to tell them but they didn't know who to ask, so they just
picked up their guns and pulled their triggers. Shot up everything
that moved. They just snapped. They were walking around with
assault weapons and a license to kill, and they just snapped. All
those people who wanted to sit at their sidewalk cafés and pretend
everything was all right had guns drawn up their noses while they
sipped their cosmopolitans. You were lucky to get out, Racine. You,
me. We were the lucky ones.

You? I thought you said you were here—the whole time.

That was a lie. Everything I tell you is a lie.

I figured.

Don't be so sure I'm not lying right now. Everybody wants to
believe the lie—I'm no different. I believed the lie when they said they
were going to *give the rebel forces* a state. And I believed it when they
said they were going to restrict the settlements in my grandmother's
garden, and the invasion—I didn't think that was going to happen at
all. They said it wouldn't. I believed it. I believed it because I *had* to
believe it—for my grandmother's butchered olive groves. I believed
them when they said they were going to save those holy cities and save
those holy people and mend history and I, man, Racine, I was
wrong. It's easy to be wrong when you *have* to believe a lie.

*   *   *

He came back over to my bed, covered his face. No weeping, just tears and sniffling. I wanted him to get out of my room. I wanted to make him feel better. I wanted to understand him better. I don't hear music anymore, even though it's still playing—my heart—overheating. I'm angry and I'm not sure why. Mad as hell, but I don't feel like I have a good enough reason to be. I'm just mad, that's all, because Manny's trying to get up in my head and whenever somebody does that—just makes me tight. I'm trying not to allow my voice to give away what I'm feeling. I take another cigarette. Can't find matches or a lighter. The candle's gone out. I throw the fuckin' cigarette down on the floor, stamp it out. Manny lights me another one with some matches lying next to the vent, cups his hands around the flame—eyes focused on me, hands it to me—his face too close to mine as he speaks.

I went to Germany once, Racine, shared this flat with a couple of art students. Americans. We shared this flat in an old bomb factory. We didn't know it was a bomb factory. Whenever we'd ask questions—what kind of factory the building used to be, the people in the management office would shrug their shoulders or say it was impossible to know anything about the building because the building was so old. It was all fixed up. They'd fixed it, fixed everything. All white. No color anywhere. Clean white walls, white concrete floors—no visible scars or nails or pipes hanging down. All new. All white. But outside, on the grounds, they'd left all the machinery intact. Outside the building, all around it were machines and former metal shops. Cleaned it all up, like it was all just meant to be metal sculpture. One day I was walking around the grounds—the furnaces, foundries, sheet-metal shops, rolling mills. I got to the old railroad marshalling yard, climbed down into it, walked along the tracks taking pictures when I heard this woman talking in German. I didn't see anybody. Then I heard the machines running—full speed, but nothing was moving. The German woman was still talking.

To who?

She was talking to me, Racine. To me. She got louder over the machinery. She was raising her voice, and then her voice was mine. I was moving my mouth, talking in German. I don't speak German. She was trying to tell me that the building had been used to make bombs for the Nazis. She was trying to tell me she worked there during the war, and she lived in a house in Oberhausen with her family during the war. Her house was bombed by the British allies. The whole town was. She was trying to tell me—she was trying to say that she was sorry. She was sorry for making bombs.

You're crazy, Manny.

I thought, maybe I was. Thought maybe I was doing too much e or maybe I was having a nervous breakdown. I didn't say anything to anybody. I'd just go back to my clean white empty room and try to move on with my life but as soon as I was in that room, the urge would come over me to run—move out of there. I'd pack up, then unpack—pack up again. And each time I decided to stay, the urge to leave would get worse . . . and that's when I realized it was a performance. A repetitive performance of life, death, life, death—there I was, stuck between the walls. So I packed up again, and came back. Came back here. Like you. Same reason. No safe white rooms anywhere.

That wasn't my reason.

We're not so different, Racine. We left for the same reasons, came back for the same reasons.

What's that?

Einstürzende Neubauten had come to a standstill. In the lull, you could hear banging coming from the riverbank, from inside the old wine cellars and storage places of the anchorage. Manny's voice played to an illusion.

Because we left something behind, Racine. Had to retrieve it. We have to stay here. Quarantined. Solitary confinement. We live here, in this building. This building belong to us now. Its botanicals and vacant lot belong to us—and the poison we breathe in our sleep. The privacy of this incarceration belongs to us now. We're willing prisoners, man, and like all prisoners without freedom to look forward to, we hasten our blindness in anticipation of dreams.

The water in the pipes start banging again, then the sound of Couchette's door opens and closes, heavy stomps jogging down the stairs, past my door, down the stairs, to the street. Her footsteps cross my ceiling, the gentle thud of her body falling onto her bed. I can hear her voice through the wall. Praying or crying or something. I wondered if she visits me sometimes the way I visit her, listening to her through the walls between us. I wonder why we stay in separate spaces, in the same house. Wonder when we'll come together. Wonder if we we ever will. Maybe separate space is easier to live in than the bed of intimacy.

I was staring into the face of the laptop, into the swirls of blue, thinking about what Manny told me about the first time he met Lucinda, when she gave him a reading. He said she'd tapped a brass bowl three times, her palms faced forward, said she prayed and told him his ancestors come to save and heal . . . to prepare him . . . told him to offer them candy—make them calm, less they bulwark him, shine a candle in their pathway . . . take baths every night for three days . . . take almond leaves, albahasca, Florida water, chunks of cocoa, and marigolds . . . cut the cocoa in five pieces, take all the leaves and put them in a pot of water . . . add the Florida water . . . mix to body temperature . . . add marigolds . . . pour into bathwater. This will keep you from harm and bring all things good.

I commanded the laptop to shut down. It asked me if I was sure I wanted it to shut down. Yes, I'm sure. The swirls vanished and the icons vanished and the arrow disappeared. The circle rolled around a few times before it went its way and the blue held on a little while longer. I waited in the blue. The blue would make the final exit. Yes, I'm sure I want to shut down. The screen went black. The surface of the case was still warm. I kept my fingers pressed to the surface until it cooled, until me, Manny, and Couchette grow old listening to each other through walls—listening for something we might've said a long time ago, like something we threw away once for no good reason at all.

In the dark of another powerless morning, we walk along the water down toward the marketplace, beyond the old power plant. On these powerless mornings before the sun, the silence hurts your ears. Silence in the dark becomes something other than itself, becomes sound again. If you dare walk outside of your safety zone into morning darkness, you walk through soft moaning and rustling grass, come upon the sound and smell of sweaty flesh, police sirens and conversations blending into distant gunshots. A voice is already at your cheek before you are aware someone is even approaching. No features are distinguishable. The course, from one place to the next—morning or night—is indistinguishable. You travel in blindness until you step into the cushion of a dead cat who has fallen off the edge of the earth, or you walk until a circle of brightness flashes in your eyes. You've come to a crowd gathered on a corner, in front of one of the vendors with an open flame. Initially, maybe, they come to buy something to eat, to cop a cigarette, or to buy some kerosene to survive the remaining days of darkness, but if someone with a hand-held radio has set it down and turned its antennae to music, barriers are broken down over burning grease. Here, people—when they are lit by open fires or candlelight—find their beauty again, like fine oil paintings, all shining in soft pastels and hues of gold. They sing songs without lyrics, speak at a different volume from a different place, as long as darkness is uninterrupted.

This morning's news and game shows blare from handheld TV radios—canned applause and bells. The listeners, gathered on a corner, savor the dull drone of the news anchor or the announcement of a prize, because they are aware that batteries die, and power can remain unrestored for days. There may be no sound at all for a while.

*　　　*　　　*

No power. They applaud when the wheel turns. Guess the answers to questions out loud. How much does the winner get? Maybe the winner gets fresh meat and produce, uncontaminated air, a brand new apartment with indoor plumbing, central heating, a front door that locks, a balcony with a view of the river flowing into forever, a basement fallout shelter fully stocked with a lifelong supply of food and drink. Maybe the winner gets his power back.

With the first light of day or the restoration of power, comes a time for pondering. Men on street corners will ponder the narcissism of men. How narcissism is less apparent in the dark.

Near the marketplace, from block to block, the earth is turned. A thousand square miles of old sewage pipes jut out like rotting teeth and the bluish gray that washes the sky is cut in half with the sharp lines of a crane that dangles over the broken bridge. Bundles of color waddle by us. They are plenteous—these women who pass you with heavy loads balanced on their heads in the dark of morning. Orange, green, ocean-blue *lapas* and saris threaded in gold; lone circles of color trying to beat the sun's first reflection bouncing off the clouds, trying to arrive at some plot of land where they can relieve their necks of the weight they carry, spread open their blankets, and display their wares. If you can *see* them scurrying along, if you can identify the color of their robes, they are already too late to find space in the marketplace.

The marketplace, beneath the remnants of the Manhattan Bridge, runs down along the East River, nestled between the old factories and warehouses, guarded by the towering metal sculptures of the old power plant. By first light it is crowded with women who have long since claimed their seats and prepared their stalls. These fierce merchants arrived sometime in the middle of the night. They have staked their flags into the cobblestone, dressed their thrones of plastic milk crates in mud cloth and heaps of heavy wool blankets. They laugh at the failure of late arrivals in Mandarin, Xosa, Gullah, Spanglish, Ibo and will fight to the death should another nudge too close to them, potentially obstructing a customer's view of their display. These women, who are already planted, descend from centuries of merchants who knew how to sit with their legs wide open, swollen feet exposed to sheets of wind peeling off the water's surface. They come prepared with homemade fans, charcoal and big cast-iron frying pots, newspaper for wrapping, toothpicks for their customers should they need to pick strings of fried pork from between their teeth, ponchos, capes, blankets, extra layers of fabric should it get too cold, umbrellas taped to Christmas tree stands should it rain.

Their merchandise is centered beneath their bellies—today's necessities splayed before you on old rugs: batteries, plastic combs, tap water in recycled bottles of Evian or Poland Springs, canned fruit and vegetables, condoms, fake gold, imitation silver and diamond-cut glass earrings with hypoallergenic posts, flashlights, kerosene, oil lamps, lighting fluid, dolls for your little girls, dolls for your incantations, photocopies of the Koran in old novel jackets, matchbooks and cigarette lighters, a mixed box of cigarettes (Marlboro, Kool, Newport, Sherman's, American Spirit—all sold separately), feminine napkins, boxes of rice, human hair, salted meats, fresh fish—whole or gutted (some of these women have set their blankets on the old pier and cast their lines out into the water, hoping for sea bass or something passable). These women call out to you—a roar of voices, each with their own melody of bargaining—throw their arms out toward you and wave heavy bracelets beckoning you to come see.

A big woman, dark in bright colors, folds her arms across a heavy bosom and rolls her eyes when Couchette asks if she had any Balinese masks, continues her conversation with another merchant in a foreign tongue, says nothing to us at all. She is not as desperate as the others. She sits toward the end of the line where Pearl Street swerves up from under the canopy of the bridge into several blocks of four-story walkups. She and the women, who set their stations along this narrow residential street, are even tougher merchants than the others. They ignore the customer, either control or withhold the tone of their voices when they are annoyed with too many questions. Should any of them lose their temper with a customer or a fellow merchant, they do it with sharp edges and blunt objects. They swing wildly in the air, overturn tables, break jars, hurl bricks. They will fight until someone is naked and torn.

Their husbands sit behind them in the doorways of the build-

ings, playing cards or dominos or just smoking cigarettes on little
foldout chairs. These men are known as the landlords of these
buildings (though it is generally understood the buildings are not
actually *owned* by them). The buildings—short, squat, post–World
War II beige squares—have been in foreclosure for years. These
landlords have simply moved their families into the tenements and
laid claim to a small block of sidewalk out front on which to set up
shop. Landlords do not fish by the pier or help their wives with
merchandise. They do not directly interact with customers. They
do not speak to anyone except the men who sit with them, or their
sons who stand close by. They've been known to kill each other in
order to acquire property more desirable than their own. They've
been known to pay off the M-16s and police officers who come
down to the marketplace when they are bored just to steal some
merchandise or take some food or beat some of the women.
They've been known to have brothers who are working for the military, and nephews who have high-profile positions in city government. They are from many different nations, but they are all very
still, very relaxed, perched on a stool in the doorway of their
buildings, behind their wives.

Visible behind these men, several young girls—about ten to
twelve years old—line the hallway stairs. Should a customer need
change, the sons of these merchants (who are about the same age as
the girls, give or take a few years) act as liaisons between their
fathers, mothers, and the customers. Should a customer need
something else, say an interborough pass, a passport, a green card,
gunpowder, a gun, or an introduction to one of the girls in the hallway, the boys are the ones to talk to. You speak to the boys casually,
they whisper something to their fathers, they come back to you and
collect the money, they return to their fathers, they come back and
escort you through the back entrance of the building into one of the
empty apartments of peeling plaster where you may receive your
merchandise or where one of the stairwell girls—picked from the
bunch who'd been braiding each other's hair, painting each other's
nails, whispering secrets into each other's ears—comes into the
apartment with a blank soft face. She is unaffected. Expressionless.

She has no emotion to show you. No sounds. No matter what you do to her, or ask her to do. She keeps something for herself.

Often, along this row that creeps out from under the shadow of the bridge, you'll see stray little boys (fatherless, motherless, homeless) running from one end of the marketplace to the other, stealing cigarettes, cursing at each other, spitting at the merchant women who chase them away, waving their penises at the girls sitting on the stairwells behind the men who send their sons after them. The girls are only slightly older than the little boys but already too old to reciprocate gestures of infatuation. The girls laugh at the little boys, who are only trying to get their attention. The little boys run in packs, with their beaten pit-bull mongrels that, like the boys, are thin and hungry and free. The dogs and the boys are still quick enough to steal a piece of meat with their teeth and escape into their warehouse hiding places. Occasionally, you'll notice these same little boys retreat into the vacant loading docks or into the darkness of the park, their dogs whimpering behind them. The dogs fall asleep next to their young masters who have parked themselves behind a garbage bin or beneath a tree, waiting for someone who needs them. The boys are smart enough to imitate the stairwell girls (who they love). They'll make no noise. Show no emotion. Keep something for themselves.

In the marketplace, fights are commonplace; a woman fights with her husband over money if she is accused of withholding from him, or if he has taken too much from her stash. In the marketplace, husbands and wives fight with fists and blades and their go-between sons speak harshly to their mothers, just like their fathers. The mothers do no take the disrespect of their teenage sons lightly. If they still can, they'll beat their sons into submission, but more often, they cannot, so they spend the day beating their younger sons, slapping them fiercely until the little boys are scarred and wounded—until they learn not to attempt the language of their fathers or older brothers. The children are still too young to understand the lesson and they are not sure how to obey the command to be silent and dry-eyed at the sudden sting of a slap. The mothers slap them again for the piercing cry that wells up from their tiny throats. Their sons will learn. Their mothers will teach them. They will teach their daughters too. In the

marketplace, mothers and daughters are natural enemies and, occasionally, you'll see these merchant women attempting to strangle their
stairwell daughters over something or the other—a muffled response,
a disrespectful sucking of the teeth. You'll see these mothers catch
hold of the throats of these girls, who are the merchandise of their
fathers, and try to strangle them or mar their faces for life—you'll see
them beat them until their daughters collapse under the final blow or
until the day comes when their daughters grow nails sharp enough to
draw their mother's blood, until the girls have grown legs long
enough to run from their mothers and their fathers and the hallway
stairs, until they learn to rip themselves away and tear across the cobblestone with the boys and the pack of wild dogs clenching something
stolen between their teeth, until these girls have finally grown up
enough to steal from these women what these women have been trying to give them freely all along—an emancipation.

We never found the mask. We searched through their poor tables
of tiny miniatures of the American flag and the Statue of Liberty.
Nothing. Couchette kept trying to describe the mask to the workers
who spoke little English. She tried to explain to them that the mask
looks like a dragon, painted red or green with gold, was supposed to
take on different characters when worn. Ceremonies are held to ded-
icate the masks at midnight in the cemeteries of Bali. Her mother
wrote her about these ceremonies. She kept saying she'd know it
when she saw it. We ran through all the tables of sunglasses, flashlights, jeans hanging from the top of tents, wooden boxes, gas
masks, cheap clocks, fake gold chains, survival kits, Chinese teapots,
feeding her frenetic thirst to make her performance piece into
something more than it was: just another tits and ass show. It's all in
her head, this need to pretend things are more than they are. It's
something I'm starting to learn about her: Everything is elaborate.
Her room, the way she dances—nothing is supposed to be ordinary.
She finally decided to make the mask herself.

As we began to leave the marketplace, I knew Couchette was about
to lapse into one of her long silences. Her head was slightly bowed and
her eyes were shocked open—stunned, as she walked quickly
through the tables, staying slightly ahead of me. This trip wasn't about

masks. It was about mothers. The mother/child conflict is embodied in a war between nations—one, a sovereign government, the other, newly emancipated and still trying to fight its way back to a time before independence. The nature of this war is an eternal psychic argument between creator and offspring. The creator can never be known or equalized, remains clothed in mystery. The emancipated off-spring will not stop fighting until the garments of its creator are ripped to shreds and the creator lays herself bare. Like the stairwell girls who have escaped the marketplace of their mothers, Couchette will run back and forth between freedom and captivity.

As we leave the marketplace, the merchants, their husbands, their sons and daughters—they keep their eyes on us, as if to say, *should anyone approach you, you know nothing about us. You have never encountered us. You do not know where we are from. You have never seen us run in the dark.*

A small square two-story building ensconced on a deserted street—one window covered in old newspaper, a bulb above a battered steel door tinting dark reddish brick harsh yellow. The Ditty Bar was a strip joint, and before that—back in the 60s and 70s—it used to be a butcher shop. It smells of raw meat, blood, pussy. Couchette said before it was a strip bar or a butcher shop it was an army-navy store and sometimes, an old brass button or a green piece of thread would show up under a table. A reminder.

A heavy spiral staircase leads upstairs to a loft space divided into semiprivate rooms; four curtained areas, each area furnished with couches and floor pillows. The speakers nailed on the walls are wired to the system downstairs, so no one escapes the music no matter how bad it is. Girls can invite customers upstairs for a private show if they want to. Costs extra. You pay the bouncer according to time spent: fifteen minutes, half-hour, hour—*before* you go. Prewar law, a private show meant customers keep their clothes on and their hands behind their back, and the girls just do a little dance in front of you. Postwar law, no rules, everybody be fuckin'. Straight-up fuckin'.

Three nights a week Couchette fondles her breasts on their small stage to Mary J. Blige. Three nights a week I spin her a wild concoction of R&B, hip-hop, old soul, or sometimes for the fun of it, hard-core break-beat classics like Leviticus and Rhythm Quest. I bring a backpack of cassettes (no turntables, no CD player). Depending on the night, the Ditty Bar could be packed with leather-jacket-wearing brothers with gold teeth and stocking caps protecting neatly braided hair, or nearly empty with a few old men with potbellies who barely pay attention to the girls swinging from the pole in the center of the room. Their system sounds like shit, but nobody really cares. Couchette loves when I play something unexpected for her, like Sylvester or the Stones. The other girls want straight-up house or

hip-hop shit, no disco, no rock. No matter how much they've made
in tips after they've done their bit rubbin' up against the men in raincoats sitting at the bar (and the young heads who never tip but
always want to take it outside), the girls still hit me off with something by morning.

Couchette breaks down the rules: in the front of the bar, the
girls can only show their titties on stage, have to keep their panties
on by law. Customers cannot touch the girls. In the back room,
behind the velvet curtain, is supposed to be the VIP lounge. Customers are supposed to be invited by the establishment to go in the
back room, but there is no establishment walking around, only a
greasy bouncer and a barmaid. Heads just walk through. In the
VIP lounge they got a stage with a pole on it like up front, and the
girls can get butt-naked if they want to because no drinks are
served back there, only soda, but if you want liquor you have to pay
the six dollars for your soda first, then the barmaid can pour some
liquor in your glass as a gift of the *establishment*. Beyond the back
room they got a narrow dark hallway with black walls that leads to
the men's room where some of the girls give head to customers for
extra tips. The *establishment* has no knowledge of this—not until
it's time to tally up everybody's tips.

Couchette says she's gonna do some performance art shit, the only
way she can make shakin' her ass worth her while, so she's been
choreographing a new dance. Borrowed a sarong, said she was gonna
start the piece off wearing the sarong and end up naked, sitting in a
tub of blue paint. (This dance has something to do with a Rastafarian drummer she was fucking once in Jamaica. They lived in the
parish of St. Andrew, beneath the curve of a dangerous highway
called Junction in a one-room concrete house facing a rapid river.
She said he fed her jackfruit, star apple, and naseberry as they
bathed in the stream that gushed outside their door—taught her traditional dances; Kumina, Bruckins, Dinki Mini. He also taught her
to smoke ganja from a bong, how to grow her own weed, and his
mother—who lived with them, three skinny goats, and four
cousins—gave her instruction on the right herbs to use for a home-

made abortion; black cohosh, quinine, etcetera. She offers this as the explanation for the scar on her stomach. She does not elaborate further. I do not ask questions.)

Couchette said she was gonna throw a little of Bali into the Jamaican mix to pay homage to her mother.

The night we got to the Ditty Bar, things spilling from her shoulder bag: Chinese fans, chalk, I was weighted down carrying cans of blue paint. In the back room girls were rollin' spliffs with the Rastas, gargling Guinness stouts. One of the Rastas was sitting on the floor in the corner, talking in low murmurs to the ugly German chick adjusting herself in the mirror.

Couchette and I rush in, the Rastas greet us with a dry *whassup*, and Couchette asks The Betty Page chick if she remembered to hang the red, blue, and green gels. Betty Page raised an eyebrow, chucked Couchette's sarong on her dressing room table, and curled her mouth into a smirk. Couchette starts yelling at everybody, telling everybody to get out of the room so she can get ready. I tell her to chill and she starts bitchin' at me in front of everybody. First time she does anything like that, just goes off, says I don't know how important this is, how necessary this is, this is what she does, dances, she's an artist and she's trying to make it right, and she needs the drummers to go check the sound, and she needs the German girl to move her shit out of the way so she can get ready. Everyone exits, I slump down in the corner and watch her cover her body with glitter.

Donna Rhea, the Australian pimp who co-ops Couchette's ass, bursts into the dressing room behind her perfume. She has this look like she doesn't want to touch anything, manages to walk from door to destination without brushing up against a single table or a chair. Her face is the complexion of a boiled egg, pulled back and sewn into place behind her ears, and tense gray hair swells into a blond wasp's nest at the crown of her head. Her black sheath dress with its thigh-high split is stretched mercilessly around the sagging pouch of her midsection. Balancing herself poorly in high heels, frosted nail tips thrown into the air, she almost touches Couchette—but doesn't.

*   *   *

Collette!

Cou—

Listen, dahling, have to talk quickly—oy think oy can pull something togetheh for you.

Look, if it's anything like . . . —

No. No. Jean-Claude—

That don't make it better, Donna.

Big big! The bridge. Undah theh bridge! Big big club, dahling! Like things used to be—such a trehgedee, you know, with that bridge being closed all this toyme, but they had this oydea—Jean-Claude and theh city and some of the Choynese buisnessmen—perfect, perfect! Not much else to choose from ef you know what oy mean. They need moy girls, want them on stages—like theh Folie Bergère! Griiiite, veeery special, oy only send moy best gurls. ONLY MOY BEST!

I mean, I'm just telling you . . .—

VERY BIG. First big party in foreveh!

They got security?

Yez, yez, of course.

I'm sayin' . . .

Theh best—doesn't it sound griiite!

How much?

Toyt budget, dahling. Toytah than furst toyme pussy—we'll wok it out—benefit for theh bridge—they're gonna fix it—so griiiite! Lots of toyme constraynts. Theh Choynese buisnessmen—so cheap and so hod to deal with-—can you do it? Under theh bridge?

Sure.

Griiiiiite! A goddess! Do you heah me? A goddess!

Yeah . . .

I clear out of the room to give Couchette some space. This dance was supposed to be her homage to her mother, then she said it was in honor of some tribe of African women she read about who allegedly paint their asses blue and use them as a sign of disdain for the observer. She titled the piece "Weapons of Resistance." Then she said it was about Jamaica and Bali and tribal rituals about the dead and there being a connection. *This is visceral, baby,* she said. *Movement theater. It's kinetic and visual and visceral.*

Sitting at the bar, smoking a cigarette, I wonder what she's ever really had to resist in her life. I order a drink from this fat chick who wears a silver ring in each nipple and one in her navel, but you can barely see the one in her navel because it's creased between two big folds of flesh.

The barmaid asks me stupid shit out of the blue, like do I know what my *source of power is,* and I don't even bother answering her because I don't like riddles. Then she asks me has anything ever happened in my life, *something really unexpected that made me tap into my power source.* I said yeah, meeting her, and she asks me do I know the difference between the *worlds we make for ourselves and the world we're in.*

About seven or eight people at the tables. Only night they'd let Couchette get away with doing something conceptual. Betty Page comes out and joins me at the bar, while the drummers go on stage and start situating the mikes and boom stands and drums, slamming their hands down on the drums to see how sound travels in the room. Betty Page whispers in my ear.

Don't give it too much thought, she's just stressed because this is really important to her, and it's not easy—the Bali thing and all that, you know wha' I mean?

You don't have to check on me.

She told you about her mother, how she died?

Died?

The Jamaicans start drumming and the lights on stage go down. I turn my attention back to Betty Page.

Her mother *used to* live in Bali, came back a few years ago to see Couchette. They weren't really talking. Hadn't talked for years, so her mother came back with the baby. Came to the house unexpectedly. No one was there. She had the baby on her back, thin woman. Chulo, him and his friends were hanging around that

day; he asked her who she was looking for; she said Saeta. Chulo
told her there was no Saeta who lived in the building. Her mother
described her, and Chulo knew then she must've been talking
about Couchette, so he told her she should wait; maybe Couchette
would be home later. He said she had tears in her eyes, started
across the street, turned around, and said, I'm her mother, then
she crossed the street over to the playground with the swings, and
she put the baby down on the ground, and she sat in one of the
tire swings, leaned back, Chulo said. Just leaned back, to hoist
herself into the air but she didn't. Leaning back, with her face
pointed up to the sky . . . the baby playin' in the sandbox, she died,
just like that. Chulo said he heard the baby crying and it looked as
if she were asleep . . . but that was it. She wasn't breathing. And
Couchette, who was just coming home, saw the crowd, paid it no
attention. I was walking up the street at the same time going
home; we both saw the commotion in the park, an ambulance
pulled up, and Chulo said, It's your mother! She looked like, like
she didn't know what he was talking about, and then the sidewalk
rumbled, like a subway passing underground, but there was no
subway.

   ?

The bridge. It came down. That was the day the Manhattan side
came down.

Couchette walks into the light, wearing the mask she made herself,
rotating her hips around in slow circles, and with white chalk scribbles words on the stage around her—identifying herself with each
marking. The light caught the colors in the mask, made them
sparkle like firecrackers. She was brewing something in the teapot,
waving it around her head—the steam trailing behind her. As non-
chalant as the drummers seemed at first, now they're playing their
asses off, summoning the Messiah. They're playing faster but she
counters it by dancing slower, like James Henry Scott and Art Pepper
draggin' out the melody. She lights a cigarette, smokes it while she
does these real slow hip gyrations, each drag of the cigarette a
painful sentence.

Her mouth and eyebrows bend head circles around her neck, hips pulling back, dances like she's all by herself, doing shoulder rolls into the air, walking up a hill, ambling steadily along a narrow path, the motion of her spine sturdy . . . high above a village of bamboo and dried grass, hibiscus, gardenia, a prayer tree, kneels down and tends to her garden; avocado, papaya, mango. Kneels down beside perfect stones of lapis lazuli and black onyx, cups them in her hands, holds them up to the light, weighs them in her palms. Prepares a bowl of fish and rice, a cup of rice wine held up to her lips, rice wine pouring down the sides of her face, and she rises, and she walks, back down the hill, moving. Bare feet— moving down a narrow path, mud splashing upward toward her knees, onto the orange-and-gold cloth pulled between her thighs traveling by the blue and silver light of the moon while the farmers of the Banjar beat their drums, alerting the community of sudden death. She visits the ruins of ancient temples with perfect stones cupped in her palms, red-brown hairless legs—whittled from the bark of the black ash, singing, *Rise Spirit Rise!*

Hidden in the pulsation of beats, Couchette and I are bewitched in the fatherland of drums and peaceful whispers announcing the beginning of a new day, and the color of sun we hear when we close our eyes is a deafening sight of music that makes us reverent. In this blinding quietness, she takes a bath in an aqueduct, copper hair closely cropped, gleaming nipples carved in perfect circles. The countryside—bejeweled with her body, a new gemstone doing the dance of the ancients, expatiating cities, cities across oceans, on a small row of wetland.

I dream a Javanese kingfisher perched on top of a prayer tree, blue wings flapping, reddish orange beak pecking insects from its chest, transmuting, just then, from bird to small girl in cerulean powder and persimmon paint, transmuting to an old woman. She is an old woman in my eyes now, naked and singing gospel songs. The winged thing flies off, and Couchette rotates her hands in circles, puts her fingers in my mouth, papaya fruit, hands and fingers and healing for the journey. I build a world around her, build Bali and farmers and birds and stones and rice wine.

She forgets herself and her questions, just floats off to the *djembe*—dark fingers cracking, soil with ancient blisters. I fondle the neck of my Rolling Rock, lick its opening, let the foam rest on my bottom lip as I watch her and her *djembe* dance to God. This conversation between us, the ancient language of music trapped in vinyl, released by the tips of my fingers, the lips of plucking fingers retreating, the changing of names played out in her body, the transgressions of men long dead foaming up and spilling over the neck of my bottle . . . pulls my way to her soul to see what can be said next.

Engulfed in music, she travels to the center of the floor, and closes her eyes, dances for me.

In the gentle light, her shoulders and back wave texture and shape. A blue bath nakedness. Slim hips and full round buttocks, inner-thigh musculature—the drummers catching the melody of her elegance, her urban black girl body mocking Balinese dance poses, trying to interpret the Legong dances of Ubud. Crude Jamaican and modern dance steps mixed with the poise of the bejeweled Legong dancer, with her head thrown back, in a pool of light, throwing her pussy out into the audience with flair, dead fetuses dropping from between her legs. Nothing need come from inside her body but an interpretive dance or a forgotten song, or some whimsical laugh at just the wrong moment. The bald girl in mask and paint jiggling her tits on stage committed suicide a long time ago. We're both adorned in masks we made ourselves, sitting pretty on our faces, dangling from our extremities, singing hymns from the third row of somebody else's convictions . . . lying to myself. We both committed suicide in our family kitchens . . . a long time ago.

The mask, its looming eyes and big red lips, leaves her face in the carriage of her palms—the ancestral ghost laid to rest. The cloth wrapped around her breasts drops around her feet, her areolas—a second set of eyes. Her nakedness—passé and strikingly unusual. A movie-star pose—except she is drenched in the light of the exotic savage, adapting the Kumina dance, speaking with her arms and legs about Rastafarian lovers, abortion scars above the navel, her mother returning from a rice paddy field, her brand-new baby crying at her feet on the black rubber carpet of a Brooklyn playground—his mother, her mother, dead on a perfect day, across the street from a rotting building.

She lifts the sarong from around her waist, bends over, exhibits her naked ass to the audience, then sits in the tub of blue. Lights fade to black. Couchette sees the irony. She dances irony on a small stage near a navy yard three nights a week.

Frederick, what she looked like?
  Who?
  Our mother.
  I don't remember. I don't care.
  Mr. Eddie say she was red. Said she had hair like us. Curly.
  So what?
  So, I just wonder sometime.
  Cuz you stupid.
  No I'm not.
  Yes you is. Faggot.
  Your mother.
  Your grandpappy.
  You don't never wonder what she looked like?
  No.
  You wanna know what I think she looked like?
  No.
  God.

WHO WAS NAHUM? THE MAN ASKS.

A prophet, the boy answers.

What do we know about him? the man asks.

Nothing. Nothing is known about him.

What does his name mean? the man asks.

His name means consolation, the boy says.

And where is he from?

El . . . el . . .

Elkosh! the man yells, He's from a place called Elkosh.

Elkosh, boy says.

Who was his message to?

His message was to Judah.

Who is Judah?

Judah is us.

What is his message to us?

His message to us is the city will be destroyed.

Why will the city be destroyed?

Because they did not know the true God.

Do not know God, man corrects.

Do not know God, boy repeats.

Who is the true God?

Jesus.

What's God's name?

Jesus?

Who will God destroy?

The city.

Who is in the city? man asks.

Judah?

We are in the city! We are in the city and we will be destroyed, the man yells.

Will God spare our lives? Will God forgive our sins? boy asks.

No, man says, there is no forgiveness, the shield of his mighty men is made red, the chariots will rage the streets and they will be like torches and none shall look back.

Mr. Eddie made us read the book of Nahum again. Always that book. Said we need to read it because it's real important and he was gonna test us about it. Last week he made us stop going to the baptist church over in Windsor because he said nobody is teaching the truth anymore. He went out back to the woods and found him a flat piece of wood, painted it white, and wrote on it with red paint, THE ONLY TRUE AND HOLY CHURCH OF GOD ISRAELITES, and nailed it to the tree out front, so everybody be laughing now when they drive by and see it, say he crazy. Next day, he don't let us stay after school for music class, because he say we gotta come home and read the book of Nahum. Won't let me sing in the school choir. Won't let Frederick study piano. Frederick didn't want to read the Bible all weekend but Mr. Eddie made us. Said we had to learn all about the fall of Ninevah. Mr. Eddie gave us paper and made us stay in our room all weekend and read and write down what we read until we could quote the scriptures out loud by heart. He would come in sometimes, draw somethin' new on the wall and pray out loud. Then he would go sit in the front room for a couple of hours and listen to jazz records, but he kept coming into our room when he thinks it's too quiet, and then he yells at us saying, Can't you see the city is falling?

God almost forgave the city of Ninevah when it repented but because they went back on their word and returned to their wicked ways God had to punish them. That's what God does to backsliders, destroys them. Then he told us God is kind and merciful, and that's when Frederick said, How could God be kind and merciful if he killed a whole city? I wanted Frederick to be quiet, like he always tells me to be when Mr. Eddie is drunk. I know the only reason Frederick is talking back is because he wanted to go swimming down by the quarry and instead, Mr. Eddie made us stay in and read the Bible all weekend long while he draws his pictures on our wall, shapes and things. He's been drawing them on our walls for as long as I can remember. Then he washes our feet in the slop bucket with soap—kneels down in front of us and cries while he's doin' it— crosses our heads with olive oil, then goes back to his jazz records. He don't know we hear him playin' those records in his room. We hear it in our sleep. He don't know. He drinks. We smell it in our sleep.

Frederick getting more and more mad at Mr. Eddie. Said he was tired of the beatings and Frederick even told me he didn't want to be saved. I got scared when Frederick said that. We were under the tree, tying a June bug to a piece of thread and Frederick said right out loud that he didn't care nothing about being saved or seeing heaven or Jesus when he died. He even said he wasn't scared of dying, but not because he believed in Jesus. Frederick said he didn't want to see Jesus. I asked him, Then why you not scared? He said *cause there ain't nothing to be scared of. A whole lotta people already done it (died) and I ain't scared to do nothing a whole lotta people already done.* I didn't say nothing else, just watch him tie the June bug to the string and twirl it around, laughing out loud—wavin' his fists around when the bug fly away. Watch him throw the rocks in the quarry, and I start to wonder to myself—will Frederick see Jesus when he die even if he don't believe Jesus is there? Or will he see whatever he wanna see, go wherever he wanna go when he die? Either way, I know he don't wanna be here, livin' with Mr. Eddie. I know he'd rather be anywhere else, even Satan's kitchen, than be here. Frederick say I'm stupid for trying to be saved like Mr. Eddie teach us to be, because then one day I'm gonna be like Mr. Eddie and backslide and then Mr. Eddie's God is gonna destroy me like he did Egypt and all them other cities.

Mr. Eddie says if we don't speak in tongues then we don't have the Holy Ghost and we're going to hell. Frederick hates that kind of talk. Hates that we can't watch TV, can't read no comic books—Mr. Eddie says superheroes are the devil's imps. Can't have no girlfriend before marriage—can't listen to music (unless Mr. Eddie play jazz) and girlfriends lead to fornication. Says our mother was a fornicator.

That's how come she was crazy. That's how come she dead now. Say
her mama was too. Say her mama not Emma. Say that's a lie. Say we
ain't no kin to him. Say, even Emma, she didn't want to serve the
true and living God. Everybody who say they are of God ain't. Bap-
tists are going to hell because they don't baptize in Jesus' name and
they don't speak in tongues, and the Church of God in Christ and
the Church of Christ and the Church of God, they all going to hell
too because they speak in tongues but they don't baptize in Jesus'
name either, and the Catholic church is the great whore of Babylon
and the Jewish people aren't the real children of Israel because they
aren't really descended from the tribes of Israel, they're all just Euro-
peans who don't accept Jesus as the Messiah, they only have one
part of the covenant, and the Sabbath keepers are the true children
of Israel, because they keep holy on all the sacred holy days and eat
kosher, don't chew the cud or eat anything that splitteth the hoof,
and they speak in tongues and they baptize in Jesus' name. That's
what we supposed to be. The children of Israel. We can't have no
friends. We can't even have friends over to spend the night, and we
not allowed to sleep over nobody else's house either. We can't have
no Christmas tree, because it's sin, and we can't celebrate Easter
with no eggs because it's unholy. He always makes me and Frederick
wear white shirts and black pants. No jeans or sneakers. Frederick
keeps his blue-suede Pumas in a secret place, says he's tired of all of
this shit.

Sometime Mr. Eddie send us out across the railroad to get him
somethin' from the market or send us over to Miss Mamie's house
across the ditch because he say she need yard work done and she
tell me and Frederick stuff about him. She sit up there, dip her
snuff, tell us how she prayin' for us and how she knew Eddie and
his sister Emma when they was all kids and she met our mother
couple of times and she remembered when Emma died and Mr.
Eddie come back down here to Zuni from up in New York and bury
his sister and closed up this house and take our mother to the
county because she was a minor, and she was crazy—and next
thing she know, years later, Eddie come back for Geneva. Say
Geneva went up there in New York and had us, died in some kinda

fire. Say we favor our mother, but she say Mr. Eddie ain't lyin'
when he say she was a little crazy 'cause she never did talk much
or nothin' but she didn't know her all that well and she say she
don't think Geneva was none of Emma's daughter no way but she
say don't say nuthin' because she don't know nuthin' about it. She
told us everybody know Emma was good friends with this woman
who was whorin' all over and she had a baby and died, Emma deliv-
ered it—say everybody know Emma raised that woman's child
after she died. She say don't pay Eddie and his religion no mind
'cause he made it up his self and that's why he crazy, but she says
he done seen some things in his life and never was too right after
the war . . . say one thing she always respected about Emma was
she ain't take nuthin' from nobody, was built like a man and she
didn't go to nobody's church and even if folk didn't understand her
she had her own way of believin' and then Miss Mamie was quiet
and she say maybe religion is what mess everybody up.

I seen Frederick smoke a cigarette before. He hide the money
Miss Mamie give us for working in her yard and he bought a pack of
cigarettes and a bag of chips in town. Then he smoked a few of them
down by the quarry. He says one day he gonna leave here, and go to
Hollywood and make it big as a DJ, like Grandmaster Flash, he say.
Or Lee "Scratch" Perry. He be listenin' to music. Go to his friends
house, they play him music. I tell him, say, music supposed to glorify
God. He say fuck that.

We're not supposed to read no books except our schoolbooks
and the Bible, because it's sin. I keep some books in the floorboards of my room. I got this one book. It's old with a red cover
and some of the pages ripped out. I took it. I prayed God forgive
me. I read the stories when Mr. Eddie is asleep or when I'm over at
the quarry. About the Trojan War and the Argive armies, and how
King Theseus—when he was only seven, slayed a lion and when he
reached adolescence—he learned the secret of his birth, and he
was so strong he killed all the monsters and beasts in his way.
Sciron. Cercyon. And he was purified of all of his murders. He was
forgiven at the River Cephissus. The way the stories sound is like
when Mr. Eddie talk about his sister or his Mama Lilly. Sound

made up. He say she descended from pirates, said she wore the treasures of ancient shipwrecks around her neck, a holy virgin, he said . . . she never knew a man, never . . . said she was dancing on the shores, dancing barefoot on the water, pulling up the scattered bones of Pirates and the remnants of great ships from the ocean floor. Say up came two big shells. She opened the first one, and in it was the seed of a girl. Emma. Opened up the second one and it was Eddie and . . . she raised them in the sun . . . gave them Jesus and room for redemption . . . promised to never let them outta her sight, but he said Lilly was like Elijah—God just sucked her up in his mouth one day. She didn't die, he said. God just sucked her up. Frederick say to me when we go to bed, Do you believe that, Racine? I say why not? He curse and turn over, go to sleep.

One time, we was at the quarry, and Frederick had got himself a cigarette. The skinny kind, smell bad. I never seen one before, but he say he got it from Pie who got it from his big brother, Li'l Junior. It wasn't like the regular kind they be sneaking. It was skinny. Smell bad. That's why you goin' to hell I told him. I told him I was gonna tell that he was doing drugs. I wasn't really. I just get scared because I know it's better to try and help save his soul than to ignore his soul. I started runnin' down the hill and he chase after me, catch me with his left hand and hook his arm under my neck till we both roll down the hill with him on my back. He hit me good a couple of times, till I was bleedin' a little from my lip, then he sat on top my stomach, laugh because he know I can't get up and he pulled out his ol' drug cigarette from his pocket and light it up. He choke a little on the smoke from the drug cigarette and then Frederick say,

Racine, you ever hear the one about niggas in heaven? Well, God had decided all the niggas could go to heaven when they die, so all the niggas came and got comfortable. Then Gabriel call up to God and ask his secretary could he please speak to Him because he was havin' problems. Well, God get on the phone—say What's the matter Gabriel? Gabriel say, Lord, I know you a merciful God, but these niggas are over here in heaven and I'm havin' a hell of a time! God

*say, What's wrong? Gabriel say, them niggas done pulled the gold up
off the streets and they puttin' it in they ears and nose. Then they
snatch the pearls off the gates and start to sell 'em to the devil's imps
for a profit. Just last night, I was blowin' my horn, practicin' my
playin' and all, and them niggers knocked me down and took it from
me and start to playin' all kinds of crazy music, clappin' they hands
off-time, all loud, crawlin' on the floor doin' snake dances, foot
stompin', spinnin' on they heads and wakin' the dead, even passed
around the hat for contributions! Now Lord, I could almost deal with
alla this . . . I got patience, like you gave me, but the angels who
make the robes are startin' to complain because they can't fit the
halos around them big ol' afros, and braids and Jheri curls and
weaves all them niggas got, some of them niggas done took to
wearin' the halos in they ears and around they necks, snatchin' halos
left and right, resellin' 'em . . . and the white robes, Lord they done
altered all the white robes, make up they own styles, shorten 'em and
slit 'em up the side, take 'em in so they be too tight around they fat
asses . . . God say, O.K. Gabriel, I hate to do it, but send the niggers
to hell. Gabriel say I thank you Lord, and he evict all the niggas from
heaven. A few days later, The Devil call God up. God answered the
phone, because his secretary had also been sent to hell with this
nigga who was her baby father (God forgave her for that) but her
baby father had convinced her to steal him some office supplies . . .
so she had to go. But that's another story. Anyway, God say, What you
want, Devil? Devil say, God, you know I wouldn't call you if I didn't
have to . . . and I never thought I'd say this, but you got to get these
niggas outta here. God say, What's the problem? Devil say, These niggas down here complain all winter long talkin' 'bout turn up the
heat, and now that it's summertime, these niggas trying to put out my
fire!*

Frederick fall off my stomach, laughin' so hard he's chokin' on
his own spit. His eyes are all red, he look like the devil himself. He
kept laughin', and I know he's messed up from the drug cigarettes.
I start to cryin'. When I get nervous I cry, and usually he whoop
me some more if I cry in front of him or after Mr. Eddie beat us,

but this time I tell him, You goin' to hell, Frederick. You sure to wind up in hell. He stop laughing, and say, *Don't you get it, Racine? Ain't no use in you always trying to pray my soul into heaven, cuz I just don't belong there. And hell ain't gonna be too happy to see my black ass neither! Niggas like us ain't got no home of they own.*

In the Twilight
of Alchemy

In that moment I lost completely the illusion of
   time and space.
The world unfurled its drama simultaneously
   along a meridian which had no axis.

—HENRY MILLER, *Tropic of Cancer*

Men in helmets dip their shovels in vats of steaming black tar, smoothing over streams of tiny black granules—paving over what lies beneath. Freshly laid asphalt spanned miles of even travel—it steamed hot and settled in, cooled slowly, covered nothing. Wherever bloodstains had soaked into the gravel, new ground had been laid. Beneath it, tunnels had been hollowed for restored subway lines long collapsed. The city made plans to restore mobility, and some of the buildings in the neighborhood were under reconstruction. Scaffolds were built around several old brownstones, veiled in a black net. Men chipped away at the cracked exterior walls, until it was stripped of its first layer of skin, then buttered these walls with globs of red-dish brown until it was smooth and flat. Transom bars, Byzantine capitals, iron crestings, lay on the curb—trashed.

Three or four houses in a row were worked on at a time, gutted of their interiors, oversized wooden multipaned windows replaced with standard metal one-over-one frames, smaller doors replaced large ones, floor-throughs divided into studio apartments, Victorian facades made to look like flat boxes. The city saw the value in these old structures, for rental housing, and there were people who had just stepped back out into the light of day—who would pay market rate. It was a slow, gradual process, but it came quickly.

Houses such as ours remained untouched . . . sleepy, dying, proud of their youth. From the parlor-floor window draped in velvet, I can see men across the street, stationed under the dead live oak, looking up at this house—men in dark leather jackets, creased trousers, their legs astride, one hand in their pants pocket, the other drawing numbers in the air, calculating the cost of cheap intentions.

DJ Shadow's "Midnight in a Perfect World" pulls itself through the crowd of homeboys with gold teeth and stocking caps stretched over perfect rows of braids. They aren't feelin' Shadow and me.

Shadow's music comes up from down the way, blowing fast and catching hold to skin. Starts in the stomach, kindles up to the throat. I throw Couchette's voice into the mix. Soft moans and sighs. Across the room, she's standing still, looking directly at me, rivers dammed up at her lids. Violation. She walks over to me. Stands there.

You know what?
What?
Let's just . . .
What?
Nothing . . . I mean . . . whatever forget it.
What?
Nothing.
What?

She's looking for landmarks of disaster. Running them through her head, trying to find cause for blame. Blame is a permanent resident in her body, constantly entertaining emptiness. Everywhere there is the opportunity, blame brings emptiness and disappointment home, furnishes all of her vacant corners. I'm all that's in front of her now, a fresh space—a new corner in which she can relieve herself. There's nowhere else to strike, no other malfunctioning machine to kick. I lay low, stay in the music, lay sitar over violin, submerge them in samples of wind, tree, sky, and rain. I sample the sound of hammering and drilling outside the window, the soft rumbling of the men across the street drawing numbers in the air. Music. In music there is no province of imperialism. No wrong, no right. In music and wordlessness, four thousand years of memory.

She fidgets again, begins to open her mouth again but doesn't, then she retreats again, not to the other side of the room but to the other side of something that misspells us. What we were becoming. It was never possible. We both know that. We don't have to say it. The music pulls a comforter of violins over our heads, refractions of distance—the sitar line leaps into a purgatory of repetitions, but the sounds they make don't make complete sentences. Not until I pull

her father's keys into the mix will the whole thing become a mono-
logue washed over in a tide of dissonance. We'd be stirred back into
a moment before now, when we were in her room listening to her
father play—when the keys stopped. In their absence, we remembered them. But it's too dangerous to do that now, pull her father's
keys into the mix. I want to stop the disc from spinning now. I want
to hear her speak now. Strings and sitar make a weak substitute for
halted piano, and music is not a substitute for language at all. She
turns away, pauses at the window, sets her sight on the men standing
across the street, looking up at the building.

Wrecking ball comin' soon.

Play it.

She finds a tape stored away in an old box, sits down, stares at it . . . hands it to me.

The B side. It's a session tape, a radio interview my father did about one year before he died.

We listen to Scott talk as we collaborate on pasta and roasted vegetables, herb tea with bits of fruit sinking to the bottom of our cups, no words exchanged between us as she stares at me. Just stares. He sounds gruff yet sophisticated. Not at all what I expected. He talks about the *death of the scene*. She is listening to a man talk from the grave. Scott is a man, lamenting the death of a day. We are a family. We've spent weeks not having anything to say to each other—unless we are in the company of others, and then it's like a performance. The words are scripted. There was a turning point. A point when honesty and intimacy clashed. She said I had no interests. No ambition. She'd never met anybody who seemed to wander through life as aimlessly as I did. As if all I needed was my records. She couldn't understand why the only time I really had anything to say was when she engaged me in some discussion about music, and then I came alive, like how most guys would do about football or basketball—with me it was always music or questions about Scott and not much else. I said I loved music. It's not that deep. She said she didn't think I loved music. I hid in music. If I loved it I'd want to make some of my own, or turn it into a career again—take it to the next level—and I said, I tried that. Did that. But when I made music, when I put sounds together, things would happen . . . open up. Things I wanted to close down. She asked what things. I didn't answer.

You don't hear truth in music, Racine.

How you know what I hear?

I listen to you . . . you're inventing something. I don't know what, but you're making something up.

Like you?

No . . . not like me. I hear truth in music. I hear things as they are.

The tape is finished. I play Don Byron's breathing—long harmonies over a whistling flute. Couchette lifts up her shirt, pulls it over her head, and throws it to the side. The scar below her navel is thick with darts on either side like a caterpillar snaking down into a triangle of hair. She waits for me to say something. The kick and snare of the drum make short, emotional statements—hits—stomps—exaggerated sighs and rolls while the piano keeps a steady melody going to travel by. She pulls a robe around her, draws the curtain on her scar. I think Jerome Harris is playing bass, but I'm not sure so I check the liner notes. I want to get to the point she's at—like old jazz heads, where you can listen to the music and know instinctively who's playing what instrument. Call them out by name. It's kind of outdated—but when we listen to her jazz records, she just calls out names, like how she says you can tell that David Murray is more influenced by Lester Young than Archie Shepp, even though Murray is from the new school but he's got that old-school way of playing so it hits you in the heart—like Young, and Shepp's got tone but she says Albert Ayler can't play sax for shit. Couchette finds a dusty paperback book of poetry by Audre Lorde hidden in the back of her nightstand's drawer and flips through the pages.

What happened to you?
What?
I want to know . . .
What?
Your body. Were you born that way?

It *is* Jerome Harris on bass. And now, there is something unsafe beginning between us. Unsafe slippery moment when relationships become too familiar and words are not spent cautiously, when too much time has been spent in each other's company and there is nothing left to discover in the safety of polite conversation or good sex or hand-holding or music. Now words have become sharp objects tearing away at top layers of flesh—until blood is drawn and bone is exposed—then words hack away at bone and this is all you have to look forward to.

I turn Byron off, clear my throat, stand up and pull my fatigues from out my ass—head toward the door. Betrayal. She recites Audre Lorde to my back . . .

> *What do we want from each other*
> *After we have told our stories*
> *Do we want*
> *To be healed do we want*
> *Mossy quiet stealing over our scars*
> *Do we want the powerful unfrightening sister*
> *Who will make the pain go away . . .*

At the landing on the top floor above, morning light and rain trickle through a large gaping hole in the roof, and the old, rusting cast-iron ladder bolted against the wall, points to the closed hatch. The ceiling is open. The walls are waiting to be climbed . . .

The abandoned bridge has robbed us of company. Manny's been back for about a week, brings storybook characters with him, from somewhere. This guy with a heavy beard and afro argues with this skinny kid about their pool game, and the bearded guy smells musty, wears horn-rimmed glasses and jeans, has a potbelly. He requested The Cardigans, I looked at him like he was crazy and he went back to the pool game, bent over the table with his butt cleavage lit by the overhead lamp hanging low. Had a slow gentle aim but hit sharp enough to tap the eight ball into the corner pocket, next thing I know the skinny kid is yellin' at him and they get loud, they push each other a little bit, turn red in the face, both of 'em got eyes like they're not sure they want to get into this . . . not sure who'll win. Who'll get hurt in the end, but their reticence is betrayed by the adrenaline heaving through their chests, and the guy with the beard falls, gets all tangled up in the Christmas lights, jumps up, swings a pool stick at the skinny guy, catches him in the mouth—right against his teeth, with a loud crack. They're both sloppy fighters. The bearded guy is awkward, no coordination, the skinny guy's face blushes red, embarrassed by his rage.

Mawepi's not here. Mawepi spends every hour she can with Lucinda. Keeps vigil over a decaying body in a white room. I know those rooms. They smell of dissolve, lack confidence.

The two guys slow down, shirts pulled over their necks, bent down, heads butting up against each other, they hold on to a collar, a sleeve, until they're weak, and calm. Release each other, breathing heavily, stagger out. I got Jay-Z, brash . . . shallow . . . combative . . . certain. I spin vinyl. Spin it for Manny's can-can girls; Sly Stone with pink dreadlocks, Nefertiti slumming alongside Harriet Tubman's layered skirts, Brooklyn gang members sporting black-orchid nail polish, Roman slippers, and names like Moon Goddess, Queen, Imhotep, Sapodilla, Pyramid, Tree,

Truth, What-Not. People he picked up in bars, from under the bridge, in the park, from wherever, all these people show up with him, looking for adventure. It's a real different crowd from before. I'm not sure if the sad-looking characters that used to be regulars at the Alibi have vanished from the face of the earth or if they've transformed into these Sandals and Wraps—but I know people are trying to come back to themselves with strange and spontaneous rituals.

Couchette finally comes in on Ely Guerra's "De La Calle" . . . walks over to the bar, leans against it. She's got these turquoise earrings that dip down her neck, this weary expression, sleepy eyes, allows herself a moment to let Ely Guerra lick her where she hurts before she tends the bar, dipping glasses in a sink of sudsy water, ripping open plastic packages of plastic cups, drawing her ear in close to the mouth of a stranger, listening to requests, accepting, rejecting . . . always the whore . . . then the square sheet of paper dissolving, and she's got these weary eyes . . . dreamy eyes . . . that want to sleep . . . and dream . . . eyes that want to find a bed for dreaming . . .

Manny runs up to his room, comes back down—distributes sheets of paper, cans of paint, ecstasy, tells me to play something dangerous. Couchette and I glance at each other from opposite sides of the room, but we don't say anything. The storybook characters finger-paint on the walls and the floor, raid the bar. I can't figure out what music to play. I'm not sure what's going on. Manny asks me to help him with the dollhouse. He wants to bring it downstairs.

For what?
The crystal ball, man.

We carry his dollhouse downstairs; it's almost complete. Manny bugs me for some kind of contribution. I don't have one. We set the thing in the center of the room; I go back to the crate of vinyl—find Serge Gainsbourg, and his African drummers. Serge's Africans start soft, patting the rim with the edge of the hands. Sly Stone throws a bracelet in, Harriet Tubman lifts her long brown skirt and shimmies out of her panties . . . red lace—chucks them onto the roof of the little house. Hands clap, applaud, heads chuck back, chasing ecstacy with gin and vodka. Gainsbourg conducts his chorus of African drummers from the turntables, kidskin and copper bell, broom, brush, sweep, and Couchette gets caught up. She throws her glance over to me, I keep my head down, she looks up toward the stairs, runs her hands along split plaster. The skinny South-African kid rips his Bretenbach poems to shreds, throws the pages in one at a time. Manny's standing on the pool table with bare feet jumping around like a monkey, mocking the drums. The Egyptian princess climbs up, penetrates his mouth with her tongue. Clack of totemic tom-toms, ancient feet, blistering, cracking dry across calfskin, steady pulse of drumming. Manny takes her, turns her around, grips her between her legs from behind, drives it up and spreads his fingers out across her midsection, gropes until he finds the zipper's pull beneath the fold on her jeans, tugs and pulls at it until it slides down easily. They're facing the savages. The savages are dancing and applauding, the totemic tom-toms play.

A Rasta cuts a piece of his hair off with a pocketknife, square, flat mesh thrown onto the miniature. Chulo pulls off his baseball cap, chucks it into the house, climbs up on the table, rests his knees on the edge, and puts his face to the Egyptian princess's crotch, pulls her jeans down to her knees, buries his face in the thick black hedge of hair. She's dark, big round belly with a protruding navel. Manny's standing behind her, holding her chin in his hand, pulling her neck, turning her head behind her to swallow the rest of her face. Her T-shirt of pyramids is caught up around her hips, wide, dark, fleshy, loose, and Chulo pulls her legs apart. She's standing astride on top of the pool table, the bulb hanging above her almost touching the black pencil line she has drawn across her lids, out toward her ears. Chulo's got his shoulders between her legs, her knees buckle, he's kneading the doughy flesh of her ass, spreading it out, Manny grinding behind her, the pink part of her inner flesh showing through a lawn of glistening foliage. I'm watching, spinning black vinyl, Serge Gainsbourg's Africans slamming into the Sandals and Wraps, high on e, gathered around the pool table, clapping and dancing. Some of them chuck a lipstick, a bullet, a driver's license, a passport, pour vodka into the hole of the house.

Couchette's face is wet again, she's backed away from the bar, backs herself past me toward the stairs, keeps a steady eye on me. The green eyes of a man are at my side. He's saying something into my ear. I turn toward his mouth, he's mumbling words . . . I can't hear them. I know his face. I look back to Couchette, the green-eyed man has my face in his hands but I turn to Couchette, she's at the base of the stairs, leaning against the wall. The green-eyed man is saying something into my mouth. I can't hear him over the Egyptian princess's groaning, Chulo's slurping. Manny's got his hand between Chulo's legs, squeezing around, finding the shape, gripping it. The Sandals and Wraps dance to Serge Gainsbourg's drums. I look into the green-eyed man's mouth . . . into his mouth, his tongue and lips and teeth make movement. Manny's high out of his mind, laughing, I don't know who to trust in the room. I'm not sure what the green-eyed man is saying to me. I can't hear him. The Sandals and Wraps turn to me; the vinyl stops. What does everybody know?

Couchette lights a cigarette, the scratch of the match against the board pops. Manny has a half-cocked smile. A roll of toilet paper from the bar unravels around my fingers, like a bandage stained in blood; it rips into a wad of softness in my grip, dissolves as it soaks in a cup of vodka. Everyone waits for me to do something with it—to make a sacrifice. I fashion a man, a boy, deposit them in the hole of the dollhouse, stand them up on the top floor. The knuckle of my thumb cracks as it pulls down on my lighter's grated metal wheel. The flame reaches the tip of my thumb. I lower the light through the ceiling of the paper mansion, onto the little vodka-soaked men. Couchette yells out. The flame catches hold of black velvet curtains. The Sandals and Wraps try to stomp out the flames; the flames catch onto paper and cardboard, melting tissue figurines into a meaningless globe of fire and smoke. Manny laughs.

Good one!

What happened to you tonight?
  What?
  You're trembling.
  No I'm not.
  Who were you talking to, Racine?
  Who?
  Earlier.
  I don't know.
  You don't know?
  Nah.
  But you were talking—as if somebody was there.
  'Bout what?
  How would I know?
    . . .
  I'm pregnant, Racine.
  ?
  I'm gonna have a baby.
    . . .
  Don't worry. I have to do this—by myself.

Her *Muerto* came down, slipped beneath the mask of the old woman, made itself comfortable in her cheeks. The loose skin of her brow tightened around the spirit that swelled beneath her pores, its elegy grumbled up from her throat through reverberating acoustics.

The van spun around the corner, stealing the corpse away from its candles and statues of saints and overstuffed chairs and cloth dolls and tarot cards and paintings of Jesus. I watched them carry the Holy Mother out of the house; I hid behind the walls from death and renovation—watched them carry a white sheet wrapped around death. The van charged away with Holy Mother in its stomach, and I waited for her to speak, to tell them they had forgotten her statue of a yellow woman guarding the entrance, one rock, and some cowry shells at its feet, forgot to collect the statues of angels with armor and spade, handmade quilts and dolls, her lime green walls adorned with murals and posters of saints, her plastic beads: peach, turquoise, jade and yellow incadescence hanging from the ceiling. They forgot to take the two huge front windows covered in velvet, her seven-day candles, her shelves and tables, her stool and the plain wooden chair in front of the altar, her brass bowl.

Mawepi called out to the back of the van, called Mother by her name, and all the neighborhood watched from their windows. All the neighborhood hid behind walls, and listened to Mawepi scream *Mi Esposa! Mi Madre! Mi Santa!* Blessed *Santa Lucinda!*

The world had no words for Holy Mothers . . . no kind reply, we couldn't *hear* the cache of translated scriptures rotting in our heads like a benign cancer, frightening us into neutrality. The world resigned itself to disbelief. The world did not believe in women who girded themselves and watched the ground open up. She saw it shift and fidget. She saw it quake beneath her steps, and she braced herself.

She saw it coming before it came, the catastrophe of years. This calamity the world struggles to resolve. She saw the incredulity on our faces, saw our eyes, as they are now, watching her corpse carried up a street of abandoned buildings, denying we bore witness to death. She knew us, and from whom we were descended . . . She spoke to the corpses beneath the asphalt as she was carted through, waved at generations of immigrants who had died on these grounds. Those new pilgrims, asleep beneath the surface who had claimed this land with a new language in dialects of bebop, slavery, polarization, Marxism, and free form. The chroniclers who came here, scripting their existence in Spanglish idioms and jazz colloquialisms. Those crude and tragic, brilliant scholars of pre-American survival and postwar mobility, those workers and schemers and Saturday night soothsayers, experimental and improvisational in skill. The corpse of Lucinda spoke to the poets, musicians, singers, filmmakers, political activists, college students, crapshooters, numbers runners, third-generation welfare mothers, actors, lesbians, bluesmakers, Middle Eastern grocers, all those who came here once with black coffee, cigarettes, and fierce discourse— erecting their golden calfs on handball courts, building their mansions in single-room flats . . . moving from one side of the street to the next with fever charging forward . . . tearing down, building up, those who came screaming from the corners with rebellion and malaise. There was born an epidemic of questioning and reinvention in the minds of those first, second, third generation American-born Latinos, Russian Jews, Irish, Coloreds—the vanishing tribes of immigrants who held fast to their statues and holy days, planted their dreams of liberty in secret places. She had been one of them. She did not speak the language of the new land, refused to learn it, pretended she had a deaf ear to its vowels . . . so the world could learn the language *she* was speaking. A polyglot of way making. She shared this talk with the bodies beneath, waved at them as her body was carted through, saw the children of the dead in our windows, staring at a van that held her corpse . . . a woman in a blue suit trailing behind with tears and mourning. Holy Mother spoke in that vernacular we were too young to understand—quietly. Conversations with the dead, the Dutch farmers, and German industrialists, the Negro laborers, Italian butchers, and Korean fruit market vendors, Puerto Rican stillbirths, aborted fetuses, AIDS victims, those bodies who once lived in these houses, those bodies who have pressed themselves into the side-walks . . . for so long, they have been the ground we walk on. They show themselves again . . . not to us. To her. These immigrants who had lived in these houses years before us, they sit up in their graves and show themselves, allow the wave of Holy Mother's passing to fan their faces.

Mawepi slowed her pace as the van turned the corner. Turned around to see how far she had come. Craned her neck to see who, if anybody, shared her grief. No one put a hand to her back when she came back inside the house, retrieved the broken statues and empty bowls scattered in the hall, trampled on by blue men with shiny but-tons. She held them in her arms and sat down on the front stoop, then she stood up . . . and walked away. No bop, no swagger. Just walked, down the street. Walked . . . away. For good. The rest of us, we slowly stepped back out onto the street, from behind our doors and windows. Filled the street, revealed ourselves to each other, emerging from our wrecked buildings. We came down the stairs, out of our rooms, from beneath the floorboards, stood on the rock-faced stone stoops of Italianate/neo-Greco row houses, leaned against iron fences with arrow rails, sat on porches of fluted Doric columns sup-porting segmental arches, leaned out of full-height bay windows with stained-glass transoms—and watched the exhausted blue suit falter up the middle of a narrow black street. We watched—motionless, stood there watching men come to us with tape measures and pencils tucked behind their ears . . . staring at our brick facades . . . planning their rituals of deconstruction. The mother of all mothers is dead.

There are things I recall . . . small moments from before my life . . . sharp images that pierce into the side of my head sending shots up the back of my neck. There are things I know from small moments in time . . . memories I would like to explain to somebody. Her. But I don't have language concise enough to explain my body. That my body is not my own. It is an unfamiliar territory, and there are unfamiliar moments where the someone I am becomes someone else. Performs other lives.

Lilly, Emma, Geneva. I know them. In my body. At any given time, always, they seep from my skin . . . and then the air is free . . . all around me . . . her . . . the her I become. The air is free, all around her except where she strains to pull it in. She makes heavy, short hollers from my throat, and her arms wreak havoc at the wind as my body falls down. Her body has become old with regret, and longing, and the hills of Zuni are brutal twists and turns of nothing. The leaves and flowers breathe dust into my eyes and up her nostrils until the air is tight again. Her chest is tight again, and the tiny room of her tiny house turns itself upside down, and my voice, tobacco husky old, calls out for somebody, anybody, but nobody is here, like my voice is not here, and time spends itself guardedly as she turns her face to the morning and darkness clears for a bird that swarms down over her garden and swoops into her house, spins up, and flips itself through the open air strangling around her body as it lay heaving on the floor . . . the third eye of Geneva's heart becomes an incubus to coral reefs and mudflats. My mother's body leaps from a small boat parked near blond sandbanks. Her body falls down, and in the process of falling, lands itself in another body, the lanky body of Emma descending beneath a glassy azure floor. Down, toward coral archways, in the company of sea urchins, snappers, and razor fish. A little girl's body, falling and welcomed in an underwater garden of efflorescent colors and strange perennials. Unusual blossoms, like herself, and the salmon house she lived in with its chrysanthemum garden so handsomely groomed. Poor, but beautiful. A young girl's body diving toward the ocean's floor, trying to inhale the scent of its blossoms without taking in water, imagining the perfume of sea blossoms to smell like her mother's neck when it was doused in hibiscus water.

Then Lilly's body ascends toward the ocean's surface, long, lean arms hang on to the side of *The Geneva* as the briny water clears from her eyes and ears, and Lilly sits at the end of the old man's small shrimping boat, Eddie and Emma attached to the tip of her breast. The old man hauls his net in and extends his hand out, lifts the heavy bail of fish, his face, a plate of burnished ochre, pushing white whiskers out of the way to introduce the few teeth surviving his gums, a smile that made her laugh at beauty in its decay. And with his smile, and her childish laughter, the translucent water hardens into a flat surface, and the long thin limbs of the girl thicken into brittle bones beneath tough cracked flesh, and the floor under the curved spine sinks into the ground, sprouts green beneath her back. Emma lay heaving in a clearing, asylumed in a circle of trees, as a gusty wind falls down, thudding its weight on all the earth, dry autumn leaves turn around husky ankles and the thing above her flaps its gargantuan wings, traveling the circumference of twenty miles six times, soaring in six directions: north, east, south, west, up, and down, until Emma is able to lift her head, just enough to watch the bird focus on something beneath it, not the decaying body of Emma, but another body beside her. An infant, Thais's daughter, fresh and new.

The air releases its hold from Emma's lungs just long enough, she washes Geneva's roseate face in cornmeal, spreads a brown blanket over hot white sand, cups the infant in her arms again, strong arms, agile, limber, hoping the air would stay this way, fresh and clean and new, and she knew it was this longing for air, the tightening in her chest that was slowly conquering her body, and she knew Geneva was not an infant anymore—lying beside her. She was fifteen. Buxom. Beautiful—red-skinned, descendant of the Pagan River.

The sun splurged its wealth of brightness in benign tones over the Isle of Wight, and Geneva turned her face to the east . . . let go of what little air there was trapped in her lungs, gave it to Frederick. Me. Fire.

These things live in the realm of my being. I don't know how I know them. These things, they belong to me. They're not for sharing.

PLAY WITH FIRE TILL YOUR FINGERS BURN,
AND WHEN THERE'S NO PLACE FOR YOU TO TURN,
DON'T GO TO STRANGERS,
DARLIN', COME ON HOME TO ME . . .

One foot tucked into the crest of a rock, the other jammed against a wedge of land, I climb the ladder that climbs the walls until I can hoist myself through the gaping hole, and crawl to a solid surface. Etta Jones's "Don't Go to Strangers" in my head.

From the roof you can see the Brooklyn grids, sectioned and wet, you can see how many buildings remain, dark . . . with big gaping holes in their roofs. You can see the street as it was. The Myrtle Avenue el with its wooden cars creaking up and down, the soldiers who run up and down the landscape down toward the water, the people who maintain yesterday's way of walking.

How do we remember?

My fatigues are damp in the drizzle of rain—more mist than drizzle—and the streets stretch out before me . . . my fatigues, green . . . darkening . . . like Eddie's military jacket . . . dark green cotton splashed with dark wet circles, unsteadily holding a drink in his hand . . . music playing . . . damaging notes . . . Scott's *Remembrance of Things Past* . . . Eddie in an army jacket . . . with a Bronze Star pinned to his lapel . . . Albert Ammons, Lester Young, James Henry Scott, playing from the phonograph in the corner of a Zuni, Virginia, wood-framed liquor house, a hard birthday cake with one lit candle on the coffee table with the phonograph . . . a prop. The music was having its ceremony, sermonizing on the turntable. Pushing through the cracks. Huge black seventy-eight, spinning around, saxophone, piano, applause. Good music and the stench of damnation.

I inhale the stink Eddie inhales from the second floor where

whores and whoremongers concoct sweat-and-come cocktails. Stockings pulled down and tangled around thick ankles, homemade
dresses hiked up over waists, greasy curls making patterns against
the walls, moans coming down. Damaging notes wedging themselves
between his gate of contentment and the wall of condemnation he
kept around himself.

Bitch thinks she can save me. Thinks she can raise her arms above my head, offer me herself, until I come back to myself. She plays Miles, pours herself another glass of Moët. She says she's finished trying to suck all the pus from my life with caring. I don't have anything to give her. She doesn't have anything left to give me. I can't be her fucking project. I tell her that. She laughs real hard, says I don't know what my issues are. It's easier this way, she says, for me to go on living in the poem. She thinks she's Jesus now, but what she don't know is I been saved before. Prophets and holy people have already been my way, and laid hands on me.

She's got her bags packed, says she's gonna buy herself a ticket to Bali to see her mother . . . soon as she can afford the ticket, she's gettin' outta here because shit is about to hit the fan. Lucinda's dead. Mawepi never came back. People comin' around the building, says it won't be long . . . they either gonna sell the building or tear it down and she's not gonna be caught ass out. She's gonna go to Bali sooner than later, she says. I can stay here if I want to, she says. She doesn't really give a fuck, she says. Miles plays. It's in line with the rhythm of existence. It's in total response to the madness.

Listen, I tell her, my eyes a devil bloodred, nostrils wide open, Miles doing "Spanish Key" on trumpet, me holding her book of *Faust*—reading out loud above the music as she smiles and dances.

> *Come or go? Or in, or out? His resolve is lost in doubt.*
> *Mid-way on the beaten trail He will grope and halting fail;*
> *Ever straying, ever thwarted, he beholds a world distorted.*
> *Burdens others with his yoke*
> *Gasps for breath, and then will choke;*
> *Chokes he not!*

Couchette is drunk on Moët, Miles is swinging some shit, and she's dancing to him. She's holding her cigarette holder, laughing at my explanations, doing leg extensions, bending her body down, swinging up with Chick Corea and John Mclaughlin. I'm yelling at her through the music, trying to catch the words by the light of the chiffon-draped lampshade, brushing my cigarette ashes off the page, speaking loud above the music.

> *Of life repining*
> *not despairing, not resigning, swept along in pained let-live*
> *Shunning an imperative, his round of durance and release, its*
> *hazy sleep, its Troubled peace!*

She laughs like she thinks I'm playing. Thinks we doing some kind of performance-art shit. I got on a pair of drawers, holding on to *Faust*, she's dancing across the room, standing on top of cardboard boxes with her plastic cup of champagne, doing rolls over couches. Saying I'm fucking up her groove. Dave Holland eggs her on. I'm trying to tell her, through *Faust*, don't be tryin' to get me to be all right! I don't know what that is. Can't be all right. Don't try to make things right. Things ain't right. We're building a house together, it's beautiful. It's got blood and piss, and that's all lovely, ain't it? Don't try and make it righteous, I can't live in a righteous house.

I take a gulp from the bottle of Moët. The Moët is pulsing through me, feels good. Cold and hot in me. Fucking me up. Fucking me up, the Möet and Miles and the way she's dancing. Miles and Couchette are playing rough. Debasing me. Bringing me down. Bringing me . . . down. Brings him down.

> *Brings him down and pins him well, and prepares his soul for*
> *hell. . . .*

Know what, motherfucker?

Her eyes going in opposite directions—Concha y Toro—Moët lips. She does belly rolls in the middle of the living room, her bald head too damn confident, condescending to me. No safety in this city. No safety.

You one trifling ass motherfucker! Took me a minute but you one triflin' ass motherfucker with your tired DJ ass!

Miles runs the voodoo down for her while she trips over herself, doing the boogaloo jumbalaya, feeling all good about this war.

You don't recall nuthin'! You don't expect nuthin'! You ain't got nuthin' to say! Woman come to save your tired ass and ain't that been done before? Where's the virtue in that shit? Where's MY reward? Woman comin' to help the man be a man, again! We been playing a very silly game you and me and I thought you knew the fuckin' rules . . . I got my own secrets, Racine. I got my own life to work the fuck out and you still ain't got no keys to open up your doors. What I had for you was a key. You know what I'm sayin'?
Nah.
Naaaah. Naaah. Naaah. Is that all the fuck you EVER have to say? *Naaaah.*

She starts laughing again, hysterical laughing from the belly, sharp and cutting like how only women can laugh—at a man, slicing into his flesh.

You ain't got no fuckin'. . . . the dick ain't alla that—never was . . . not even down through the ages . . . and you ain't even got no balls!

Slicing. Slicing.

I'm givin' you a chance. Well, I'm givin' MYSELF a chance now. I growin' this baby inside me, and I'm gonna give my goddamned baby a chance. We don't need you. You—you should go, go somewhere and find yourself somebody.

I thought I did. She doesn't hear me when I say it. I'm not sure if I've said it.

*   *   *

I can make love to myself . . . love myself . . . touch myself . . . face myself . . . woman can touch herself and be all right . . . she can . . . we can . . . create nations inside our bodies—you know how to do that, little boy with no balls? . . . do you . . . Racine? Know how to touch yourself . . . no you don't . . . you can't . . . not even with your own music let alone some Faust shit!

Slicing. Cutting. Ripping. Shredding.

It was all very intriguing for a minute but only about a minute and we on the fuckin' sixty-first second now and I'm bored, darling— BORED! With you, with my father's music, with Art Pepper, with—
    Lying to yourself?

She wavers.

She's dead . . . right? She's not in Bali. She ain't healin' herself in no rice paddy fields. The bitch is dead. Been dead. Died in the gutter. And there ain't no baby inside you. You can't have no baby— you're empty inside. Gutted.

Leaping across the boxes at my throat was her appreciation of the poem we're living in. The lamp falls down. The ashtray turns over. A glass breaks, bleeding Möet all across the floor. Hurling our bodies into the shower was an ovation, Yeah, we got beauty . . . no power . . . got music and it keeps snapping us back . . . trips us out . . . music. Turning the shower on her jolting body was my way of saying, we're drunk and I love you. We're holy and I know you. We're fucked up and I need you . . . You made me catch the Holy Ghost with your invective sermon . . . with your leg extensions and I need you to stay a little while longer, in this house, we've built. Stay.
    The baby powder spills, the toothpaste glass shatters, the towels are tangled up and twisted, perfume falls all around us anointing us in fragrances. I stumble back to the living room, pull out my thing, let go a stream of piss aimed at Miles and Scott and Pepper, and

packed suitcases and she's throwin' wet fists and wet kicks at me
from behind, draws blood from the nape of my neck, her teeth sink
into my waist, and I am now all kinds of motherfuckers who had to
get the fuck away from her and—hallelujah—hands to glory—she
pulls me back, her body stumbling through the doorway, pulls me
back, both of us falling into the bathtub, water showering down, a
thousand acid spangles raining over bald beautiful brown incredulity
. . . us all wet, my body pulled down on top of her, she's Muhammad
Ali all over me, sharp blows, dizzying, the spit from my mouth a
shade of dahlia, her face, a keen resignation, our kiss—forced.
Teeth grating against teeth. Applause. Yes. Amen. Thank you. Yes . . .
Please don't. Don't leave. Not now. Please. And I thank you.

Miles plays "Sanctuary." We sleep in holy slumber, rained on.

Manny held a Gitanes packed with dreams. We pass it between us. He sat himself in the window. The cars were going. Everything was going and my eyes started going, retreating . . . The music chugged along, traffic got heavy outside. Trucks and cars honking their horns, whizzing by, cans clanging against each other. She's leaving . . . after the party under the bridge. Tomorrow. She's definitely leaving.

Manny had come back from a long stay nowhere. With a freshly shaved head, sat on the floor of the parlor room. Empty. The turntables, the mixer, the jukebox—gone. Stolen. Escaped sometime in the night. Manny climbed onto the pool table, swung from the light box above.

It never bothered you, Racine?
What?
You never asked me questions about it.
What?
The soldering irons. The dreams.

What I was hearing, what I was hearing was . . .

The interpretation of a dream isn't a dream. The logical and the rational are obstacles—moral conventions. There's no such thing as two and two. When you saw me you *had* to see me. Had to see this house. All of it, in all its despair . . . new to you . . . rebuilt for you. You were new too, walking on the streets of this city—revisiting ancient roads, where your body is scattered. Pieces of a body scattered.

I was hearing his voice introduce me to the house, that first day, that day he showed me around, that night, when I had been walking, just walking, all over, wherever, and I had wound up in Brooklyn and didn't care how, and stopped in front of a vacant lot.

I kept walking, made a right at one corner and made a right at another corner and made a right at the next corner so I should've been making a circle, a perfect circle of, should've wound up at the same vacant lot, but then I couldn't find that lot. No vacant lot anywhere, I had imagined it, but I hadn't imagined it, it had to be in the middle of the block because I hadn't made too many turns or anything, but it wasn't there, and I walked up another street.

There was this diner with a steel gate pulled down and I had passed that before and here I was walking by it again but I couldn't find the vacant lot to save my life and then I paused underneath a dying tree and there was this old building across the street and this olive-skinned guy with curly black hair leaning against the banister and the guy with the curly black hair started talking to me, describing what I was seeing in some kind of architectural language . . . *oversized windows with exterior shutters . . . four tall Ionic columns supporting an entablature surmounted by a pediment decorated in a Greek fret . . . eight-paneled double-leaf doors of mahogany opening into a vestibule with plasterwork of urns overflowing with anthemions and garlands, and each room has an elaborately carved rosette of plaster, and on the parlor floor, some of the original ornamental plasterwork survived to climb twenty feet above light and dark wood floors. Romanesque encaustic tiles of inlaid earthenware lay before a grand fireplace of alabaster carved in swirls of angels and curves of sparrows with grape seed branches in their beaks. A decorated arch introduced the reeded pilasters of a winding staircase.*

But where it gets crazy, Racine, is we compete with ourselves to see how far we can go with . . . our new way of seeing . . . before it all implodes.

Manny . . .
What?
Why'd you tell me that story . . . the boy . . . on the roof?
Why not?

But it's a lie. You made it up.

No . . . no . . . I didn't make it up.

You didn't?

No . . . *you* did.

Why did you say a boy died if—

Like what I was saying about this war. It's not over because it never really started, did it? Nobody's sure. We know something happened, but nobody's sure what, or why we're in, and not knowing is like being stuck between walls. There's something on either side, but you don't really know. The boy didn't die. He climbed the stairs. He was locked in a room. There was smoke, but he got out—didn't he? He survived, didn't he? You find a place . . . you build a house . . . you make a dream . . . you call for company . . . company in the middle of a dream . . . search for pieces of your body, scattered on the avenues . . . beneath the highway . . . in the darkness . . . where automotive angels roar above your head . . . birds and angels . . . The weaker ones have no dreams . . . no escape from their crumbling buildings . . . do not survive slanting streets . . . they die by fire . . . fall to the ground with their hands to Jesus, they lose their footing and bash their heads against the rocks . . . get cut, get shot, come to be rigor-mortis sculptures growing from the earth in a piss-stained darkness. We are not one of the weaker ones, Racine. We are blurred figures of acetate brown nudity framed in slabs of concrete and wire mesh. We are lies. Beautiful lies.

I spit a couple of times, my chest tight with blood-speckled phlegm, and move away from him. Move toward a boy who disappears into the abyss of a vacant lot with monsters. The monsters return to the light of the side street before he does, galloping up the road with grunts and grievous laughter. The boy reemerges. Limps by, palms bleeding. Whimpering. A girl dances by the curb, cedar complexion soaked in a citrus glow pouring down from the lamppost. A little girl in a purple dress is bent over a blue Chrysler, negotiating price and performance. The Chrysler's radio booms beats mixed with strange chords. The girl's stomach rolls counterclockwise parading for side-street browsers. The soldier in the Chrysler sucks his teeth as the car pulls off into a dense coppice of trees. The girl dances—an equinox celebration—sits on horse-head gate at the entrance of a mansion . . . a gargoyle discerning spectral forces. She is protector of vagrants meandering the elysian fields of our vices. She is leaning against a wall, watching blurred figures jaunt above me, flashing over. By the wall and gate, on the other side of the street, imps rush by with mescaline, allowing the ecstasy of the moon to flash a green haze across their faces.

I wobble down a bicycle path, further into darkness. Glance backward. Follow. Branches scrape against my cheek, a flash of light is cast against a rail. I lean against the rail, dry heave near the bushes. Move out into the light to find a safe place. Behind a well, in a cluster of bushes. Safe, in the solitude of bushes, a rustling. The moon is full. Lick it. Lick the bowl of the moon. Fire on my tongue. Spontaneous combustion. Flesh, and building, burning in the basket of an oval sun. Tiny cigarette sings, like Mary J. Blige. Throw up. Try to stay awake. Rustling of trees and bushes. In the clearing, two boys. Two boys in the alcove moving further into the rambling intervals between seconds. Move. Out of the park, up the street, gliding. Down. Cold steps. Rush of a sound breeze, motion of air, colors of steel forcing through—magnificent rumbling. I'm bleeding onto my shoes. The warehouses leak smoke shaped like abstruse trees, looming over the river from an exorbitant hill. Their leaves are air carriers, guiding me through apartments of retrospection, a chariot of prisms passing through siphons. My mouth pulls back behind my ears. Find the train station. The train. That train to glory. My head threatens to rip itself from my shoulders, influenza of questions boiling between my ears. This motion . . . *Paris will be a safe place . . . Paris or Lyon.*

The train is coming—yellow card. Find it. Slide it through. Descend onto the platform. Locomotion. Doors open. Fall into the fainting seat. Two boys run through. One in white shirt and black pants, a Bible under his arm, one taller than the other, smoking a cigarette. The one with the Bible says, *Jesus saves.* The one with the cigarette calls the one with the Bible a *pussy. Stupid pussy boy with Bible.* Conductor yells, first stop—Zuni . . . Stop the train! It's moving too fast. Not safe. It rushes through the tunnel. Rides. Does not stop. Carries me back. Locomotive shift to rapid speed. Ride. This train to glory. Ride this train. This train to brother's cracked skull. Ride this train. This train is bound for glory. No winebibbers and no backstabbers on this train . . . The train stops. The old man with the Greek cap gets on. Says, *You know the truth you cannot speak, a grief common to all men.*

IF YOU DON'T KNOW, YOU SHOULD ASK SOMEBODY.

Somebody what?

About everything. The fire in Brooklyn. The musician, you and Frederick asleep on the floor, Geneva on the couch, the fire coming out of the fireplace. Why she didn't make it.

He said she just didn't wake up in time.

Racine . . .

What?

Why do you believe everything he say?

I don't know . . . have to.

EDDIE TURNS HIS FACE TO THE WALL, TAMBOURINES CLANGING ALL around his head, Church Mother kneeling beside him screaming in his ear, clapping her hands, organ playing loud, Eddie walking up and down the aisles with his hands thrown up in the air, crying. Old church mothers kneel, tongues at the altar, preacher in a white robe, olive oil, choir clapping and singing. Eddie, sweating and crying and singing, Scotch on his breath, gray hair turning white, deacons holding hands in a circle around him, on his knees at the altar, his hands, his ear, his eyes, closed, he doesn't like his eyes closed because he can see the dream again. He opens one eye. There's the walnut casket and there's Frederick lying beneath sheer white muslin, he closes his eyes and claps his hands and pulls his ear away. The Church Mother yells, Tell Jesus all about it, baby! That's all right! Hallelujah! His hands, his eyes, talk to Jesus. Says, Lord, will it be all right if I change my name?

MR. EDDIE DON'T SAY MUCH TO ME SINCE FREDERICK DIED, UNLESS he's drinking and sometimes he wake me up in the middle of the night with liquor on his breath and pull me outside and we walk through the pine barrens and it's dark and I don't have nuthin' on but pajamas but he take me through the pine barrens over to the quarry where Frederick died and we kneel down and he make me read the scripture out loud and he sit on a rock and drink. He sit there, then he say outta nowhere, I'm stupid and I was born in sin, and I say but the Bible say we was all born in sin and he say the only reason he's raising me is because my mother's dead and he didn't want no responsibility of no two children and he should've just left us in New York where we was born, up in Brooklyn where our mother died, but the house caught on fire and our mother died and he came on back down to Zuni with two boys thinkin' he would return to the house he was born in but then he say the house is filled with seven more spirits more evil than the ones that was already there, and then I don't say nuthin' but then I ask him to tell me again what happen to our mother and like usual he won't say nuthin', he won't tell me nuthin' about my mother except that she's dead, and then he say Frederick was hardheaded and wrong for running away and that's why he died, that's why he fell in the quarry, and he hope don't nobody think he did it, pushed him or nuthin' 'cause he would never do that, and don't we know he loved us? And ask it again, don't I know he love me? And I was trying to say yeah I know it but I was nervous and nuthin' came out, and he start crying and take another swig, and . . . I didn't want Frederick to leave. I asked him not to. I prayed for him. I asked him not to make trouble. But he did. Last night, I had the dream again, 'bout the woman, and she standin' in the darkness on the cliff where Frederick fall from, a bird flying around her head.

THE PHONOGRAPH PLAYED ITSELF A PLAINSONG ROOTED IN A COM-
plicated theory. Barrage of bullets coming down to him, coming
at his ears, melodic maneuvers skillfully advancing. Masked
notes, hard to dismiss through the nebula of compositions in
blood. Music of roll call, alarms, taps eulogizing days of soul sim-
plicity. Honorable discharge of notes, coming at his eyes and
glass, medley of piano and saxophone hurling around his chest
decorated in a bronze star hanging from red-and-green-striped
ribbon.

Hard whiskey and humid air turning in the soldier's eyes,
Eddie's collar wide open, inviting a northern breeze. Tight air
pushing at him through the cracks in the walls of an old house in
a wooded nowhere, surrounded by loud crickets coming over
from the Antioch swamp, longleaf pines surrounding a feeble
house built back from the main road. You walk through the pine
barrens, walk just to the left of white sands until you come to a
cart road, you follow the cart road and cut through an extensive
depression until you get to the end, until you get to a little old
house made of thick hand-hewn timbers interwoven, joined at the
corners in a cross notch, clay mud filling the spaces between the
logs. A house one-story high, two rooms deep, two rooms wide,
big black potbelly stove in the main room, a square brick fireplace in the back room, the occasional whistle and thunder of the
Norfolk and Petersburg railroad line. Return of the prodigal to a
Zuni dirt road. This dark corner of the earth. Home.

COLORS—ROUND BUXOM SOFT, RINGING INTO STRANGE UNFAMILIAR places. The same darkness. The same unfamiliarity with quiet. Horns and chord progressions, progressing into purple darkness. The same quiet sameness of a Zuni night. The once fertile flesh of the earth was imperturbable beneath the sun, moon, stars—all luminaries. Vines and weeds replace rows of fruit and vegetable, once neatly planted in miles of flatland. All things had changed. All things were as they have always been. The myth of memory is elaborately colored in gothic lies. A thousand hills curve into narrow paths—too narrow a path to revisit.

A little girl in a woman's body sits in a quiet chair. A little girl in a quiet purple dress, round, buxom, skin the color of Zuni dirt, her hair—a quiet purple night. The little girl wears no shoes. Dark wet earth splashes up around her ankles, clumps between her toes, her purple dress is wet around the hem. A girl, in a room with an aging man in green, sits in a simple chair. The old man's green jacket, green pants, creased, small green hat, are unfamiliar to her. The old military fatigues are hunched over a simple chair across from her, unable to look at her.

The old man's graying beard and dark face, wet with inconsolable weeping, embarrasses the little girl. The old man is spinning an old shiny black record—his ear inclined to it—spinning the King Cole Trio and Harry "Sweets" Edison. The aging man—almost forty—arrived in a blue Chrysler. He pulled up to the house and drove over the front lawn. Drove over the earth where pink hydrangeas grew in spring, trampled peppermint and dandelion beneath his tires, stomped big black combat boots into the house, into the clean room, stomped the clean rug with mud, breathed whiskey into pure air. The young girl, barely fifteen, sits in the living room. The body of her mother lay center. The girl watches the old man she does not know and glances at a photograph on an end table by a window; a young man in a suit with a hat, smiling, skin the color of unending beauty. The girl looks back to the thing in front of her, dazed, ear inclined to a phonograph, listening for some clue as to what went wrong.

The man wriggles a bit in his tight green chinos. He'd walked along an empty navy yard, through the empty barracks and warehouses, saw a small shop on a narrow street with a little bulb above a door. The man behind the counter smelled like all the folded green wools and cottons and brass buttons of forgotten heroism. *What do you want? We're closing. Closing down. What do you want?* The old man looked to the shelves of folded green, half-priced heroism burst from his eyes.

Now he looks to the body of his sister in the center of a room. A room he grew up in. A room he does not know. Looks again to the young girl in purple who is supposed to be his sister's daughter, a girl he does not know. Looks to her breasts and her hair the color of Zuni, and he looks to a photograph on an end table of a young man, smiling, skin the color of wishful thinking. He looks to the wood-slat walls and listens to the branches as they fall from the live oak tree onto the zinc roof above his head—looks to the road that cuts across the field of cornstalk, remembers laying the last thin layer of roadbed over subsoil. Trowels and shovels. Remembers coming home from war, the young man in the photograph stepping off a train, walking a familiar path toward the house he'd grown up in, toward the well and the zinc roof.

A young soldier stood in the center of a wooded nowhere, feet set down on a half-paved road . . . red dirt covered in sand, limestone and black granules. Materials thousands of years old, used by Romans to seal aqueducts and reservoirs, Phoenicians for caulk, Pharaohs as mortar to join rocks along the banks of the Nile.

Roads to Babylon on which his sanctified body was breast-fed by an unsanctified woman from down Florida way. Mama Lilly. Unsanctified. She had given birth to a girl and a boy without a husband . . . met a Prophet. The Prophet told her she needed Jesus. The Prophet took her and her children away from the bones of her great ancestors who lay on Florida's ocean floor—shipwrecked pirates, escaped slaves—away from a twelve-mile rock in the middle of the sea. The Prophet brought an unsanctified woman and her two children back with him to Zuni. Mama Lilly walked her children through pine woods looking for herbs and berries. She walked until she walked away. Left the children to raise themselves.

A young soldier turned toward a house he'd grown up in, then turned to walk another path—toward another house where melodies and women commingled with bathtub gin, where a woman walked up to him in ankle-strap shoes and a tight purple dress with sweat stains, pressed black hair curling back into itself. Black bangs and one braid down her back. She sat next to him fanning herself with a newspaper, picked meat from between her two front teeth capped in gold, sipped his drink and marked his glass with bright red lipstick—held his cigarette between two battered fingers, took a drag. Her black bangs stared into his profile, a face without rules or pretensions. She smiled, crossed her legs and adjusted the rhinestone resting in the slope of her breast—agreed with herself; his dusty red complexion reminded her of his sister Emma, who was handsome, like a man. Strong. The way his eyelids sloped down—Emma when she was languid, sitting on her stoop grinding herbs into a wooden bowl. Rough. Emma's hands mulling over her breasts, between her legs. His hands, her hands, hewn from mountain rock or hardened lava. Hands that could explain the scarcity of love.

She cuddled up under his arm, pushed her thigh against his thigh, dismissed all recollections of the boy who grew up with his twin sister in a clapboard house. She put her mouth to his neck, betraying his sister's mouth. She pushed herself closer to him and ignored proclamations she and Emma had made. Proclamations meant nothing in the dark with Ben Webster and Lester Young. Emma's hands and Emma's breasts meant nothing now. Now, she could not even remember Emma's breath, Emma's mouth, birthroot, cranesbill on Emma's shoulders.

The young soldier is home now—fresh from war. Already he is floating away from the bathtub gin, already drifting on a light-wave backward—beyond Normandy and the Rhone River valley, beyond the cities of Lyon and Ste. Mere-Eglise, falling away from defensive action and schemes of maneuver—his date of induction and his date of separation—already swimming out of his medals and his uniform, dissolving into shapelessness—drifting up above the liquor house onto the zinc-roofed shacks, already aiming himself upward and beyond it toward a breeze that takes him back to the Dragoon forces moving up the Rhone River valley, toward Lyon, back further to the 818th Amphibian Truck Division, to the 752nd Sanitary Company, to the CCC camp in Yorktown, Virginia—back to the small Zuni schoolhouse and the piece of slate he carried with him from a string every day. The honorably discharged soldier's body is already twelve again, stripped down to its nakedness.

A wave drifts the prodigal soldier to the quarry, and he hooks onto a passing thought, toward smooth red nudity. He'd spied on little girls as they walked home alone, up Zuni dirt roads; lured their innocence down into the quarry—performance of conquering—the beauty of nakedness in combat. Resistant pubescent bodies. He loiters in the explosion it inspired, tenses at the shrill of little-girl screams.

The young soldier draws down to Hades, wafts to the prayer room where he fell on his knees and prayed to God the Father and Jesus the Son—the soldier lingers in the Holy Ghost that entered his body then, the presence of the Lord and the fullness of tambourines that protected him from cruelty.

YOU STILL PLAY PIANO? SHE SPOKE, SAID SOMETHING. SHE SAID something, the plump woman in the liquor house, with a purple dress and gold teeth, said something in his ear that brought him back down to earth, softly—and he looked to the lipstick stains on gold teeth. He knew the form of her body, had seen it before . . . bulbous violet rolling from side to side. Bathed by his sister in the tin tub set in the middle of the room, boneless and shiny—covered in white foam, Emma's hands, rubbing big fat shiny purple breasts— Emma's hands and Emma's mouth on this woman's breasts. This woman he saw walk down the road once, this woman he wanted to meet. This woman Emma ignored, as if she didn't see her at all.

He fled Zuni and joined the CCC camp. He was drafted into the Sanitary Division. He was in the 818th division—preparing to go to war . . . learning to pave roads for military aircraft. Emma was home, mentioned this woman in her letters:

Thais—you remember Thais live over in Ivor? Used to visit me sometime before she married. Move on up over there near Newport News? Thais came back to Zuni. Thais stayin' with me for a spell. Thais fell sick. Today I went on up into Portsmouth. Lard and spignut, dandelion and lobelia seed, turpentine and beeswax, put it on Thais chest; Thais doing fine; Got your letter today say you comin' home, Thais and me gon make you one of her pies. Me and Thais doing just fine.

His regulation green cotton suit enveloped in reefer smoke, Eddie thinks about what Emma said as soon as he got off the train—*You look troubled, don't look right in the eyes . . . the war over, when you gon' take off your uniform, Eddie? Remember Mama Lilly's recipe for healin' wounds? Take baths every night for three days and say prayers, take equal parts almond leaves, albahaca, Florida water, chunks of cocoa, and marigolds, then cut the cocoa in five pieces and take all the leaves and put in a pot of water, then add your Florida water and mix to body temperature, be sure to add your marigolds last, pour the whole thing in your bath water, and this will keep you from harm and this will bring all good things to you, and this will help keep you whole.*

No recipe could calm his spirit. No weed or root could pierce through the images ripping through his skull of bullet-torn bodies draped over rocks, headless torsos he once called friends. Only the liquor and Lester Young could do that now—ease him—they come with him wherever he goes, from the bandstands of the Golden Gate, to Jock's Place. Eyes wandering through his hair, his face, proud uniform. He was forced to fight a new enemy dressed in silk on the front lines of Minton's, and the Celebrity Club, at Sunday afternoon jam sessions, with Sonny Stitt's playing, Claudia MacNeil singing . . . the holy-roller soldier boy in northern bars and ballrooms . . . Harlem gals in rhinestones and fake ermine . . . red fingernails digging into his back too damn hard, taking him in like he was the devil, clawing at him, civilian number runners and Yankee punks exchanging insults and shoves, civilians who'd never ducked Normandy bullets, or German mortar shells . . . never emerged from the hedgerows, advancing through St. Fromond.

Civilians lived in free-style nomenclature; they demanded his uniform fall away, demanded he sit down at the piano and come up with compositions in blood. They knew he had Avery Parrish's riffs in his fingertips, he knew he kept Cow-Cow Davenport, Jimmy Yancey, and Pine Top Smith in his head. He knew eight beats to a measure, they knew he was waiting to bleed them a river, and change his name.

THE OLD MAN, ALMOST FORTY, TURNED HIS FACE BACK TO THE phonograph, turned his back to the cold gray thing on a cooling board in the middle of the midwinter's living room, The body in decay. Scratches in the cedar wall near the kitchen's entrance, sorry curtains veiling windows, forced his mind toward his bruised fingers—too many years. He licked the thick cracked leather coating his lips, caught a quick glimpse of a yellowish tone dulling his complexion in the mirror on the wall, could smell his own internal organs sending up a stink through his mouth. Fifteen years.

The old man turned his mind back to the black disk spinning in the liquor house when he'd held a glass of bathtub gin in one hand, and with the other—wrenched the fat girl's legs open, pulled back the veil of purple, surprised her body, pushed up between two wet walls. The tips of his fingers touching where earth meets water. She playfully punched his shoulder, but no one else in the room noticed his hands wading in the pool between her legs, and she never attempted to remove his hand, and he stared at the black vinyl disk with the eyes of a dead flounder—wondered how a dead fish would look in an old military uniform? Could the sharp creases of green on regulation trousers stand up to the currents of living waters, or would the fish have to find its way inland? Would it have to dry itself off, and prepare itself to die? Would it have to be scaled, so as not to snag the fabric? How would it look then, dead flounder eyes wide open, mouth and gills puckering for air?

The woman moaned softly and took another sip of his gin, sat there, in an awkward position, his arm under her legs gaped open, dress hiked up to the middle of her thigh, green army jacket arm vanishing under purple silk, rough twinkling sliding deeper into a ditch, digging up under dark wet earth. His middle finger, sliding back and forth between a tight hole. He was drunk but he'd seen things. He'd been somewhere, outside Zuni, Windsor, Ivor, Suffolk, Portsmouth, Richmond. She groaned softly, laughed a little—left her legs limp, tugged her dress over her knee just in case, sipped his drink again as he dug deeper, gripped his crotch sheathed in regulation green, concealed, becoming more apparent—a weapon for later.

She finally pulled his hand from up under her dress and said, *I read some uh 'dem postcards you sent home to Emma.* He sat there with the eyes of a dead flounder drying on an embankment.

She looked in her handbag and held a mirror up to her face, should he come to himself, and she saw that her hair had shrunken into her scalp and the only thing saving it was the rhinestone hair combs she had on either side of her temples. She took out a tissue and pressed her lips against it, wiped away the residue of reddish brown on her two front gold teeth, straightened her pearls and dabbed her face, took a swig of whiskey and crossed her legs so Eddie wouldn't feel like he had the right to get up inside her without even saying anything nice first, then contradicted herself and uncrossed her legs, waited. His hand reached over and rested on her knee, and he glanced at her with a casual smile, like Clark Gable's in the movies, quick but at least it was a smile, and at least he looked at her. His flounder eyes were slightly out of focus, and his fingers found their way between her thighs again, and she said, *I didn't think you was comin' back at all,* and she repeated something she'd said earlier, a whisper, repeated a whisper he'd heard before, an invitation to leave this place we are in—an invitation to go to another place where we can be alone.

The old man thought to himself, where is the place I can go where I am alone, without yesterday or tomorrow, without Emma dead in the center of a room in a house I grew up in, without photographs of myself in a suit of death, without a fifteen-year-old girl who does not speak, without a Bronze Star hanging from my chest?

EDDIE TOOK A SWIG OF JOHNNIE WALKER BLACK, WATCHED EMMA'S waxen skin asleep on a cooling board, covered in linen gauze—fifteen years ago, he had not come walking across the threshold of their tiny clapboard house, he rolled thunder on a bed of wild mushrooms and wet grass, under a live oak tree, whiskey spilling over clumsy thrusts: an offensive action of forward movement, engaging the enemy. The enemy groaned discomfort, defended space with mobile action. The soldier destroyed all cohesion—peer left, jab right—operated with surprise and shock action, manipulated and maneuvered the body until she was disoriented. Pushed her face into the wet green, deep into the cool damp brown—gripped her by the back of the neck, pushed the face deeper into soft wet humiliation—lifted her purple veil. Rend the veil. Rend the veil twain. Push. Further. Permanent rupture. Infiltration—opening of engagement. Surprise action. Defeat. Meritorious achievement. Freedom from fear and want.

Thais lay beneath her assailant, trying to decipher the night's conjugal dance of ripped stockings, and fallen government chinos. Emma knew Eddie was asleep on Thais's purple breast like a newborn after suckling—her grunts had inspired colors other than the sameness of the Zuni darkness droning itself above the countryside of poor niggers living and dying, coming and going—working and praying and dying and fucking—on the same path they always have. The same path Emma trod, the same sleep Emma slept—dreaming of a sky that never changed colors, one great and powerful heaven looming over the topsoil blanketing turnips and ginger—reaping a new crop of purple dresses and government chinos. One same God. One same blessing—from a reliable sky. A sky that never departs.

But morning came, bringing with it the same transparent blue, blushed with an approaching storm. A Bronze Star and a military duffel bag were hoisted onto a Greyhound bus bound for New York. A ripped violet sat against a well behind a wood-slat house with a zinc roof. A woman in broken pearls who had betrayed love for the invasion of her body sat, spitting out tiny bushels of tobacco stuck to the edge of her tongue, and fifteen years ago, Emma turned herself up toward an approaching storm, accepted quietly to herself that Eddie wasn't coming home, and Thais wasn't coming back. The date of separation, when everyone had departed to go to some corner of the earth, where they could be alone, and change their names.

EDDIE LIFTED THE BODY ONTO A WHEELBARROW AND CARTED IT UP through the wooded hills. Geneva followed, carrying a shovel and toting a chicken-feed bag filled with a few of Emma's belongings. Eddie looked to the girl. Knew she hadn't come from Emma, she'd come from Thais. Geneva removed the contents from the burlap bag and placed them several feet away from the body, placed a broken string of pearls on top of Emma's body, waited for Eddie to dig the grave and cover his sister with earth, another attempt at erasure.

Did you know that Longfellow lived in a great mansion full of beautiful thing? Kong and Bali . . . and his wife caught on fire in their mansion. Longfellow's wife ran through the halls trying to put out the fire until she died . . . Longfellow could not save her.

Before we leave for the club beneath the bridge, she stares at the postcard of Scott on the refrigerator door, tucks the photo of her mother in the pewter frame from her vanity into her costume bag. Turns back to look at us in the mirror.

There's something about fire. Fire's coming our way, Racine. Wrecking ball comin' soon. You can't live in the dream forever.
Yes I can.

What's left of the vinyl is packed in a crate, she's got all her gear in a tote bag slung across her chest. Buja Banton's "Shiloh" plays from the taxicab's back speakers, and she rests her head on my shoulder. Regret sits between us. With regret comes a new fear, that we can no longer cohabit the bed of intimacy—not with each other. Not with anyone. This failure is the final failure, convincing us of our daily will to end all new beginnings. Love will have to find another employ, and the void we've widened in ourselves will forever be the window through which we breathe. The sacrifice is air.

I never knew him, Racine. Never got the chance. She left him before I was old enough to remember him. She said he had started drinking heavily after his twin sister died. She said he had a daughter somewhere, in a sanitarium or something somewhere down south. She said he always felt guilty about that. Then, one day, out of nowhere, he brings this woman home who he said was his daughter.

Full-grown woman. I was just born, I don't remember her either, but my mother said she was weird. She acted like she was ten. She never talked. She got pregnant and nobody knew who the father was. Got pregnant again, and my mother . . . she didn't know what was up. Suspected him—that maybe he was sleeping with this woman he said was his daughter. He denied it, but she couldn't trust him any-more. He'd started drinking, reading the Bible, drawing on the walls, dismantled his piano and used it for firewood. They were about to lose the house. Electricity was off. It was bad, she said—so she left. The night she left, the house burned down. They only found one body, the woman's, never found him or the kids. He just van-ished. When I read in the paper that the house had caught on fire again, years later, that they'd found the body of an unidentified man—something told me it might be him. He'd come back home. Maybe he was looking for me. For us. But we were long gone by then. She was in Bali by then. I never forgave her for leaving him, Racine. I loved him, even though I never really knew him. Not know-ing him makes it worse. I love him even more. I don't think I ever loved my mother. I couldn't wait for one of us to die, so I wouldn't have to live with this feeling of not loving her. She's dead now. I love her now. Now I can, but it doesn't feel any better.

The cab swerves to miss a wall, curbs at a cavernous vault of stone; a cathedral or vampire's tomb beneath a bridge, with lights casting neon colors against fifty foot walls. A long line of people snake around the anchorage. Police and M-16s guard the perimeters with assault rifles firmly in hand, flashlights beaming down from heli-copters circling above. Couchette tries to roll the glass down, but the handle is missing. She leans her face closer to the glass.

Touch my stomach, Racine. Our baby. Feel it? It's ours, like the house. Let's keep them forever, Racine. Our child. Our Alibi.

The driver's already yelling at us in some Middle Eastern language so I slip him a ten to shut his ass up, but he just gets louder. Couchette finds five singles in her purse and he licks his thumb counting out loud in English. The wind whips around, comes up strong from the the river. From where we stand, on the edge of the island, the bridge towers over us with American flags and lights strung across it. Where the bridge is broken and dips down into the river's basin, a sharp shape protrudes from the water, climbing up beyond the roadbed, scaffolding cutting against night—cranes dangling in air. It will be completed.

Jean-Claude, a tall skinny French guy with pockmarks and a cig-arette twisted between his lips—dark pencil-line suit and slick black hair—is standing outside without a coat, talking into his cell phone. As soon as we pull up and he sees Couchette's face in the backseat, waves his hand. A few guys in muscle shirts run over and open the door. Jean-Claude kisses her on both cheeks, says some-thing to her, she says something to him, I hear my name—an intro-duction. He says something to me—I don't know what 'cause I'm too busy trying to open the trunk. The muscle guys whisk Couchette inside the anchorage with a few other girls who were already waiting at the curb to be escorted in. Jean-Claude talks on a cell phone, watches me out of the side of his eye. The cabdriver wants me to hurry up and get my shit out of his trunk, but some of the CDs have scattered and are tucked beneath a spare tire, tools, containers of oil. Jean-Claude waves his hand again and somebody runs over, lifts the half-filled box of CDs out of the trunk and barks a bunch of people out of his way as he heads inside.

Behind two metal doors, Tribe Called Quest's "Jazz (We've Got)" echoes out to us in the cold river gale. I slam the trunk closed and the cabdriver pulls off, then I turn around to introduce myself to Jean-Claude, who is arguing with some of his workers, ordering them to check people properly for guns or knives, gets another call on his cell phone, disappears behind the gray metal doors protected by another guy in a muscle shirt.

Between the base of the bridge and the huge river that blends into the opacity of sky framing Manhattan, an interminable line of fanatics threads across the wet cobblestone. They attempt smiles, anticipating the warmth of rituals inside the vaulted cave . . . des-perate for it . . . hungry . . . facial muscles flexing and pointed with

intention against an early and bitter cold. Silver-banged girls with
black nails, unshaven boys in business suits, drag queen conceptual
artists with glow-in-the-dark paint spread across the flat canvas of
their foreheads, waiting for ambient beats, leaning against brick
walls where projections of distorted texts are manipulated by com-
puter geeks with green hair and blurred eyes, high on e; the offspring
of an inconvenienced middle class stained with the slippage of real
property value in designated war zones, displacement—and the
humiliation of government subsidies. Some of them have endured
the impersonal hospitality of hotel bedsheets and tiny scented soaps
wrapped in plastic, and their parents wait for the glory days of government budget surplus and tax breaks, and even though some of
these young people still sport tattoos and piercings from bygone eras
of vanity, their most permanent marking is unseen on the surface of
their bodies; brothers, cousins, neighbors, friends, lost to cleverly
disguised bombs and land mines in Kandahar, mothers and fathers
lost to the nudity of bare existence, where everything that is super-
fluous and false is stripped away, and all that is insufficient in love
blatantly reveals itself.

These young men and women wait for admission to the anchorage without conversation, like children lining up for lunch in a class-
room, poised, with washed faces, clean teeth, combed hair, but they
are thin with hunger for the careless apoliticism of their youth. Their
tongues are swollen with the unwelcome knowledge of the Pashtun
and the Tajiks, and some of them are first cousins once removed of
the Uzbeks, some of them have been encouraged to forsake the
despised religion of their fathers, and the despised culture of their
people.

Some of these—should they speak—will proudly sport adapted ver-
naculars, will practice an American polyglot of tonality—pitched
high—harmonizing in agreeable keys, will change chords on certain
vowels and attack consonants in similar ways. These girls sport
stringy hair, teased up in an eager rush, fold tiny arms across crumpled
dresses, packed away too long. Their coats are flung over their arms,
or bundled in the embrace of their escorts, and their young flesh shiv-

ers in the cobblestone-river cold without complaint, soliciting the attention of the doorkeeper—maybe he will see the protrusion of nipples, the turquoise and amethyst glass pasted to inverted navels, the architecture of young naked bodies beneath dresses from another time, when these dresses were frequently worn to parties such as these, when the fabric seeped from their skin and left little to the imagination. These young girls, who have gilded their hair with silver or gold and glittered cracked lips a bright vermilion, sparkle and tremor in the disconsolate light of a Brooklyn waterfront, turning their minds to the luster of the huge vacuous space inside, beyond the metal doors, a room with fancy light projections and a designer sound system, where every young woman is Alice again, in a wonderland of light, and every young woman and every young man can celebrate the harsh transition from childhood to adulthood. Where they are all rich and beautiful and young forever, and youthful abandon translates into an existential necessity.

Some of these pedestrians with wool caps pulled down over skin too coarse for their youth, with dark sunglasses further obscuring their vision of night, have not bathed with tiny scented soaps wrapped in plastic or rinsed their mouths out with complimentary mint-flavored solutions. Some of these young women entwine dry unruly tresses into synthetic extensions, braid the strands tightly to withstand the severity of their lives, and they did not unfold last year's silk dresses or iron out the creases. Some of the young men escorting these young women wear nylon scarves tied over their heads, their chests are zipped in goose-down, some of them have never knotted a tie around their throats, have never had an occasion to, have never seen their fathers do it, have never seen their fathers. They come like me, in vintage fatigues, thick leather boots fastened and laced around their ankles, have smeared a thin layer of joy across their faces. Some of us have no illusions about the reflection of light cast against bare brick walls, and we do not wait in anticipation of our imaginations, and we do not lament the fall of buildings, we feel no violation, we have no blame, we have no Jesus, we just want to feel the vacillation of a massive subwoofer beneath our feet, we want it to jar us into a dance, a memory in sequence, something we can make sense of.

Ray?

He slams his hand down on my shoulder, grips it tight and tugs it back and forth. Claims me. Green eyes inspecting, trying to find someone else, someone he used to know. I am standing inside, by a stainless steel bar, watching a mass of heads moving, and a moth or something—out of season—flies around my face. It lags behind, has lost the trail of creatures who go wherever creatures go when first frost arrives. I study its flight, the flapping of its wings. My hand eases up, fingers erect and huddled together, eases up slow—gravitating toward the moth, stalking it, easing up over my head, then slams down on the stainless steel countertop, trapping the thing beneath.

Ray, it's so good to see you, man!

Peeling my palm carefully away from the surface to study the corpse; small translucent wings flat against its body. Briefly, the moth survives the assault before acquiescing to death. The wings rise up a bit, stand straight up. Death. Death rises from the surface.

Ray, how are you?

I ignore the voice calling my name, recognize another face in the crowd—a shaved head moving through the crowd. Manny. He sees me with his half-cocked smile. We're miles away from each other, but I hear the smile—cast-iron pipes, old watches, bottles. *You ever wanna burn the world away, Racine?* No explanations are necessary. No explanations about now. Now can't be explained.

Ray? Can I buy you a drink, yes?

*   *   *

Once I saw the world from a glass window that looked out onto Yankee Stadium. I saw something beyond the bowl of white with blue letters—saw something else just beyond it, saw the world from a window, climbed out of that window to get a better look, leg first, then arms and head . . . until my whole body became part of what I saw.

Ray?

He knew me before that, knew a body and a name that used to be mine. Once we knew each other in rooms with windows and books and conceptual drawings on its walls. Once, we knew each other in geometry classes and auditoriums. We wore blue jackets and gray pants. His parents paid for classes. A scholarship fund paid for mine. A better chance. He played the cello. I would see him, in his cello classes, sawing a stick through a tall wooden body. I liked the sound of it. Sat outside the room of his cello classes to hear that sound of sawing, and he saw me crouched on the floor outside the room, almost asleep, the sound of his cello in my ears. Once we walked to the train together, every day after school, beginning the day he found me sleeping with the cello in my ears. He took the train downtown, to Manhattan, to Riverside Drive. I took the train uptown to the Bronx and Yankee Stadium. He went home to a father who was a diplomat or something, Iranian or Palestinian or something and a mother who loved cats and took English lessons to subdue her French accent. They spoke French, all of them, and when he went home he went home to French food and a French father who laughed and kissed him on both cheeks and a French mother who laughed and took hang-gliding lessons. When I went home I went home to a woman who was not my mother, who did not work, who had been contracted by The City to take me in, who received a check for taking me in, who never called me son, and I never called her mother, who was old with black bangs and two gold teeth. I have never called anyone mother or father. I have never been called son. I have never been kissed on both cheeks.

Man, it's good to see you. My god, Ray, you look good.
Yeah.
You play music here, yes?
Yes.

Once, he invited me to take the train with him downtown, to
Riverside Drive, to an apartment building with twenty or thirty
floors and marble hallways and a doorman. To meet his father, who
sat in a room with walls of books and kissed him on both cheeks,
and his mother, who was listening to her English tapes in a sunken
living room, kissed him on both cheeks. We talked in his bedroom,
with framed posters of KRS-One and Public Enemy and an original
painting by Jean-Michel Basquiat, and he played his CDs of Slick
Rick and Prince and said he hated playing the cello and he didn't
have any friends because his English was not that good yet, and I
said it wasn't bad—he had an accent, that's all, and he told me he
and his mother had just moved to New York from Lyon to be with
his father, and then as I was leaving his mother invited me to come
back the next week for Christmas dinner and I told Miss Thais, the
foster lady, I had Christmas dinner plans, and she said that was
fine because she didn't have any plans, she never did, and she cried
. . . and I took the train downtown—from Yankee Stadium to Riverside Drive, and a big park sprawled out before a tall beige building
with windows the size of doors, windows draped with elegant fabrics, layers and layers of fabrics, a building with stone eagles and
sharp triangles carved on each floor of a twenty- or thirty-story
building with a doorman, and Phillipe and his mother and his
father were kissing everybody on both cheeks, everybody they
knew in New York and some relatives had flown in from France
and everybody exchanged boxes wrapped in fancy paper and everybody laughed and Phillipe's mother went to the big tree in the
sunken living room and reached into the pile of boxes beneath it
wrapped in fancy paper and checked each of them for name tags
and settled on one and handed it to me and I opened it in a chair
in a corner while everybody they knew from New York and some
relatives from France danced and sang and drank wine and ate

cheese and bread, and it was a tie. I had never worn a tie. I wasn't
sure if I had ever worn a tie. I couldn't remember. I couldn't
remember anything before the police, and the brown blanket
when I was twelve. I couldn't remember ever being in a room with
everybody kissing and hugging and exchanging gifts on Christmas.
I couldn't remember. I didn't want the tie. I left.

I press my thumb down onto the moth, smear it against the hard surface of the countertop, until all the parts that were once its body
become a fuzzy brown line. A signature of death. He keeps talking
and follows me as I make my way to the DJ stand. He is so glad to
see me he says, Nathalie will be so glad to know that I am doing
well, that I am still doing my music, he says, and his mother, she will
be happy too. She was upset with me, but I shouldn't think anything
of that. We should all just forget about it, he says. She will be so
happy to know that I am doing well, that I am resting. That I am
being cared for. He will call Nathalie tonight and he will call his
mother, and he will tell them he has seen me, and he asks me if I
ever received his letters, did they give them to me, and he asks me
did I ever receive the money he sent. He sent me money. He is sorry
he couldn't come sooner but he came as soon as he could. My
friends called him, and he came. He was pretty mad at me as well,
I must understand that, he says, it's understandable, he says, but
that was before, no one is mad at me now. They all understand, he
says. It all makes sense, he says, and he is so glad to see that I am
doing well and he asks me if I would like him to get me some water.

Nah.
Nathalie was worried, but she will be so glad to know you are
doing well.

All of us, together—cast our eyes over our shoulders toward the river,
toward the channel of water moving seaward, moving beneath a
bridge that attempts to stretch across it, half a bridge attempting to
cross over incoming waves, waves making sandbars beneath the surface—coming closer to shore, we hear the sandbar collapsing

beneath the surface, and a fiery current recedes from the shore, outward, foaming at the mouth, rippling inland toward the ugly new buildings erected too quickly, proving too much, cast our eyes toward the ugly new buildings, beyond them . . . toward the old buildings . . . the ones with shattered windows and smoked walls, and histories. We are aware. Our awareness is already swimming across the cold river . . . toward the mainland, and we climb up and gather around a wound—we peer into the wound with our awareness, that gaping sixteen-acre hole waiting for reconstruction . . . and already some of us . . . we do not want anything from forever. Just a little piece of yesterday. We do not want anything from forever. Nothing at all . . . everything we once wanted from forever is everything we have . . . now.

I never dream of faraway places. In Paris, Richard Wright resides under the stairs at Père Lachaise. No coon boys are celebrated in the floral arrangements of le Parc du Luxembourg. Richard Wright resides under the stairs in the graveyard. Bound. Masked. Dark marble slab. Edith Piaf sings arias to concrete mansions there. Jimmy Morrison entertains generations of daily visitors who decorate his stone with gardenias and rituals.

I flip through my shit—gonna start with some Arvo Part classical music shit. Gonna mix it over some Beta Band shit. Couchette throws herself into the aggregation of sinners, dances elevated on a small platform in sequined panties and no bra, red and green lights cast onto the brick wall behind her, bass line pumping through. Couchette's neck rises high above her shoulders—kinetic sentences of ragged ambulation, completing herself in a streaming consciousness of beats. Pulling herself through the eye of a needle: woven fabric of movement. Brushing waltz pageantry. Frail fiber of communal lore. She enters the circle with bare feet, shoulders celebrating what she thinks she is about to know. The people surround her. They clap and holler, shake their beaded instruments, wave their incense around. Couchette floats out into the deep wave of bodies, splashing in the current of hands. She turns toward me . . . *Racine* . . . waves toward me with liquid fingers . . . *Racine* . . . invites me to dive in, swim out, where the water is cool. I remain on the periphery, standing steadfastly on the rim of normalcy . . . behind the turntable, one ear to her soul, the other to the headphones, watching . . . still . . . waiting for safety . . . for things to stop moving so fast . . . I never follow people into dangerous places . . . *Racine* . . . casual observer, scanning down from the top of the hill, into the lake, water splashing against rocks . . . she notices the emerald eyes and black hair beside me, speaking in my ear. . . . A certain glimmer in her eye. Mischief. Sarcasm. She sees me from her perch where she is mounted high, sees me without permission through people dancing with bestial turns. Couchette sees me, she has found a connection to me, an emerald-green-and-black clue. Longfellow's wife caught on fire in their mansion . . . Longfellow's wife ran through the halls trying to put out the fire that caught hold to her flesh. That's how we die. In buildings that burn down all around us. We run to escape buildings, with flames scorching our backs. We run across bridges that stop midway. Couchette looks at me, with small embers shooting from her scar. There was a baby. A baby boy. There was another baby. Another baby boy. They are gone. Her children are gone. She is gone. The crowd cages her in, she cages the emerald-and-black jewel of a city in her hands.

How's the movie, Phillipe?

The movie? The movie did well. Nathalie is singing now. She would think that you would laugh, Ray, if you knew that she is singing now. She sings well, Ray. She has a small voice but it sounds good and she's making a record. I will send it to you. When you are ready, Ray, you should make music for Nathalie.

He's here to make up with me. He's been here a week, a whole week. He's here to see me. He's here to see me be weak. God it's so good to see me, be weak. We should *do music together again*, he says, when I am *ready*, and he laughs. Nathalie. *She doesn't sound bad, she doesn't take any of it seriously* and she would think that I would laugh if I knew she was singing now. Do I remember? Do I remember? Do I remember, when I made her sing, when we laughed at her singing. *She would sound great over beats and dis-*

torted instruments and strings and samples, like what Serge Gains-bourg did with Bridget Bardot, but with heavier beats. Says he wants to *program beats* with me again, *mix it to some live instrumentation,* asks me if he makes another movie, will I score it, asks me if the food is good here, if they're treating me well here, asks me do I remember anybody from Lyon. His friends. They've asked about me. They wondered if he'd heard from me, after I left. They were so sad to hear . . . I left.

Once, I got on a train and went downtown and got off where the buildings were tall and the park sprawled out across the street from the buildings. I would walk up to his apartment building with the doorman, and stand there and wait for the doorman to see me through the glass door and unlock the door, and I would stand there and tremble as the doorman in his crisp green suit and green hat trimmed with red rope looked at me with one eyebrow arched. I would tell him who I was there to see, that I was there to see Phillipe Lanceau. I would say it softly, with neat diction, and the doorman would pick up a yellow phone and dial a number and I would tremble with fear. Perhaps I might be arrested if no one on the other end picked up the phone, or if no one on the other end claimed to know me. I would tremble, thinking that I might be arrested for having wasted the doorman's time, for having boarded a train in the Bronx, for having gotten off where the buildings are tall and the park sprawls out before the tall buildings. And once the doorman had said my name into the phone, announced me as a visitor and hung up the phone, I made an attempt to walk toward the elevator. But the doorman in the green suit called out to me, echoed through the acoustics of the marble hallway, and he made me sign my name in a red book. A book with columns. I would have to write my name and the name of the person I was going to see, even though he already had that information . . . but I would have to write it down. And I would have to write down the apartment of the person I was going to see, and the time I arrived at the building, and there was a column for the time of departure. My hand froze there. The pen paused in my frozen hand, because I did not know what time I would depart. I had not thought of it, had not planned it. And I thought now I would be arrested because I did not know what time I would depart, could not predict or promise it, and the doorman looked at me strangely and lifted the pen from my hand and I pressed a brass button for the elevator to take me away from him. Another man swung open a gate, a man who sat on a small metal stool, and I stepped inside and he swung the gate closed and the doorman called out to him. Told him what floor he should deliver me to. Told him what apartment I was going to and the name of the resident in that apartment—*Lanceau*—but there was no need, and I trembled thinking that I had better not get lost in the hallways of this building. I had better reach my destination because the doorman had told the elevator man where I was going and I had signed my name to it, and I would be arrested if I had falsified that document.

Ray? Are you feeling okay?

Once I had entered Phillipe's apartment, when nobody was home— just him—he and I, we would play my tapes of Guru and he would play me some of his father's vinyl, Miles Davis and Etta Jones, the piano and the flute . . .

> *Build your dreams to the stars above,*
> *but when you need someone true to love,*
> *don't go to strangers,*
> *darlin', come on home to me . . .*

We had this music in common, and *Hustler* magazines in common, and we both fell in love with the same girls on the same pages with big tits and pink nipples and red hair and tiny panties snatched between their legs—daughters of Zeus. We would marry them one day. We compared our first crop of whiskers and pubic hair—jerked off on the pages of *Hustler* magazine, made bets to see who could shoot the furthest—shared his father's hashish, choked when we laughed—all we had in common, a moment when it seemed as if we belonged to the same world.

*   *   *

Ray, would you like me to . . .

But when I emerged from the train, back in the Bronx, and walked the city steps littered with beer cans, and waved at Pie and John-John who played stickball against the wall of the bodega, and once I walked up the walkway to the tenement building I lived in where a hole on the door indicated where a lock should be, and no intercom system or yellow phone or doorman intercepted my entrance to the building . . . and once I pressed the button for the elevator, waited to hear the cables move . . . and once they did not, and I walked up to the sixth floor, put my key in the door of the woman with shiny black bangs' apartment and followed the sound of Etta Jones blaring from the living room, saw the shiny black bangs sitting on the worn sectional with the glassy eyes of a flounder, a stiff Scotch, smiling at me without her front gold teeth and said, *Did you know I was your mother's mother, baby?*

Phillipe belonged to the world. I belonged to something vaguely similar to it. A poor imitation.

Ray? Racine?

Bare breasts of the tropical coon tickled against the Sankofa bird perched on her finger, fruit spilled from her cupped arm as the marines arrived to pick and pluck, suck and claim. Smiling with big-teeth faces. Marilyn's cigarette man in pink and yellow. Albert Ammons, long dead. Lester Young, long dead. Freddie Hubbard and Harry "Sweets" Edison are remembered in glistening teeth and gleaming eyes. No romantic music beaming from the boulevards of Paris. The movies lied to me. The movies we saw together when we were kids, the ones with subtitles, they lied to me. I'd come all that way. Left the dying corpse of a woman in a hospital room attached to wires, left the apartment with Yankee Stadium's lights glaring through the living room window—left it furnished and dusty with closets full of her dresses and my shoes and her lipsticks and my junior high school photos—left it unlocked and took a plane all the way to Paris at the invitation of a best friend who had lured me there with romantic notions of a utopia. An elysian field.

I will try to see you one more time before I leave New York, next week? Okay? I will try to come back. Would you like me to come back? Would you like that?

At any moment, tears. At any moment . . . none. Arid eyes waiting for rain. The body is weighted down with shit. Weighted down. Ten thousand one-pound bags sacked across our shoulders, our feet sinking when we walk, but at any moment the head can detach itself from the body and swirl up to Jesus, only to be thrown back down again and crack hard against the pavement.

Ray?

The boy, wandering away from fire, was sinking down. The people who watched the boy gadding down vulgar streets with fumes emanating from his jacket . . . they had no reason to take responsibility for him. To claim him. Women do not remember palms groping their vaginas, or penises in their mouths. There were no words spoken in hallways, anywhere, the night he was conceived, this boy walking away from fire with smoke coming off his shoulders. No music played anywhere on earth the night he was born, this boy in a brown blanket sitting in a police station without words. No record of the sky turning any color other than sky. No swelling stomach of a young girl. No screaming from the ears, no elevation of feet. No white sheets smeared with red and clear white and me.

Phillipe.

Yes, Ray?

You remember the book, the sound, the image?

I don't—

Champs de Mars. We were a family. We—we were gonna be famous, man. The music. We were gonna make it—the music. The music for the movie.

Ray, I don't . . . would you like to step outside with me, Ray? For some air? We can go to the garden, for some air.

We jumped off the bridge together near Pont Alexandre III. *Tou-*

jours content! Jamais malade! Jamais mourir! I was the one betrayed,
see?

The chair falls from under me, metal legs scrape against the tile,
falls—loud, they've got me by the arms . . . I could've not said anything. Could've just played the music. Stayed in the music, in the
rooms I was building for myself, but he kept pushing it. Kept pushing
it, and now—what's funny is—I'm laughing so hard, my eyes wet—
they overflow. Rain and laughter. I'm hunched over a big wooden
plank, my stomach muscles contracting, and I can't stop laughing at
that crazy shit, and I'm peering down into the dark black water that
blends with the sky. I'm laughing and looking at the sky and the water
together, how they frame the ugly new buildings of Manhattan. I turn
around and look at the ugly girls and the ugly boys standing on line,
these girls and boys who are just stepping out into a world in recovery,
who have just recently turned on their television sets again to watch a
situation comedy or a music video, have been inspired by inspirational
news anchors and the return of designer fur coats, have just begun to
return to the frivolity of life, of fashion, of Hollywood movies and
mixed cocktails. Today, maybe for the first time in a long time or
maybe for the first time ever, these young men have knotted ties
around their necks—aiming for the perfect triangle and the perfect
dimple, have returned to their rookie positions and starter salaries,
returned to oak-veneered desks in glass skyscraper office buildings
with walls of windows, and some of them have just shaken hands with
important men for the first time—firmly—cupped their fingers around
the important fingers of veterans of business whose alma mater is the
same as theirs. Some of these young men with buzz cuts and fresh
growth on their chins have neither secured nor returned to employ-
ment or graduated from the Ivy League universities of their fathers—
rather some of these young men in the company of a girl without a
coat, standing on a line that coils around a vacant livery stand and a
closed bodega on a cold cobblestone street beneath an abandoned
bridge, are just waiting for admission to a party that will transport
them to the normalcy of abundance and privilege.

*   *   *

From inside the anchorage, a boom resounds—an explosion, spitting out fire and black dust, pieces of brick into our backs. Manny. *You ever just wanna burn the world away?* I turn around to see a mushroom of fire and black smoke expand into the sky—an umbrella of fire and black smoke. A whirlwind of screams and motion, people running in and running out, the M-16s lie flat against the cobblestone, shots are fired—the helicopters swing their searchlights through the air, one falls from the sky into the river—another explosion. Everything is blown away. The music. Plans for renewal. Couchette. I run toward the anchorage, try to push past the rifles and bleeding girls in ripped dresses—ashen. I try to push past heavy steel doors, shredded and hanging from their hinges. I try to get inside the cloud of black smoke to find Couchette—to retrieve my body. My body is inside black smoke. I want my body back. I want all the pieces of my body back, scattered somewhere on the road from Troezen, but they've got me down, holding me sharp against the ground. Phillipe is yelling, doesn't want them to handle me too roughly, he says, it's all right, he says, but they've got me flat on my back and all the boys and girls are screaming and running past—hair aflame. They've got me down on the floor, firm hands to the back of my neck—like the doctors and nurses, and someone is muttering something and someone is calling out the names of meds: Prozac, Risperdal, Paxil, Ativan, Haldol . . . and the big buxom woman screams, Haldol! and Phillipe is yelling, *I didn't mean to upset you, Ray. I didn't mean to upset you . . .* as if he is oblivious to the explosion. Sirens yell out, only for a second—there is no music. But DJs live in rooms. Rooms they build for themselves. We are self-sustaining, like the other young men and women who stand on line, the ones who have never known privilege and abundance, who have not fallen far from where they always were, who know nothing about the blank checks the government gave to bail out small private businesses, who had no sufficient papers and no valid criteria to qualify them for emergency assistance, who have never stood on line with a copy of their mortgage and unpaid insurance bills and unpaid property tax bills expecting to be rescued, who were not displaced when their historically hazardous environs came within close proximity of enemy lines, who were not given a hotel room to recompense the nuisance of crisis. These others who were standing on line, anticipating a ritual of rebuilding . . . stood in line with their lives.

We are the same survivors. We know how to dance. We just want to dance like the dancers in basement studios who wear sweat and kente-cloth *lapas* and strike their palms against kidskin with the umbrage of assassins. We are ready to climb our legs up each other's bodies in an unholy convocation. We want to inhabit an efflux of internal sound sprung up from pelvises and toes, the dance of limbs bending into connection with other limbs, the sudden impact of limbs building temples with combative huddles, with inhalations and exhalations that disconnect the body from the spirit and accelerate the being off the surface of the floor, want to send each other into flight and cavort with each other in interactive shapes that morph into psychedelic pornography . . . adjoining maneuvers restricting certain mobility, our weight falling into the ground until two bodies become one body, and three bodies become a thousand keys linked without a chain, the bump and grind of unlocking doors that protect us from the inhibition of abundance and privilege.

Racine? Can you hear me? Nod if you can hear me.

Some of us come with tambourines on our backs, we make noise, come with a reservoir of spit floating beneath our tongues, we are spirited . . . we foam at the mouth, knowing we may not survive until morning, because some of us have been injected with too many things that bid us sleep . . . we come with too many pills . . . we come without birth records, photographs . . . reasons for the demise of our brothers . . . no buildings, no radicals, no countries to blame for our atrocities . . . we bear the heat of naked flames. In war, we are clothed in brilliance, and we have no further explanation for our anger. All the words wash away from the pages in war. War is not unbearable. What is unbearable is the absence of mirrors.

Count backward, Ray. Ten . . . nine . . . eight. . . .

The bridge has fallen into the embankment—all its bodies trapped inside. The anchorage collapses, with pieces of me trapped inside. She is gone. Couchette. That object resting in her palms like a floating skull falling against gravity. That part of me is evaporating in the cup of her hands.

Racine?

I don't feel like talking . . . I don't feel . . . like talking. I don't feel . . .

It's just the Haldol.

Nah . . . it's you. You. You, with the questions, and you don't play it right. You don't play it right. Like, look at the glass. Look at that glass, what's in the glass?

Water.

The liquid . . . the sea is in my glass . . . enormous body of water in my glass . . . the bridge.

Is that what you see?

I see it like it was.

What was it, Racine?

Dead. She was dead.

Who was dead?

Eddie said she gave birth to us, never raised us. Said she was crazy, she in the crazy hospital. Said that's where she belonged. No pictures. No stories about her. Nothing.

How come you don't just make up stories about her?

I did. I do. No, I mean . . . I don't make up none of the stories. He told me the stories . . .

But none about your mother.

Nah.

Never?

Never.

. . .

. . .

Zuni?

Don't start.

He fell, right?

. . .

From a cliff, right?

Yeah.

Was it an accident?

. . . Eddie . . . took me on the bus, to the building.

What building?

In Brooklyn.

Why?

I don't know. It burned down.

And?

The blue men took me to the social worker.

Yes?

She brought me to Miss Black Bangs.

Then?

I lived with her. Thais. Geneva's mother, but she only admit it
when she—

And?

The dreams. The medicine. The swelling between my legs.

Yes?

Phillipe. I met Phillipe in school. He was my friend.

Yes?

We grew up together.

And?

He left.

To go back to France?

Yes . . .

Miss Black Bangs . . .

She died.

Were you there when she died?

She was in a bed, she was three pounds, rotting flesh, her hair
was white in a bed, and she had tubes strung up her nose, jabbed in
her arms, and the nurse kept coming in and going out and sometimes she would talk to Thais and say *Enjoying your visit with your
son?* She couldn't say yes or no, because she had tubes in her
mouth, she only had one eye left, she never called me her son, never
introduced me that way, I was just this kid she fed and played

records for. I was this kid who hated when she drank, because she felt bad about Eddie, felt bad about Geneva. I was this kid who made these weird sounds and had weird dreams, she was not my mother, I was not her son, but I was the only one in the room and I . . .

What?

Left . . . because she was gonna die . . . and everything I never knew about myself was gonna die with her . . . I couldn't stay for that . . .

Go on.

He said I could stay with his mother in Paris . . . she wanted to see me . . . Then I could take a train to be with him and his girl-friend. In Lyon. Said we could make music.

Make music.

That's right . . . that's what I said . . .

And? What happened when you went to visit Phillipe?

They could see it.

See what?

Something was wrong . . .

What?

. . . don't know . . . can't remember.

Let's start there.

Where?

. . . Let's go back.

How far . . .?

How far back would you like to go?

I don't . . . know.

I'll go back with you. We'll go back together.

You got the advantage over me. You always did.

Why do you say that?

You knew this city, before its reconstruction. There was a city here, once. A city with a name . . . the city of Racine. I tore it down, built it back up from the scraps. Recycled the tendon, the tissue, the marrow, rebuilt it. First I walked the pace of disbelief. Now I walk the rim of normalcy. No need to excavate further. A man died, that's all.

EDDIE SAT IN THE ROOM IN FRONT OF THE FIREPLACE, IN FRONT OF THE DYING FIRE. Sat in a brown leather chair with a glass of Scotch in his right hand and a Bible in the other. Ruined body of rage, complacent. He sat receding from the room, the house, the city, music, sat staring at an elaborately carved fireplace of alabaster with sparrows carrying grapevines, and angels strumming mandolins, and he leaned toward the fire, took the heavy wrought-iron poker in his hand and jabbed the logs, lifted one log from the bottom of the pile, balanced it on the sharp tip of the poker, and tumbled it to the top of the pile, lifted it again, and propped it up in the wrought-iron grate, so that there would be air between the top log and the ones that lay dying beneath, and he jabbed the logs until they shone brighter, until a tiny flame kindled and grew again— breathed in the small space he'd made for it, until the tiny flame grew tall enough to catch hold to the log propped up on an angle, and he splashed a little Scotch into the fire to encourage its growth, and the tiny flame awakened into a larger flame, exploded with ferocity, and the embers beneath the grating rolled out onto the blue-stone hearth and a stream of black smoke escaped from inside and blackened the face of angels, rose up to the crown moldings twenty feet above the heart-pine floors, and bright orange embers popped out and fell onto the wood slats at his feet, seared into the grooves, and Eddie watched it burn into the floor, watched little streams of smoke rise from every piece of bright orange ember scattered about the floor, tiny pieces of sun burning into wood, and Eddie turned his face to Geneva, asleep on the couch with her thumb in her mouth and her left tit hanging out of her pink blouse, and the yellow from the fire made her skin look redder than it was, and he looked at Frederick in his flannel pajamas spooned in the crest of her stomach, asleep, but opening his eyes, and he looked at the baby asleep on the big pillow on the floor, and more embers popped out of the fireplace, leaped beyond the bluestone hearth, onto the heart pine, and more smoke rose from the alabaster to the plaster molding, and somewhere, there was a bang, from somewhere, a bang, from outside or downstairs or heaven or hell, and Frederick opened his eyes, saw the raging fire that had been encouraged to grow, the drunken Scotch-drenched fire, escaping its place on the wrought-iron grate, between the walls of brick, behind the alabaster birds and grapevines, saw it grow large and step out into the room, put its arms onto the walls, its feet on the floor, its head rising to the plaster crown moldings, and Frederick screamed *hot mama hot* and Eddie turned his face back to the flame he had given birth to, the only thing he had sired that he could be proud of, and it moved toward its father, kissed his shin, and Eddie jumped back when the kiss stung, jumped up out of the brown leather chair when his child moved toward him with open arms, and he grabbed Frederick in the arm that had held his drink and grabbed Racine in the arm that had held the Bible, and his third child, the fire he had given birth, picked up the Bible his father had dropped, turned the pages with its hands, each page burning to ash, the words of God charring before they could be read, and Eddie bolted from the room, his child growing too big for the room, growing rapidly, the appendages breaking glass out of windows, knocking down lamps and drapes, and Eddie screamed for Geneva to waken as he ran into the street, and Geneva remained on the couch, curled, asleep, dreaming of Emma, dreaming of a house as large as a foreign country. She opened her eyes only once, to see the fire that resembled the face of Emma, welcomed it, extended her arms, and the third child Eddie had made leaned in to the girl, accepting her embrace.

By day it was a road, a long line gashed up the shaven earth where daily travelers have stooped wearily alongside the trimmings of grass and slept unbothered, others have dashed the scorching trail without stopping—waving lazy palms at passing trucks and field hands picking through the groves. By night, it was an anomalous staircase steeped toward an uncertain destiny. A path your feet had to know better than your eyes. He ran it. Photographs of shortcuts and landmarks flashed vivid colors in his head, but the world around him was one shade of darkness. Land requiring visceral exploration. The first mile, up the gravelly course, was aimless. The feet ran with the speed and clumsiness of a boy outrunning ghosts and ghouls and God. The second mile, through the serrated colony of cornstalks, was pursuant. He was heading toward the hill, the tree, the rock, the water; the place he knew.

Frederick hooked onto a branch and hoisted himself up into the densely wooded area, voyaging through the second city beyond rows of maize. He anchored himself onto a huge rock and propelled upward, embracing the limbs of trees and crags of clay. He climbed until he'd navigated himself within plain view of the lake below the cliffside. Footed on the hem of the wooded hill where the earth folded and plunged down into a gorge of rocks bathing in fresh water, the defiant boy pulled back his robe, positioned his fist at his hip, and rested one foot on a sure foundation. He was that explorer of social studies textbooks in helmets and velvet vests. This was *his* land. He knew it even in the disguise of darkness. He would always know how to find it, a place he loved. There was no light anywhere else in the world comparable to the silvery needles darting through the thick of trees at night, sparkling diamonds in the places where water met stone, with its mystical harmonies of hidden creatures.

The live oak was just one hill below him to the right. Frederick climbed down toward it with careful footing. Beneath the oak's awning, he sat in the cradle of its stump and invented a plan: by morning he would run down to the railroad tracks, the point between Zuni and Portsmouth, hop onto the train's side like the escaped convicts in the movies do. He'd stow away as far as Richmond, maybe farther . . . anywhere he could smoke a cigarette, fuck a girl, spin music and get famous, send a car back to Zuni to get his little brother. Get Jesus out of his little brother's head. Racine's not gonna make it with Jesus in his head. Racine's not gonna grow up and be no kinda man in that house.

BLUE MAN WITH SHINY BUTTONS TALKS TO BOY IN BROWN BLANKET. BLUE MAN ASKS BROWN BOY, DO YOU KNOW YOUR NAME? Blue men have come to boy in chariots with torches of red that raged through the streets with the noise of destruction. The blue men have come in their chariots in the middle of the night, have covered the boy in a brown blanket, and more chariots come, and a building burns in the distance and chariots of red come with water but God is destroying the city of Ninevah and the blue man asks the boy, *Do you know your name?* Boy wants to speak, but the boy is too scared to speak. Too scared of speaking. But the boy tries, because maybe there is forgiveness. Maybe the mighty blue men of God will bring forgiveness if he tells them his name, so boy tries to say his name but he can only make himself say *Ra—! Ra—?* blue man repeats. *Ray? your name is Ray?* Boy is frustrated. Wants to say, *no, that's not my name. Please tell God I want forgiveness.* Boy keeps trying to speak, and his chest feels heavy and his body jumps up and his arms flap up and down like wings and out of his mouth comes a hawk hovering over a fire in a burning building, and boy has no control over his body. He falls and flaps his wings and the blue men try to hold him down and they yell out to each other and to the boy, all he wants is to tell them, to say—*my name is Racine,* but what comes from his mouth is the sound of an earsplitting bird, flapping its wings.

WOMAN WITH BLACK BANGS WEARS A TAN RAINCOAT AND BLUE HAT, seems out of place in the white room of stainless steel cabinets, and flat bed covered in clean white paper where the boy lies back, his legs dangling off the end—pants pulled down around his sneakers, a huge stainless steel lamp aimed at his genitals. Swollen. The doctor's hands are covered in little white latex gloves, fingers lifting the boy's penis to inspect the swollen scrotum beneath it. Woman with black bangs interrupts the latex inspection.

Social worker woman say she gonna come by and check on him. I told him he need to wear a hat, this weather changin' every day like it do.

Doctor says nothing. Boy says nothing. The mention of a hat and the changing of the weather seems out of place in the latex room. The boy is worried because he's missing school today. Missed all of last week, but today is important. Today is only a half day because of English competency tests. Only freshmen and sophomores have to take the competency tests. The boy is a freshman. First year of high school. Should be a sophomore, but there are no records of his elementary school years and he got left back in junior high. The boy is a freshman, the boy is competent and smart. Knows he's smart, even if he doesn't talk much. Wants to prove his competence. Hopes he doesn't have to stand up again—not until the pain goes away. Hopes when he stands up his jeans aren't wrinkled because he'd ironed his jeans carefully. They had perfect creases in them. He used steam on his sharply creased jeans, used the steam iron and spray starch. The steam iron had a little orange nozzle and you could squirt water onto the fabric as you ironed. Steam would come from the little holes underneath the iron, and he would push the orange nozzle and the iron would spit water onto the edge of the jeans and he pressed the iron down hard along the edge, dragged it hard and slow, then sprayed the starch on the place he had just squirted and steamed and pressed the iron down on the little white beads of starch until it sizzled underneath, and he dragged the iron hard and slow again and he hung his sharply creased jeans carefully between two heavy coats so they would stay flat. That was last week, before he got sick. One ball is swollen, the size of a golf ball. The other is flat, deflated, empty. The flat deflated one was swollen first, but Miss Black Bangs didn't take him to the doctor, made him stay in bed with fever and pain—gave him soup, played her records. Then it went down, deflated, and the pain was gone and he was ready to go to school again but the other one swelled up, to the size of a golf ball, and the fever came again, and he couldn't walk because it was heavy and pulled down and he stayed in bed and watched TV and thought about the bottle of aspirin on the nightstand, thought about taking the whole bottle but then remembered the girls in his freshman homeroom who said he was cute even if he's quiet, Antonia, Latrice and Kyndell and Deidre. He had hung out with Latrice before, and her brother Oscar. They had hung out down on 170th Street at a place called Merit Farms where they ate hot dogs and drank orangeade, and then they went to get Kyndell who lived in the projects on University Avenue and they yelled up to her window and Kyndell came down in a tank top and terry cloth shorts, and they went to Latrice and Oscar's house, he gave everybody a beer and passed around a joint and they all got high. They had invited him to go with them to Long Branch, New Jersey, to the Haunted Mansion amusement park, but he got sick. The foster lady made him soup and made herself a drink and played her records and checked on him every now and then, complained that he didn't listen to her when she told him to wear a hat and a scarf. That's why he's sick now. Said she didn't want anybody from the Social Worker's office sayin' she had anything to do with this. She made herself a drink and she made him soup and he lay in bed until the pain got worse and the fever got higher and he wanted to take the pills, all of them, and she made him get up and get dressed and made him walk, slowly, until they caught a gypsy cab down by Yankee Stadium. The cabdriver played a mixed tape of old songs, "Between You, Babe, and Me," "Good Idea, Let's Dance," "Super Sperm."

What's that you call it again? What you say he got?

Orchitis. Inflammation of the testicle. Can be caused by virus, bacteria , infection. How long did he have fever?

Week or two, off and on. Doctor, I told him to wear a scarf around his neck.

A scarf has nothing to do with it, if you had taken him to the hospital sooner, it's possible we could've reduced the swelling and saved the testicle, but both are destroyed now and I'm sure the sperm cells have been destroyed.

Boy remembers something someone said once, At least now *the cycle is broken.*

Hippolytus
at Versailles

. . . There are fools
Who hang close
To their original
Thought . . .
(I mean I think
I know now
What a poem
is) a
Turning away . . .
From what
It was
Had moved us . . .
A madness . . .

—LEROI JONES, "Betancourt"

She kissed me on both cheeks, she's happy to receive me. The red car hurls around corners barely missing dogs and their walkers—my luggage, slapping up against my chin at every turn and bump. Mme. Marignac attempts a smile. She and Phillipe's father are divorced now. Phillipe called. He will be happy to receive me when I arrive in Lyon. First I must *see Paris, yes? I am a man now,* she says. She beams with joy, laughs at how she still remembers me from when I was a kid. Shy. Quiet. *The most beautiful complexion of red dirt after the rains.*

The red car pulls up to 20 West Guynemer, Garches, near St. Cloud, just outside of Paris. A little gingerbread house in a little gingerbread town. She jumped about to get my luggage, with the energy of a rabbit on amphetamines, and I thought to myself, as she turned on the lamps in her living room, she's probably uncomfortable—this man in her ostentatious living room, this man who was a boy the last time she saw him. And now, he's completely unlike anyone else she's ever met. Or she thinks I'm completely ordinary, common maybe. Perhaps there is nothing portentous about me at all. Claude Luter plays "Down by the Riverside," from her record player. Transparent hospitality drizzles over politely seated bodies, fills the lagoon between us in her flowery little living room, decorated with statues of angels, with armor and spade, handmade quilts and dolls. The walls are painted lime green, plastic beads . . . peach, turquoise, jade and yellow, hanging from the ceiling, two huge front windows, covered in thick black velvet. Seven-day candles on shelves and tables and against the walls, there is a cat. The cat is a fat iridescent blue, stalking about . . . watching over her master. She curls around her legs, stares at me. Claude Luter and Pavarotti play from the small record player near an arrangement of dried flowers and freshly picked vegetables. The cat is uncomfortable. Phillipe's mother looks the same.

Blond hair parted on the right side, black at the root, cut in a sharp angle just short of her ears. She looks older. She shows me to my room, another small flowery room of green and yellow scattered across pink, French doors that open out onto her vegetable garden.

It's been some time since you've seen Phillipe, yes?
Since high school.
Yes, you had some problem, yes?
    . . .
You mustn't think badly of it. My husband was very fond of you, Racine. He thought highly of you, we all did. He was very angry—
Yeah . . .
I am so happy you finally responded to Phillippe's letter. It was such a long time before you responded, yes?
He sent the letter to . . . to my foster mother's address in the Bronx. I'm not living there anymore. I only got the letter recently.
Oh, of course! Yes, and so . . . where is it that are you living now?
Here . . . there.
?
    . . .
Did he tell you about his father?
Yes.
It is better for me to forget about this thing . . . well, we were already divorced by then. We must move on, yes?
Yes.
It has been hard on Phillipe, his father being so publicly humiliated . . . ruined . . . they took away his job, not because of the . . . uh—
Drug possession?
Not because of that but because of what he taught.
?
The fall of great empires, this is not treason. Well, if there is some parallel between America and the fall of ancient empires— maybe it is true what he finds in history, yes?
Yes.
Yes, and so . . . maybe it is discrimination, because he is Arab.

Well, it is a school with so much money, spoiled sons of rich men—
I hate to accuse of these things but, well, you of all people must
understand this discrimination at the school.

I understand.

Phillipe is not in touch with his father. It is a shame. I don't wish
that. Phillipe is not in touch with me very much, either. Occasionally. I think, maybe, he disapproves of the man I am seeing now, but
I must live for myself, yes?

Yes.

He is different, Racine. So much sadness, I think. Very serious
with so much sadness. His girlfriend, well . . . very nice but no . . .
uh . . . substance. Perhaps, I think, seeing you will bring him some
happiness. He has changed so much. No friends. The two of you,
were good friends, yes?

Yes.

He has told you of his film, yes?

He asked me to do the music.

He tells me nothing of this—

The producers flew me in.

Oh . . . well . . . well it is good. The two of you will be together
again, making music, yes?

Yes.

In the morning, we rise early, run all over Paris, reading maps, return
to her gingerbread house in Garches, rye bread, wine, cherries, and
strawberries on the table, neatly assembled, and perused by the cat.
She speaks of hypocrisy and evil. Every night, the same conversation.
The cat knew the scope of my discomfort.

I am so sorry, Racine, to hear of your . . . eh . . . your mother.

Foster mother.

So much tragedy in our lives always, yes? You will survive it, yes?

Her eyes turn red. She is *so sorry. So sorry to read of the things going
on in . . . in the world . . . but liberty is its own enemy,* she says. She
cannot *condone the death penalty for traitors.* She cannot *condone*

racial profiling. There are *Christians in Pakistan on death row for blasphemy against the Prophet Mohammed. Religion is evil. God and the Devil follow you wherever you go. Each year, the Shias mark the decapitation of Mohammed's grandson, Imam Hussain, with self-flagellation. This is silly, yes? They take knives, tie them to chains, and beat themselves, this is silly, yes? Taliban soldiers were shot by American troops and thrown into wells with bombs, this is cruel, yes?* She had relatives who were killed in Oradour-sur-Glane, *ten days after the Allied invasion of Normandy. They were gathered into barns, shot, burned. Evil, yes? The wars we remember most are our own, yes? What is anybody really doing to . . . ensure safety? Remembering is a social act. It is triggered by something. Racism. Préjudice. Religion. I dislike religion. I dislike the Hassidim. It makes me cry to think of it.*

Her eyes brighten, delighted to see Fannie stalking the table, licking cheese from my plate, then her face shuts, her hands massage the arrival of a new thought into her temples . . . *Several of my cats have died . . . So many cats, she says. I think a neighbor killed one of my tabbies when I was a young girl living in Strasbourg.* She refreshens my cup with hot tea, her eyes becoming portals of rare vivid colors. *A cruel little boy who learned to hate the Jews killed one of my cats. I found another one a week later. Wet and weak. Living under the house. Perhaps she was escaping something. Something terrible. A boy's cruelty. I fed it. Nursed it. Until it was fat and happy. I promised it tomorrow. But it was not long for us to stay in Strasbourg . . . We kept moving. My mother, my father and I. We kept moving. We had to move quickly. We were Jews. Jews had to hide. We had to convert to Catholicism. The day before we were to leave Strasbourg, my father took the cat by its tail and bashed its head onto the side of a rock—just once, then tossed it into the brush. He'd left her in her misery . . . She suffered so . . . for a long time . . . dying. I watched her hind legs lose ground. Too weak to lift her head to sip water from the bowl I'd placed by her side in the night. By morning she died. She died very slowly. For months we hid ourselves under the house of a family not far from Strasbourg. Like the cat, hoping no one would take our heads and bash them against rocks.*

*   *   *

Claude Luter plays on without the benefit of Joe Newman or Freddie Hubbard. The cat apathetically curls itself around itself. Mme.'s face becomes an open wetland overflowing its banks. She excuses her face from me to run her bathwater. The aroma of lavender salts returns with her to the living room. She speaks one last time before retreating to the sanctum of lavender. *I hope if I should die, I will not suffer. I hope when you should die, it will be pleasure. I hope you never meet anyone who should cause you harm. I hope you should never learn hate so much that you should cause cruelty. No one should have to suffer . . . No one.*

The 95 bus on rue Auber to St. Germain des Prés—too many big restaurants serving pork. Behind the Panthéon they smoke and dance. Père Lachaise, the graveyard. I feel at home among the dead, my back rests comfortably against hard granite. I search endlessly through the maze of tombs and crypts, and granite stone statues of ballerinas who died early. Jim Morrison's grave is covered in flowers, as is Isadora Duncan's. Richard Wright is buried in a memorium at the base of the wall under the stairs. I bend down to see the words carved on its facade. Buried under the stairs . . . No honor for the expatriate poet here. In shop windows shiny black porcelain dolls with looming chalk-white mouths and grotesque eyes. Thick heads of hair, wrapped in red scarves. They are too expensive. 1,750 francs.

Outside a small café I order the only thing I can understand, *omelette fromage,* and tea. My postcards are stained with tea—Miles Davis and Billie Holiday—smeared with a little egg, and a bit of ketchup. A young soldier sits near me, reading my postcards over my shoulder. Shiny black, looming blood lips and fluorescent eyes. A beautiful dark man. Beautiful dark Bronze Star at his chest. A strange odor emanates from his shoulders. Vodka spittle, or nasturtium, a familiar stench.

Wash your hands, Racine. Ninevah is falling.

Waited for Phillipe at Gare Lyon Perrache for over an hour. I was sure he wouldn't come. I was thinking that the whole thing was a huge mistake. He said we could make this music for his movie. Ambient shit. Said he had a Pro Tools setup and turntables, built himself a little studio, said we could make beats. Tracks. He said we were a team. We could do this together. We're gonna make beats. As soon as his girlfriend picks me up, my whole life is gonna change.

Nathalie interrupts my tenth cigarette and anxiety. She walks right up to me, kisses me on both sides of my face and explains in crude English that Phillipe is at work editing his film. She takes my hand and guides me out of the station. Nathalie borrows a cigarette and steals a light. Her smile, a sweet perfume. Thick waist and large breasts, plump thighs pulling through an opening in crescent-moon-patterned silk. Her body generous, her hair catches the scent of the Saone River. She offers to carry my bag. I refuse. She smiles. We shift in photoplay progression; camera panning the river, glistening over conversation. Mingus plays, words dissolve and become images. Thilly Weissenborn's nude Balinese virgin hung over Phillipe's bed-room. We made jokes about the virgin. Planned a strategy for music, collaborated on beats and sounds, submerged ourselves in images and books and dreams. Imagined a world that reimagined music that reimagined us. Mingus's bass extends to us a medley of that room, where Phillipe and I would be famous. The press will follow us, push cameras, and microphones, up our noses. They'd want to take pictures of the sweat gleaming from my jaw, capture the imprint of my penis pushed to the side—a pendulum swinging from a bestial frame. My turntables in motion, my band behind me at the press conference of fame—my huff and growl in harmony with the bass line. Piano out. The vacuum of paparazzi chatter filled with bass and horn, my speech for the camera without pattern or preconceived chord progression. My existence is a crime in their city of opulence. We're gonna make beats and new music, together. Phillipe is gonna make me famous with his movie. Mixmaster Mike, Quentin Tarantino, sound, image, sound . . . a place to be.

Nathalie and I move into the nakedness of Montée de Chazeaux, rue de la Bombarde. Past the Cathédrale Saint-Jean. Along the Saone, an opal jewel on my arm.

> You . . . had nice times with Mme. Marignac?
> Yes.
> She is . . . political, much political talk, no?
> Yes.
> Did this make . . . eh . . . for you a bad time?
> No.

We turn a few more corners, tri-level shops with more distorted faces on postcards like at the Bibliothèque Forney, on rue du Figuier in Sully-Morland; the smiling Negro, the thick-lipped African coon erasing himself with soap, the topless tropical whore welcoming her marine lovers.

> *Pour faire de beaux voyages*
> *Et apprendre un métier*
> *Engagez-vous dans la marine.*
> *Engagez-vous voyages.*

Their small apartment overlooks the Saone River, one window facing the steeple of the St. Jean Church. Nathalie pours wine and entertains me for several hours while Phillipe continues to cut film in his studio. About an hour later, Nathalie and I are already drunk, my imagination soaring above reality. Nathalie and I have a private game. I pretend to teach her new English words. Nothing words. "Mee-wee." I am laughing at the joke, and she is laughing at the phonetics of new American words.

Bon soir, Racine.

Phillipe walks into the kitchen, hair tussled as always, green eyes piercing through a firm handshake. Formal. We hug. I'd forgotten the mass of black hair, uncombed. The beautiful green eyes. We do not know each other. Not anymore. Not really. I don't know these people. I don't know anybody anywhere. They speak French to each other, I interpret the exchange in my head. *There is nothing much to eat, Phillipe. I tried to research where to purchase pig guts. I didn't go shopping or prepare anything. I was here all day, making myself beautiful for you.*

Fuck him, darling. I don't even know him. We went to school together, in New York. Calls himself Racine now. I think he loved me, once. I must've been drunk when I invited him here—he'll be gone in a few days.

Phillipe! Speak without emotion, he'll know we are talking about him.

I am sorry to have left you alone with him for so long. I forgot he was coming until this morning. Did he touch you? Did he say anything inappropriate? Did he look through your handbag or take advantage of you?

No, I'm all right, Phillipe, but he looks at me funny . . . I don't like the way he smells. Look at him. He has a distant stare, mumbles to himself. I think his mind leaves him.

He kisses her gently on the mouth before he speaks to me again.

Shall we have dinner out?

Yes is the first and only thing I've said . . . at all.

Nathalie's clogs clack against the cobblestones—galloping horses on Place Benoît Crépu. She throws her hair from side to side, a long blond burden, it gets caught between her lips. We drink some more at a bar near the church in the St. Jean district. We are drunk, and a woman is in a hospital room somewhere in New York. Something that used to be a woman is in a bed. Chapped. Sour. Silent. One eye to the ceiling. You're supposed to sit there, and look at it, with flowers. She can't see you or smell your flowers anymore . . . you wait. Sit there with all your unanswered questions. Now that you have composed the questions in your head, you're supposed to sit beside a bed and watch the source of information slip away. Then leave. Walk down the stairs, hand in the visitor's pass, smoke a cigarette on the sidewalk, walk to the subway. Catch a train somewhere. Paris. Lyon. Somewhere.

We continue drinking and laughing and smoking. Phillipe and I tell Nathalie stories about junior high school, cello playing, and girls in magazines. We talk about music. We browse through the passageways, old tunnels used by sixteenth-century silk merchants to avoid the rain, World War II Jews to escape Nazi soldiers. We go to bed late. I drift off to sleep in their living room, in Lyon. I am somewhere I've never been before where a river lives beneath the window. The bells of the St. Jean Church ring me to sleep in a place I've never been before. A place I know, bells ringing me into somewhere.

Nathalie sleeps later than I do most days. Both of us waiting for Phillipe to come home before we begin drinking. They fight a lot. Fighting and lovemaking. Nathalie is always crying, Phillipe is always indifferent. Always scribbling notes to himself and drawing lines through his screenplay.

The first week, I take two long boat rides in the park of the golden head. Sleep on water. Haven't met any of his producer friends yet, who want to finance our record label. His studio is under construction. I haven't seen his film yet. He hasn't introduced me to anyone yet. I go for walks, in parks. I take boat rides. The boat walks steadily across the water.

In Nathalie's absence, Phillipe and I share a bottle of red wine and light candles. He plays Stravinski, I show him the drawings I've done in charcoal on discarded newsprint. He loves my sketches of Nathalie, and the words I write across the drawings. He says he remembers me making drawings like these when we were in school . . . scribbles, like Cy Wombley, he remembers the stories I used to tell about them . . . about young women dying in rooms with birds, and drunken soldiers . . . I was so intense, he says. There was something *profoundly intense* about me.

Life takes us many places . . . yes? It is good to be alive now, Racine.

I'm not alive. I try sometimes, to be alive.

Still intense!

You want to ask me about it?

About what?

Nothing.

*   *   *

He doesn't understand. He starts calling out names of kids who were in our classes. Asks me if I've heard from anyone, seen anyone. Asks me about my foster mother, about the last time I saw her . . . the day I walked out . . .

Can I tell you something, Phillipe . . . I need to tell you . . .
What?
. . . Hard to explain.
What?
I met my brother.
I didn't know you had a—
I'd forgotten him, too, see? No—really. I had forgotten he ever existed, and there he was. Clear as day, and it was like . . . There was a story in the Bible about God destroying a city. I used to read it all the time . . . God was going to destroy a city and there was no room for forgiveness.

Danger makes footprints. Digs into the mark. He's playing with the candle flame on the kitchen table between us, rolling hot wax into balls, very delicately, as if something might break.

I don't think I understand, Racine . . .

Morgana King steals our attention. Phillipe lets out a sigh that changes . . . no . . . *releases* the mood; a condolence. He walks over to his CD pile, tries to find Jean Lee with Ran Blake. Her first album. He can only find Jean Lee singing the words of Charles Mingus, the spit drying into white pearls at the corner of her mouth. White pearls spilling all over our shoulders. Phillipe relaxes into the couch and watches me watch him. He lights our cigarettes in his mouth, like in the movies, except I am not cupping his hand to protect the flame from the wind, or some shit. Green eyes. Curious face. He is afraid.

We fall asleep listening to the Pogues and Ra Digga. Phillipe across the couch, me on the floor by the stereo. I hear Nathalie put her keys in the door, close it behind her. Instinctually he jumps up from the couch and goes into the bedroom. I hear the bed creak inside the room—my eyes give up on me, and I dream of a dollhouse. We will all dance and live in this dollhouse together.

On what I expected to be an uneventful morning, washing glasses and scraping up hardened wax from the night before, I heard them whispering before either one of them had even stepped out of the room to wash or take a piss. Phillipe emerged moments later, closing the bedroom door behind him. He tightened his robe around his stomach, paused in the narrow hallway when he saw me sipping a cup of coffee on the couch, acting like I was part of the furniture. Still and indifferent.

Nathalie laughs like the alabaster goddesses on TV in lamé gowns with suicide endings. The ones on movie screens—who smoke from expensive cigarette holders. I drop onto the couch as if there is nothing left in me except the need to be free from myself. I'm confused. Where the fuck are the movie producers? I want to be crowned with gladness. I want the legend of heaven when I die. Jesus is a glass sky. I am deaf and mute with only the vain traditions my elders have taught me . . . Inherited ignorance. Phillipe, I don't trust the green of his hair and the black of his eyes. Lips, teeth, spit. Nahum is right. All the world is a kingdom of wickedness.

Racine? Are you okay? Would you like me to call Phillipe?
Nah.
You are sure?
Yeah.

We drive to a club in Villeurbanne. *Maison du Livre, de L'image, et du Son.* We're supposed to have drinks with the label heads. The producer people. They want to know me. He's gonna tell them all about me, and I'm gonna produce records and be a big star in France or some shit and maybe start my own label and build my own house, a house as large as a foreign country and Geneva will be there and Frederick and me.

A scrawny French waitress with rotting teeth serves French fries, fried clams, and beer. A woman in sequined dress sings torch songs. The patrons are all in their twenties, T-shirts and jeans. A rowdy crowd. Tame music. No risks . . .

We eat clams and French fries and drink beer at a table with three of his friends. One has oily brown hair. His girlfriend has a Farrah Fawcett flip and no bra. Her girlfriend is fat, seems to know Nathalie very well. I am introduced very briefly, cannot remember their names seconds after the introductions. They talk and laugh in their language. A woman on a small stage sings torch songs. She sings "Summertime." Phillipe asks me if I know this song. His friends ask me if I know Spike Lee. I try to talk business. Nathalie laughs her alabaster goddess laugh and flings her hair, sucks her Marlboro butt until the cinder's bulb becomes a holy luminary. Someone asks Phillipe about our friendship. They wait for a story. Phillipe digresses into memory—a validation.

Racine and I met in school, we were about thirteen I think—very rich, private school in New York full of American brats. Racine got in on a scholarship.

Nathalie interrupts with her hysterics.

Phillipe, tell them—the story of the paper!

*   *   *

Phillipe is hesitant. Quiet. Not sure of their private joke now. The guests are waiting for a story. The singer keeps singing her torch songs about love—sloppy, and prone to danger. First time love, unbalanced. Songs for the brokenhearted.

I was telling Nathalie about my father's class and your paper, Ray—
What paper?
The paper you wrote.
I didn't write any paper.
Well, yes . . . I suppose you are right. You didn't!

An old man is at a table by himself. He wears a black Greek fisherman's hat and horn-rimmed glasses, like Phillipe's father used to. The torch singer is singing about Poseidon, and Zeus. About the heavy load of loathing. She's singing about boys who fall in love with rooms crowded with books, warm sprawling apartments, with Christmas trees; she's singing about a boy who fell in love with his friend and his friend's mother and his friend's father, about two boys who practiced their turntable skills imitating the scratches of the X-ecutioners. She's singing about boys when they are young and sloppy, before they grow up and become men. She's singing about strangers who used to be sloppy and in love with each other. Nathalie and Phillipe take turns telling their story about me.

My father was teaching this sort of thing—
The late Bronze Age—
Dorians in Peloponnese, this sort of thing.
Even the plays, Euripides' *Hippolytus*, Racine's *Phaedra*—
Well, Ray was fascinated with Greece and so forth, which is very funny when you think about it—

I'm shaking my leg, uncontrollably, my cheeks deflate when I pull on the square. They're poised, cigarettes reaching out across the river, dangling from bent wrists.

*   *   *

Why? Why was it so funny?

. . . Well, I thought my father's class *was* boring.

Because you didn't know what your father was talking about?

No . . . I just didn't care.

About your father?

No. I am talking of the lesson.

I still don't get the joke.

Nathalie tucks her hair behind her ears, refreshes everyone's glass. She moves with the tiniest gestures, like Phillipe's mother—stands up to pour more wine into my glass, does it so slowly, sits down, her ass suspended a thousandth of an inch above the chair. But Nathalie is too young to be Phillipe's mother. His mother's face has inroads and culverts carved around the mouth, across the forehead, under her neck. Phillipe's mother's hair is bronze, the color of an epoch. Her face can't lie, and she's perpetually on the verge of tears because of it. Phillipe hates his mother because he hates his father. He hates his father because Phillipe doesn't know how to travel through the archeological excavations of Akrotiri, the earthquakes of Thera and Crete; he's never taken off all his clothes and nose-dived into a volcanic eruption, or walked barefoot across the remains of a suspended bridge, all the way to the end where it cuts off halfway across the water—he's never peered over the edge. Nathalie smiles at me, as if to say—*no harm meant here.* I don't believe her. Her face is not as honest as his mother's. She encourages Phillipe anyway.

This class, for me, was a noonday sleep but for you, Ray—

It was what, Phillipe? For me it was what?

Ray, do you remember that paper you wrote? . . . we had to write these papers, yes? I was having a terrible time—but Racine . . .

Phillipe coughs up a little beer, crying with laughter. Every time he tries to speak, he doubles over, a vein juts out on his forehead. Nathalie laughs, looks to me—looks to him. Their friends laugh because there's nothing else to do right now.

*   *   *

Ray wrote about . . . he wrote—

He chokes on spit and beer, slams his knuckles into the table. The torch singer is singing "My Mother's Son-in-law." The trumpet and cornet harmonize with perfect syncopation. Keep it bouncy. She makes her voice thin, whiny. Bats her eyes, does a little dance with her hips. Comédie Française. Phillipe is dangerously close to dying. Takes a swig of water and laughs about that. Tries to light a wet cigarette. Laughs about that. Calms himself enough to finish his sentence.

We were supposed to write about the ancient city of Mycenae and so—I didn't care about this and I told Ray we should—we should present our paper together so—Ray comes—we come into class with two—with two turntables, like Lee Scratch Perry—I've got on the gold and the hat, the Kangol hat—Ray's wearing the sunglasses, we're standing like this, he's—he's scratching the music, I'm rapping about the invasion—of Mycenae—up in flames—*Puh-puh-Pylos*—everyone is looking—Ray and me, we are rapping about the—*inva-va-va-vasion*—my father, oh, my father did not think it so funny, and one of the students made fun, yes?—said something and Ray didn't like this, and so he walked right over to him and punched him, a big fight—papers flying all over—

They laugh. They repeat my name over and over again through laughter; *Racine.* Pronounce it with a guttural *r*, a soft *a*, a long final vowel . . .

You remember this, Ray? You stood up and—

The laughter erupts again, spills forth from all of them. The laughter of ridicule and loathing. They laugh at Racine—born of an ancient religious order, subject to an extreme doctrine of predestination and original sin, laugh at his mother, his father, his grandmother who raised him. They are hysterical, laughing.

*   *   *

And Ray took it sooo seriously. So seriously—

We were subject to persecution—laugh. For falling in love—laugh. This little religious boy from this disrupted, dysfunctional religious family—what right did he have to refuse predestination? What right did he have to reinvent what had already been made, and ordered? Laugh.

    Racine!
    So funny! Racine, that's so funny!
    And he—he sang a song!
    He what?
    He sang a—
    No!
    He asked me to—
    He what?
    Asked me—
    And you did?
    Yes!
    What were you?
    I don't know—I don't—
    It was—
    No!
    Racine!

Hyppolytus falls weak to the ground, under the glare of Zeus. In this city he has no right. He turns back to God and all the saints—devout. Refuses to reinvent destiny. Refuses to reimagine what has already been imagined. What right did he have? Laugh. We finish several pitchers of beer, and even more bottles of wine and Nathalie's crescent moon begs me to sing something, anything—to drown the torch singer out.

Mon ami des États-Unis va chanter pour nous ce soir!

    One of dese mornings you gonna rise up singing
    Spread your wings and take to da sky

But until dat morning—there's nothin' can harm
you . . .With Daddy and Mammy standin' by.

Phillipe spills his drink into the lap of an Algerian. Does not apologize, he's too drunk, too busy applauding me. He's laughing too hard. The audience is applauding me. I'm going to be a huge star in France, and I will build my own house and sing out my dreams. I take a bow. The Algerian pushes Phillipe, who pushes him back. They fight. Everyone fights. Beer spills. I am singing. Nathalie screams at the sight of blood trickling from her nose. An alabaster goddess scream pulled up from the crotch, erupting from the top of her head. Holler. There is beer on my face, blood on my lip. Nathalie pulls me out of the club. A doll in her care. Phillipe throws his chair, spits his last *fuck you* for the night—finds Nathalie's mouth in the dark backseat of the car.

João Gilberto, "Aguas de Marco" and "Undiu." Gilberto has become the chief magician of gin and wine. Presentation of continuous action. The reel is rolling: Nathalie and Phillipe disappear into the bedroom, remove their clothes. Laughter turning into yells. She escapes back into the living room naked—my camera pans her sallow face, wet. Blond hair pasted across nose and lips. Free breasts bouncing—wide hips. Profuse body, giggling—letting me in on half of a bedroom joke.

He is terrible! Terrible! He is not like you. Strange and brave. He does not laugh. He does not really understand your metaphors. He is afraid of you, you understand? He can not sing! I am not afraid of you, Racine. I am not afraid.

Phillipe calls out from the bedroom, *Nathalie, reviens, laissons telles banalités!*

We fall quickly. A movie-star scream spears out into the gardens. We are drunk. Very drunk and I thank them for asking me to sing, and Nathalie laughs and says *we did not ask you to sing. We did not ask you to sing. No one asked you to sing. You just stood up, and you started singing.* She laughs. I laugh. She says I started singing and I threw my glass against the wall, and Nathalie demonstrates with laughter. She throws her glass against the wall, gin splattering on her shins and stomach, screams above João Gilberto—a movie-star scream in black-and-white traveling to the St. Jean church just outside the window, bouncing back to broken glass. Manic amblers, drunk with wanderlust, disquiet the cobblestone square below—yell back to our open window, return our caterwaul with hardened symphonies—a dissonant yowl probing the chasm of what makes sense.

João Gilberto screams. Albert Ammons screams. Bud Powell's symphony of insanity at the Club St. Germain screams. Richard Wright removes himself from under the stairs. Cats with broken skulls, murdered by Catholic Jews, remove themselves from under rocks for the thing called love that ruptures and pains the bearer, nappy uninvestigated past, for the ghost of drunken torch songs for sinners. Wail and ball for the girl who wants you to touch her in places you are afraid to travel, for the mystery of her body, for the complication of language. Mothers unrevealing, in the lifelong process of abortion, drink and dance and die. Wanderlust! I've survived! I'm in another part of the world and nobody at the St. Jean church rang a fuckin' bell for me today! Can't the world hear me surviving?

With a calm cigarette and fresh drink in hand, the black of his terrible hair and the green of his opprobrious eyes are engaged with my banal display of rage. Phillipe takes pleasure in the score of the coon, the debutante, and the village idiots of the St. Jean square, our screams pouring over nebulous laughter. Pan: broken glass, two naked bodies. My body is fully clothed, arms wrapped around their waists, their arms wrapped around my shoulders, our breath wrapped around each other. Maybe, I think, there is a chance that we will stay together. My eyes are unsure and full of hope, like the child I was in the home of strangers . . . eating meals at the Empire Revival–style dinner table, haute cuisine and Venetian plaster, hoping to remain . . . humbly requesting acceptance. The screams Nathalie and I now share are contracts binding us all together. I'm blessed, with a refuge in their arms. Our feet bleed across the floor: blood-washed tile. *Pas de trois sur les verres cassés.* And I am happy. I am filled with gladness. *Bon Ami—Poupée Nègre.* But the people in the courtyard below are silent now . . . our feet cut, blood streaming across the floor, we are hushed. I ask him out loud, *Are you afraid of me?* He looks at me with the green of his eyes.

No, Racine . . . I am not afraid of you.
Then I want to get to business, Phillipe.
What business?
The music for the film. I've been here over a week now—
Ray, I . . . don't understand you—music for the film?
You asked me to come here to score the movie, right? You asked me. We were supposed to talk to the producers tonight. Right?
No.
Don't FUCK with me! We were supposed to talk about my ideas for the music for your movie and I just want to know when the

FUCK we're gonna get to that! Huh?

Ray . . . I never asked you to make any music for my film.

Yes you did! The producers paid my way and we were supposed to—

My mother paid for your ticket, Racine. When she heard you finally called, and when I told her you sounded like . . .

Like what?

Nathalie moves toward me, lights a cigarette, hands it to me. Her hair is all wet, my hand is shaking, she is not afraid to come close to me. Phillipe has kept his distance, has not looked me in the eye, but she sees me—she comes close to me, speaks to me. Carefully.

Racine, did Phillipe tell you about his film? What it is about?

No.

Phillipe steps toward me. He keeps a careful distance. He averts his eyes.

You know the story, Racine. Hippolytus. It's about Hippolytus, expelled from the house of his father. He has been mutilated by Zeus on the road of Mycenae. His body is scattered in pieces between two cities—Troezen, his city of shame, and Athens, his city of integrity. He's looking to avenge himself, and gather up all the pieces of his body.

Does he, Phillipe?

I don't know . . . I was hoping *you* could tell *me*.

His green eyes move in close. He slips his hands behind my back, pulls himself into me close. Nathalie stands by the kitchen sink, watching, crying. Phillipe grazes my ear with his bottom lip, my shoulder is wet with his whispers, *What happened to my friend?* Two porcelain green basins fill up with water. *What happened, Racine?* he says. *My friend is gone. What have you done with him?* He's holding on to me to keep from falling, I can see the reflection of his back in the wall mirror across the room. I can see my own reflection too. I can see my face.

My face is vague, drawn—older than it was the last time I looked. My complexion is not the color of anything. My fatigues . . . are fatigued. Phillipe leaves me in the mirror . . . like the Israelites. Like Frederick. I can see his moderately quizzical eyes tell me I am welcome to sleep in the living room for just one more day or so . . . and then I will have to leave. I will have to leave.

I barely notice the naked old woman dancing in the corners. She recites the name of the club we've just returned from in Villeurbanne—

Maison du Livre, de L'image, et du Son. . . . *House of Book, Image, and Sound.*

I am the doll I've been trying to find. Looming white mouth, hideous eyes. I am looming white mouth and hideous eyes, singing myself to sleep. Body draped across the couch, palms and soles of my feet ripped, spilling bad blood. The old dark woman has returned. I try to make the room stand still to see her clearly, but the room turns. She turns. She is dancing from drooling lips, ajar. João Gilberto is quiet. The pedestrians are quiet. Phillipe and Nathalie are quiet. The ghost dances. The only sense of continuity.

Tonight I will not dream of alabaster goddesses and coons. I will dream of hibiscus underneath the live oak tree, Frederick's head, and the bitter dance of a naked old woman, beating out one word over and over again— *survive.*

Paris is as cold and gray as I'd left it. Standing on the rue St. Jacques, behind the panthéon near the Sorbonne, a blithe crowd of teenagers stumble along the sidewalk, caught up in the nirvana of monstrous giggles. They are good subjects for charcoal on paper. Teenagers in a dream—distorting instinctual fantasies. Public dreamers disguising fantasy with mechanisms of reality. Manny would draw them in bold circus colors and they would fill every corner of his canvas. Every corner except one, where a small figure is crouched down, an indiscernible object in the corner of the canvas overwhelmed by woebegone circus tones . . . words painted across a depressed backdrop: MISCREANT, DAINTY, RETROGRADE, VITIATED, LAPSED, SINK, SLIP.

The night is arduous. My pockets are virtual. Virtually empty. The air is damp. Tobacco fumes in strangled garments, spilling from an indifferent duffel bag. I have just enough money for cigarettes, several drinks . . . maybe another cheese omelet in the morning . . . not enough for a room tonight. In a small underground bar, I listen to the Doors, Ray Charles, Aretha Franklin, and chug carafes of sangria. This glass? A refuge in ice. Someone is sipping syrah rosè, staring at me from the bar. Talks to me but the eyes do not see me. They do not speak. Eyes crossing the room, buying the next round . . . invading my privacy, follow me out and watch my color cast onto the sidewalk. *I have no name. I am too high for you to touch,* but this someone would like to kiss my holy lips, taste my tongue's palate of mortar and stone, this someone leads me to rue Dussoubs.

    Tu es très beau . . . Si sombre et si beau . . . Inhalation . . . In . . . So high . . . Too high for you to know . . . *Beau comme les photos . . . Tes yeux . . .* Your eyes . . . *Est-ce-que tu la déjà fait avec un homme . . . Restes avec moi, çe soir?* . . . Going down by the river . . .

Demain, je partirai, restes avec moi çe soir? . . . Pourrai-je te toucher? . . . Si beau . . . down by the riverside . . . I will return to the open field of furtive turns.

Someone touches me softly, then moves away. She is walking. Moving. The lilac bleeds into the dark black hair painted all around her shoulders. She is young. So young. A child. Young. Thick neck. Wide nose and thin lips. She is red with thick black hair and she is moving all around me. She is moving. All around the bed, and there is another woman. In a white shirt and long skirt. And she is young. So young. *Is Artemis, the goddess, present in this place?* And there is another woman, with huge hands and she is tall. The third woman is so tall. So much taller than the others. So much older. Older than her years, it seems. They are moving. All around the bed, all around the room. In different directions, with a sense of urgency. I can smell the flowers and earth. It is hot. Very hot. My body is soaked in sweat. Sweat or water, water coming from my flesh–with the smell of sea salt or ocean. *Oh heavenly breath of fragrance.* The three women are moving. Moving all around my bed, and one is so much taller than the others. *Even in my pains I feel your presence, and my body grows more light.* The smell of sea salt and blood coming from skin . . . Soaking into the sheets.

The cat welcomes me back with apathetic stillness. Night brings frigid air and darkness into her house. Mme. Marignac is not home when I let myself in. A bowl of fresh tomatoes stacked in a wicker basket on the table. A lampshade draped in lace is lit in the corner near books and record jackets. This house is cold. Masturbate in front of the cat. Shower. Lavender soap lathers my contemplation. Fuck this. I'll see if I can stay here a few more days, see if Mme. can find me a job, or I'll wander the streets and figure something out. Sing songs from the corners for spare change. Do tap dances. Eat a tomato. Smoke a cigarette. Drink a glass of wine.

As I settle into the small bed in the room that opens out into the vegetable garden—I hear Mme. Marignac enter the living room and greet the cat. Mme. Marignac opens the bedroom door without knocking.

You've come back?
Yes . . . I . . . Uh—I . . .
I did not think you would come back . . . here.
Yes. I—
How did you get in?
I—
Phillipe called me, he said you left Lyon . . . he said the two of you had disagreement.
Oh, I was hoping . . . Because I was gonna—
But it is . . . it is not possible, Racine. You should go.
I was hoping . . .
You should go to the hotel. In Paris. To see if they have rooms. Yes?
Oh . . .

A Japanese man in a navy worsted-wool suit stands behind her. He is short and severe looking and peers at me without much facial expression. I am unable to escape myself. They stare at me without words. Me, lying in her guest bed, lying in her bed in my undershirt only, the quilt pulled up to my chest. Mme. Marignac and the man in the navy worsted-wool suit linger. The cat stares at me from the doorway, Marignac's hand still on the knob. I'm definitely not welcomed, and the last train from Garches to Paris has already left. No money. Not enough to stay in no hotel. Some kinda way I'm gonna have to lug my shit all the way back to Paris tonight. Hitchhike or some shit.

You will get dressed now? Yes?
Yes.
You will have dinner with us, first, yes? And I will take you to Paris.
Yes.

Tofu, tomatoes, wine. The Japanese businessman speaks to her only in French. Speaks French with a Japanese accent, and she speaks to him only in Japanese from a book she keeps nearby. He looks at her. She looks at him. Phillipe has told her we had a disagreement. He has told her I am not that boy he met, who fell asleep to his music. He has told her something is wrong. Something is terribly wrong, and I imagine a world where bridges reach across empty caverns and fail to connect themselves to land. He has told her that I have little regard for the impending death of my foster mother, and ghosts follow me around. He has told her that I sang in the choirs of the Pentecostal churches. Sang in the choir on the day of my brother's interment. Sang on a bus, leaving Zuni forever. Sang all the way to an abandoned building. Sang with my brother's corpse on my mind. Sang while a Brooklyn mansion burned down all around me, and fire caught hold to the flesh of a Prophet. He has told her that I will keep on singing, making the notes up as I go along. I will just keep on singing until there is no more war in my body.

I think she is telling the Japanese visitor that I am about to entertain them both. She says this in French. He looks at me and cracks a
forced smile. I wonder if she has also told him I took money from
Nathalie's nightstand, and I used Phillipe's credit card to buy myself
a ticket from Lyon to Paris, that I live in vacant buildings in New York,
and I have so much music on my mind . . . my vacant house is littered
with music . . . I wonder if she has told him that I shower in old fire
hydrants, do my laundry in church basements, steal, borrow, beg . . .
without giving back . . . I *should* sing now. It's appropriate. It's a way
of giving back . . . and she will not call the police . . . as long as I
leave . . . as long as I sing.

Luter plays "Down By The Riverside," "Summertime," "Nobody
Knows the Trouble I've Seen." I am standing in the middle of the living room floor, under a paper lantern. The cat is curled around a hand-
painted floor pot, relaxing in the shade of its ficus branches. The
Japanese businessman, tie tightly knotted at his throat, lights a cigar
and crosses his legs in an abundant red velvet chair draped in yel-
lowing lace doilies. Mme. Marignac sits opposite her guest, in an elaborately carved wooden chair upholstered in yellow silk. Claude Luter
plays. They are waiting. The Japanese businessman, the old Frenchwoman, the cat. Eddie, Frederick, Emma, Lilly . . . Geneva.

I am standing in front of them, singing in her living room, barely
audible above the music. She turns it down. She wants to hear me
clearly. Every crack. Wants the humiliation of this recital to be clear.
I sing. Hoping to get a ride into Paris tonight. Knowing I cannot stay
on her couch, and I cannot hitchhike my way across a broken bridge
back to reality.

The room is tight. Cramped. Mme. Marignac sits, ankles crossed,
arms folded. The Japanese businessman sits, eyes focused on nothing. One hand cupping his crotch, the other hand gripping his wrist.
Holy Mother lies across the floor, a cold blue corpse . . . waiting.
Geneva sits with her head in Emma's lap . . . a teenaged girl. A young
girl who has given birth to two children. Two boys. She does not
know where they are. They do not know where she is. She does not
know what they look like. They do not know what she looks like. She
looks like Lilly. She looks like Emma. She looks like sky veiled across

Brooklyn in a time of war. I dream a mansion. A papier-mâché mansion full of rooms with beautiful furniture. There is a rug hanging on the wall from India, with a thousand stories woven into its fabric. There is a lamp, fifteenth-century I imagine, from Indonesia. Mahogany tables layered in veneer decorated with hibiscus and tulips. A copper-top coffee table from Morocco—holding silver and porcelain cigarette boxes. A marble fireplace, six feet high, with marble from the halls of Hippolytus. I escape into the garden, away from the old Frenchwoman and Japanese businessman, climb over their bodies, operatic notes falling over glass, ashtrays, hiking through forests of red carpet. I leave them by themselves, leave the song behind to entertain the cat's attention.

My wife, Couchette, has caught on fire in the parlor. She runs through the halls, her body aflame. I could not save her. I have received forgiveness. I am in the garden, running through Irish yew trees. I am hiding in seventeen garden rooms, running from upper terrace to lower terrace, running one third of a mile down a path connecting sixteen acres of garden. Olive trees trimmed like Chinese lanterns, redwoods, California native oaks, two hundred and ten upright yews surrounding me. That's not me singing and dancing in your living room. It's a body that looks like mine, but it is not. I am outside, in a magnificent garden, playing. Can't you see me? Free. My mother is dressed in a lilac gown, and she is dancing in a ballroom seventy-five feet long and thirty-two feet wide. Twenty feet from marble floor to elaborately painted ceiling.

Nahum forgives me. My wife and I are dancing together. My wife has a beautiful bald head, and she smokes cigarettes from an elaborate holder and her name means a place to dream. We dance to Mary J. Blige . . . crystals from the chandelier reflecting little shapes on our shoulders. John Coltrane's tenor sax, Lee Morgan's trumpet, Jimmy Garrison's bass, Jill Scott at the microphone . . . Rza . . . I am shining beneath a chandelier that once hung in Versailles during the signing of the peace treaty. The fireplace was lit twenty-four hours ago for us. My mother, my brother, and me—we dance in the external rooms of the state gardens. We sleep together on the floor of the ballroom with marble from the halls of Hercules at Versailles. We reside in a tower built of reinforced concrete with brick veneer—the steps are white Italian marble. I do not know the words to any songs ever sung. Scagliola columns support the heavy weight of my shortcomings. Walls wainscoted in white Italian marble, floor designed in a Venetian mosaic, heroic-sized windows, a serpentine staircase winds to Jesus. We climb . . . we climb . . . my brother, my mother, and me . . . God forgives me with gladness. We dance in a mansion somewhere. A place I have never been. A place I know.

Mme. Marignac stands in the doorway, her Japanese businessman still seated inside, with the cat in his lap. She has a look of concern on her face, as I walk down the path toward the train station to Paris.

Where will you go to . . . Racine?

. . .

. . .

I've been to the city of my integrity. I think I'll return to my city of shame.

Tonight Mr. Eddie come into my room and said I was cursed and the devil is trying to make him feel like it's his fault Frederick dead and our mama is crazy in the crazy hospital, but he rebukes Satan for the liar he is. Then he said I have to leave here because he's not gonna have this seed of wickedness in his house. He said he's sending me away . . . tomorrow. Said we gonna take the bus to New York and then he gonna call the people and they gonna come and get me and put me in a home for the wicked. Says we leavin' right now, just me and him, and I best get ready so he can take me back to New York to the group home and the social workers where I belong because we was more trouble than it was worth and ain't had not a goddamned thing to do with my brother runnin' away and fallin' off that cliff in the middle of the night and then he say we he gotta make atonement for Emma's body. I look around the room and I see my books and I see Frederick's clothes still folded on the chair and his good sneakers by the window and I see the road outside the window, with the moon lightin' up the path and I can see Frederick and his orange T-shirt climbin' out the window tellin' me I better not say shit and I can see that orange T-shirt runnin' up the hill toward the moon. I was reading my Bible, I was reading the book of Ninevah about how God say he was gonna destroy the city because of the sins of the people and I remember how Frederick say he don't care nuthin' 'bout heaven or hell and I remember how Mr. Eddie say sometimes God gotta destroy the body in order to save the soul and I remember seein' that orange movin' toward the moon outside the window and next time I see Frederick he in a light blue box and now Mr. Eddie takin' me back to New York which is all Frederick wanted to do anyway, if he had just had the patience of Job—if he could've waited.

I get dressed quick, look around, see what I can take with me because he keep yellin' saying we don't have no time to pack nuthin'

or take nuthin'. Say we leavin' right now. Say we gonna take the
Greyhound bus to New York that passes through Windsor, and then
he gonna call the people and they gonna come and get me and put
me in a home for the wicked. We walk up road, only light is that
moon that Frederick said leads you back to home, and I remember
him with his orange shirt runnin' up the road and me readin' the
book of Ninevah about God destroying the wicked and I remember
climbin' out the window and following behind him. I never follow
him where he goes because he goes dangerous places, but I follow
him up a long line, toward the hill, the tree, the rock, the water. And
I wonder if God understands. I sing songs about Jesus, and Jesus
lead me back down the hill, toward the trail through the dark where
Frederick is. Eddie pull my body up the road, but my soul walks with
Frederick through the cornstalks. And I wonder what God knows.

THE BOY SAID NOTHING TO THE MAN ON THE LONG BUS RIDE FROM Zuni to New York . . . Just focused on the parade of trees and thick forests lining the highways. He never asked to use the bathroom—held his water in until his stomach swelled and his penis stung. He would not even look at Mr. Eddie, who sat beside him in the aisle seat—sweating and sipping from a wide metal flask trimmed in brown leather.

Racine thought mostly of Frederick, and tried hard to remember the details of his brother's face. The exact timbre of his voice, the way he smelled last year when their bodies folded together in the dent of a winter's bed. Staring out the window became a private game, the object used to see his brother's face crystallize in the foliage of passing trees. But details were vanishing with the miles beneath the wheels. The burden of remembering was becoming too much.

Eddie propelled up Eighth Avenue against smoke clouds, skipping through tornadoes. He held on firmly to the boy's wrists, dragging him behind as they dodged cars moving up the street, and hurried past movie marquees. Eddie averted his eyes, pulled, pushed, directed with tugs and yanks. He slowed down when he approached two police officers at the entrance to the subway, then charged down the stairs with great motivation. Beneath the ground: a city. Lower chambers of urine and unrepentance. Eddie sat Racine next to an old man in dirty yellow pants, sleeping on the platform's bench. The train took too long. Eddie paced steadily across the platform and kept peeking up into the void of the tunnel, hoping to see some light come shining through. A light that would snatch the boy from his seat and pull him down into the hole. Away.

First a vibration came, the rumble of something in their feet and shins. Then a small stream of yellow shot up the steel tracks, alarming rats and other vermin, who scurried through puddles under the broad cliff of the platform. A reverberation came from a great distance—resounding a holler—of earth cracking open and swallowing skies. Racine's head lowered toward the brown bag in his lap, he pulled it closer to his stomach for comfort. The old man quaked, just a bit—Eddie stumbled back as the team of dark metal came surging through the tunnel. Open doors, an invitation. They are devoured by the beast.

Eddie threw the boy into a corner seat and leaned against a pole. The train pulled off, traveled through more darkness, swallowing and purging strangers at various stops. A violent wave snatched the veteran soldier forward. Eddie tries to balance himself, the pole aligned with his spine, and he looks down into an unmarked grave. Another gust of wind snatches Eddie to Frederick's body lying in the bottom of the rock quarry—and the eagle that perched on the mound, clawing at the earth as they exhumed Frederick's body, and the voices of those who said Eddie killed the boy, or said the boy was only trying to escape— ran across the field up onto the rocks and fell down into the hole.

The train stopped again, and they leaped out, Eddie's hold on Racine's wrist—climbed more stairs and stepped out into the light of more darkness. No movie marquees. No women in torn stockings. No police. Huge buildings with broken windows. Isolated structures, beaten massive structures, built tightly next to each other. Every space, taken up with buildings sucking in and breathing out from empty doorways.

Eddie's nails were digging into the boy's upper arm. He continued to pull and shove—causing Racine to trip over himself. The shopping bag ripped under the boy's stumbling feet and all of its contents poured out onto the street. Racine lay facedown, the underside of his hands trickling beads of blood mixed with particles of glass. The bag's contents were spread out before him: two apples, an orange, the Bible that he shared with Frederick, three broken race cars, his favorite book; a collection of Greek plays. Eddie looked down at the hard red cover of the book that the boy kept hidden underneath the floor boards of his room. He did not pick it up. He just looked at it—open to the lamentation of a king, betrayed by God; *my crimes from this time on exceed all measure! I breathe out hypocrisy and incest every breath. My hands are swift to seek revenge—are homicidal—ache to steep themselves in blood of innocents!*

Eddie gripped the child by the collar of his windbreaker and held him firmly, carrying the boy away from relics of cognizance littering avenues. Eddie mumbled things that made no sense as they approached the four-story building at the end of the street. Their steps sank into soft beds of earth, crossing over a vacant lot to get to the other side of a horse-head gate. Eddie paused, looking up. The building wasn't itself. In the time it took to burn down, swallow a life, and spit out Geneva's charred remains—in the small window of time it took for him to become, and then mourn the silence of James Henry Scott, to collect himself and manage his return to Zuni with two little boys, in the time it took them to grow legs, for Frederick to sneak out of the house, run up into the hills, and slip from a cliff, crashing his head down onto the rocks below, in the time it took them to retrieve his body, to sit with police and coroners, to get the boy's body to a mortician, to buy it a suit, to pick out a light blue casket trimmed in white, to bury him, to pack their things, to buy a ticket for the bus and come back to the city, in that short eternal moment of time—a four-story building on a Brooklyn street gutted by fire, waited patiently for retribution; everything he had. Everything he knew. The sins of the father, visiting the son.

He pushed the boy through the doorway, stomped up collapsing stairs, ambled through corridors of wet wood and chunks of plaster. Trying to remember his way. A half wall tricked him into a wrong turn, and a flight of stairs dissolved beneath him, temporarily hindering his ascension. He opened a door to see the remains of putrid green wallpaper.

A large gape in the ceiling introduced the stars, consistent with his recollection of things.

Eddie propelled further into the years he'd spent in this house just after the war. If he dared peek in the pantry he'd recover the bottles of liquor he once stored there, and if he walked into the larger bedroom he'd smell forgotten women with big thighs. The walls would not lie for him. Eddie stood still, recited a scripture out loud—*Cursed shalt thou be in the city! Cursed shalt thou be in the field! Cursed shall be thy basket and thy store!*

He turned to Racine, and poured a libation of whiskey from his jacket's flask onto the floor—*Cursed shalt thou be when thou comest in and cursed shalt thou be when thou goest out!* Eddie's trembling fingers searched his pockets for a cigarette. The perspiration dripping from his brow kept quelling the flame every time he struck the match. After several tries, he placed the soggy cigarette between his lips and protected the small fire in the cup of his hands.

He held the flame up to get a good look at the boy: the thing sin had produced. He observed the boy until he felt the fire kindle his thumb and he flung the lit match on the floor, landing it on the line of whiskey. Then he watched another fire begin; a purifying flame that promised to erase all the mistakes of before. This time it would. As quickly as the flame traveled across the floor, Eddie threw the boy to the other side of the trail of fire and slammed the apartment door shut behind himself. Racine could hear Eddie's heavy shoes banging down the broken wooden steps. *Does my son know I am his father? All sin, selah. Does my son know I love him? All wickedness, selah.*

Glancing up from the small vestibule below, Eddie hoped this time the walls would burn to the ground and become a pile of nothing behind him. Seated under the stairs on the ground floor, he gripped a broken strand of pearls in his fist and took a small sip from the old leather flask, then emptied the rest onto himself, positioned a fresh cigarette in his mouth, and lit another match to sear the world away.

THE BOY STOOD PARALYZED, HIS EYES SHUT TIGHT, TRYING TO SEE the face of Frederick clearly. The details blurred. He wanted to run through the growing wall of fire, out of this room of smoke and burning wood. He wanted to retrieve his things from the street. But his legs would not move, his feet had no feeling. His heart punched from inside his chest. He wanted to get out. Far across the room, a figure moved against a wall with the umbrage of fire. A bird, ten feet tall. A woman. He couldn't see it clearly but Racine knew something was there, and his heart punched harder, fighting the way his voice wished it could.

The figure danced against the walls, gulping the air, and a dam burst open between the boy's legs. A flood of urine gushed down . . . The cars. The doll. Frederick. *I didn't even do nothing. I'll be saved. Forgive me all my sins.* The foment of the birdwoman ushered him through the torching gate toward a clear hallway, down the stairs, beyond the burning vestibule, and out into the vacant lot. The bird-woman watched the boy sprint out of the yard, then commenced to dance from floor to floor, in every corner where flames lived and smoke arose, until heaven broke open and water poured down.

He pulsed forward and away, the building a castle of urgent flames thawing his back. Racine did not look back and he did not hear the sirens blaring in the distance. He searched the pavement for the things he'd left behind, but the streets were bathed clean in the downpour. The avenues would not return to him his life. By the fifth block of the journey away, he'd forgotten what he was looking for, and dreamed of a mansion: a safe and beautiful place to play in the privacy of dreams.

The hours passed. The fire quelled. The building remained. The landscape of day tinted in sunlight. His name. His possessions. The night before. He was just a boy for police and social workers to rescue. A boy for sheltering and self-invention.

FREDERICK WAS ASLEEP ON A ROCK, AND THEN THE EARTH TILTED and explosives burst in rapid succession. Bombs landed on his face, blasting orange and yellow against a field of black in his sight.

Instinctually, he threw up his arms as he awakened to shield his head from the crashing force of ammunition. His eyes had no chance to focus and his mind could not alert itself into defense as readily as his body needed it to. The outbreak of heavy blows came in legions within the span of seconds, and a mighty force lifted the flailing body up off of the ground. Frederick's voice blared at the brink of powerlessness, at the point of fear, upon the realization of imminent defeat. The alarm called out long and hard as the weight of arsenals hoisted him off the cliff, up into the lap of air. His unfocused eyes pulled open wide, his back acquiesced to gravity. The legs kicked and the arms flailed, reaching for something to brace against—his head whirled beneath his legs and aimed his body down toward the lake rocks sparkling diamonds. Eyes finally focused, on the jagged rocks coming toward him, and in that instant he felt as if he were not falling down. It was the lake that was falling up to meet him. The alarm did not quiet until Frederick's head timbered against the boulders below. Then there were no sounds except the mystical chorus of forest creatures and the splashing of fresh water against the rocks and the broken body splayed among them.

Cartography
of Invention

Real invention consists of
Making something out of nothing.

—JEAN RACINE, Preface to *Berenice*

Yes?

The building.

What about it?

. . .

Racine?

. . .

The building . . . what about the building?

I found it. Went to it. When I came back. After the war.

What war?

My own.

And who was there?

Everybody. I made a world. Friends.

Who?

Manny. Couchette. Lucinda. Mawepi. They told me all about the boy. The boy.

Who killed the boy? Do you know, Racine?

No.

Yes . . . yes you do.

He was in the building. The boy was in the building. On the roof. The boy is real. The building is real. Death is real. Nahum was there. He could tell you.

What?

The river gates are thrown open and the palace collapsed. It is decreed that the city be exiled and carried away. Its slave girls moan like doves and beat upon their breasts.

You came back to the city, you were wandering, aimlessly, and you saw a building. You were in the building by yourself.

No. We were all there.

You were there for a long time alone.

Nahum was there. The boy was there and . . .

Go on. Start from there, when you came back from France.

I came back to the city. Came back to the city and she was already dead . . . the foster lady was already dead . . . no use in tryin' to find her grave . . . I went lookin' for a building . . . a sure foundation . . . Huddled in the alcove behind the brick wall, they were all there. All the people I never knew. All the secrets I can't solve . . . they were gathered around the window, sitting on the ground, trying to catch a breeze. I recognized some of them from tenement stairwells, from park benches and warm grates above subway stations in wintertime. We were the same. All of us. They were trying to hold on. I was trying to let go, but we were the same. All of us. Trying to protest and stand fast and bring life back to our lives. Victims of war. Soldiers without an army. You understand?

Go on.

The frame was leaning. The eyes and mouth—covered. Large wooden boards nailed across the windows. A thick chain pulled itself through a tight hole in the steel door, anchored by a huge lock. Debris cluttered in front of the building and along the alleyway. The door at the top of the side steps had also been replaced with a steel slab, knotted with chain and lock. The building had a terror frozen across its facade—so tightly chained and locked and nailed shut. Waiting to be destroyed on death's row. The street was quiet, its neck torn open: silent. No need for the sidewalks to testify of tribes and settlements come and gone. Something came to me from the side of the building. The walls were trying to speak. The alleyway appeared to be clear, except for the garbage living there. I remained standing in front of the four-story building. I didn't move. I'd come to offer tears and rotting flesh. I was ashamed.

Of what?

Myself.

Why?

I had not become a soldier in army of the Lord. I had not slain the minotaur . . . There were people. People I knew. Manny, same color of red earth like Frederick, running through the trees. Couchette, dancing by the riversides. Mawepi, fat blue cat. Holy mother. All of them. We were a gate, arms braided to each other, locked. People knew we were there. They could smell us, catch quick glimpses of figures moving in and out of the black hole—and that was okay. We wanted them to know. We wanted them to trust our presence, and aid us with sandwiches and spare change. We weren't squatting. We were occupying. The black hole was our barrack, and we were soldiers, hooking bulbs and hot plates up to the streetlamp, sharing our food, our works, our bodies. We were there to protect the ruins of our temples. Waiting for the next invasion. We recruited who we could, and ran it down to them like this: It's wartime. We're arming ourselves and avenging the abduction of the queen, our sacred lady. Armageddon. These are the last days, and we need soldiers to help forge a tomorrow. The ones who could hear us, stayed. Others moved in and out. I didn't feel good about that, didn't want this to become some hotel and shit—but the others, the ones who were there before me, had no problem with it. Said we were forming a community, and in a community people move in and out. They argued that a movement had to be about just that, coming and going. Then more people joined us. They came without cause or knowledge of our struggle. Just came for shelter during the rain.

Then the cops came, like I knew they would, and tried to chase us out of there. They always came at night, in twos or threes at first—while we slept in knots, everybody was either too sick or too fucked up to keep watch. They came with flashlights to burn our eyes, and a couple times a few of us were injured; got bloody lips and battered faces. Got dragged out of there by our hands and feet, and thrown into the back of their cop cars and driven away. The rest of us hid in corners and blended with the darkness, learned to scurry under openings and slide our bodies between the cracks. We were the ones who could survive, and I believed we could still take back the building and demand the return of our mothers. Though my body failed me, and my throat was tight, I traveled the city by day— seeking new recruits for the struggle . . . some to replace the afflicted and those taken into captivity. But they came with apathy for the cause. Came for the drink and the dust. My spirit was weak, my flesh was failing me—I succumbed. Our army became a frail thing, unraveling. The cops returned, with new sheets of metal and blocks of wood and nails, kept hammering away—trying to shut us out of there. But we found other ways in. We moved from the basement to the upper floors, and slept behind the back bar, on the stage, beneath the floorboards. I wanted us to be an army. Resilient. But I knew we would lose this battle if we didn't watch our asses, if we didn't stop with the lying. The fucking lying! I was trying to be captain of the army, kept yelling out loud: *Remember it in the music! The music will save you from your sins!* But after a time the others didn't care. I was trying to be a captain. Trying to ride my horse, with an army behind me—but it was no good. No good. They stopped hearing me.

There were people who left their children, and came back after a time to retrieve them, whores bringing their clients, bruised men who beat bruised women, falling into a drunken stupor across my chest. There was no community. No tribe. No army. Just a gathering . . . of garbage. A heap of twisted flesh with twisted stories. Babies, and mothers and fathers, just a mass of bloodlines distorted. A crowd . . . a mass of distorted flesh all around me, in a building ravaged with vermin and rotting wood. Just another place to be.

They wouldn't stay awake, kept falling asleep, like the disciples on the Mount of Olive, and I was—begging them to take watch sometimes. And finally the cops (The Pharisees) came again in scores with guns and fists and flashlights, and somebody— crouched down beneath the upstairs window with his friends. One of them had a can of gasoline and somebody else had matches and empty bottles, and they threw a torch at the flashing police cars parked outside, yelled when the flames caught on to the hood of a car and raged. The Pharisees pulled their guns, we were all inside—panicking—but this one kid with bluish hair and dirty face kept throwing things from a side window and I kept yelling: *Halt! Cease! I have not called fire! I have not given you instruction!* But nobody heard me or knew me or cared, I was too high to speak clearly, and this woman climbed out of the basement window to take charge of things. She climbed out murmuring to herself; fucking kids! All uh yous . . . I knew her—these streets were hers. She'd inherited them from her father and her mother, and their parents who came before them. She climbed out of the hole to talk. The cops were aiming their guns and calling for backup. Their guns had no discernment. The cowboys were having a good time. I knew then that they were planted. They were secret agents, sent to con-found our mission of saving, men in suits who wanted The Alibi to be destroyed.

I heard the woman trying to speak, even laughing a little at the ridiculousness of it all—her words unclear, her balance unsteady (she'd just scored, I think, yes . . . We'd just scored with her old man on the roof before all of this went down) and she stood up in the alleyway and came out from the alcove, hastening toward the police pointing her bottle of beer, and then I heard another firebomb. I could see from the cleft in the wooden slats that woman's torn body falling down—quickly, as if a magnet had sucked it to the sidewalk. The bottle of beer crunched beneath her drop, a dark red syrup and thin white foam spilled out from under her—moving slowly in one expanding circle encompassing the pitiful corpse. The whole neigh-borhood came out to witness the battle. There were cameras and cars lined up and down the street, and I knew then that the earth here was no longer sacred.

My voice wrung itself from my throat and leaped to the killing ground below. A strained holler aimed directly at the riddled remains of the woman, washing all over her. Clean. A sanctification. The cops kept yelling at us through the bullhorns, *Come out!* They were increasing by numbers, their guns aimed toward us—their flashlights and shields . . . And Mawepi started yellin' back about how the cops had just killed the old lady. She was crying from the rooftop, and I was hiding in the cracks with the rats. I could hear the cops pushing people back, away from the building—trying to control the crowd, saying we were extremely explosive and armed. The scribes were recording it all word for word in small notebooks, standing next to cameras distorting images of us for the world to see. No! I want them to hear me. I want a voice for hearing! We're here to protect the walls. This is our home, you took it away. You came with your money and guns and destroyed the legacy, tore down our idols. Again! Ripped the queen from her sacred throne, and hushed our rit-

ual of being. And now you kill one of our elders. And now you tell
the people from across the street that we are *other*—you strategize to
diffuse and separate us from them, who should join us! We're not
crazy—we're just mad. All of us. Even if the reason for madness has
changed with the pulse and shift of days—we share the temperament of airless living, and we are all armed with a rage and madness
more fierce than guns.

The cowboys made another bomb, and smashed it against the
wall. The fire poured out of the windows. The cops tried to rush in.
A fire truck alarmed the world of the holocaust bursting up from
the tar beneath, blasting away at nothing until an exhausted beam
relaxed beneath the floor and bodies came hurtling down. A human
torch consumed itself on the pavement below. Those who
remained in the building came choking out for air into the arrest-
ing arms of policemen. Couchette vanished, dancing into blue suits
and shiny buttons. The firemen, with bullish hoses and slaughter-
ous axes, hacked away with more malice than the searing flames. I
was still inside, crouched down, looking for a cool place, a low
place. In the middle of the bonfire, my body became paralyzed by
something. A hint of something in the luminosity of searing sparks,
and strangling vapors. The alpha of thought dinned, my legs
moved to an exit. The fire traveled up, from the floor below, sirens
hollered out. There was no way to walk down. Fire veiled every
doorway, window. I escaped through a curtain of smoke, up the
back staircase, to the second level. And then the third. Fire alarms
screaming. One more flight. No smoke. Top floor, clear and quiet.
Everything—dissolving.

I pushed open a heavy steel door at the far end of a room. There
was a large gape in the ceiling, a wide open space of what was once
rooms and hallways. The Prophet was seated at the opposite end of
the room. On this floor, above the fire, where Nahum sleeps, there is
a single naked bulb dangling from its cord, giving off no light. The
moon helps sometimes. It is a place to die in the last term of purgatory. On this landing, nothing was wrong. It was a floor I'd never
known, but I knew it better than anywhere I'd ever lived. Knew the
stairs. Every turn the walls made, every fragment of glass. Nahum

coughed into the air, filthy hair violent and distressed like his eyes. He sustained my breathing with a tonic of lobelia seed, garlic, parsley, and licorice root, sweet wine and rainwater. *Frederick? Is my brother here?* No response. All things were calm. Yes . . . This was a safe place; hub of the believer living in exile waiting for the great destroyer to come. A salty sea sigh was breathed onto the back of my neck. She had come back. The woman from the train over the bridge. She was beckoning me to dance. Our bodies bent and crossed each other, moved in slanted angles, rising and falling, dancing gingerly on the deaf ears of Nahum's head. *Do you know something? Tell me what you know.* My tears are hungry. Her dancing only hints at information. Nahum folded himself into the scriptures, inquiring truth of the pages, embracing the night's metaphor. The prophet hushed me with kisses to my neck and fingers. Nahum took me up, my feet elevated above the ground . . . carried me to a room. A quarry.

The little boy. He was there. In his white shirt, with his black pants and his Bible. His hands would not steady themselves. They were stricken with tremors, as were the legs. Blood rushed to the heart, and the heart banged adrenaline beats long after. He peered down long from the place where he'd found Frederick sleeping. Peered down long at his brother's body on the rocks, everything black . . . dark . . . and he wondered if God understood this violent act of consecration. Understood that all he did . . . all he was trying to do was . . . he'd navigated his own way up the road, through the hills in order to reckon with a wayward soul. Reached out to his brother with all intentions of stirring the boy to wake . . . accusation and fear of abandonment in his touch. He wanted to convince him to return home. To obey the word of God. To avoid wrath. His palms nudged, then slapped, then pulled—quaking Frederick out of his sleep—and with one sudden motion, the boy hit him with a rock, and the body twisted itself from under the tree and over the hill. Was that God he saw in the anonymity of night? He wondered, as he tripped back down through the country roads lapsing into blindness . . . journeying back to the house, back through the window, back to his bed . . . falling back into a sleep of complete innocence, toward forgetting. . . . Falling asleep, forgetting, a broken body splayed among the rocks.

In that room . . . there, cradled in the arms of Nahum, I saw him . . . the little boy with his white shirt and black pants and Bible. He was just a boy. He was a boy like I had been once . . . He was my age when I had been that age. He was memorizing scriptures in the corner of the loft, his body supporting a voice in thin strains. His church was that corner of the room, without members. I joined him there—he wore a clean white shirt and black slacks, creased. We prayed together. Only us—

The strangers remained seated apart from us with folded hands . . . Watching. We spoke tongues into each other's hands. Fingers voyaging eyes, nostrils, lips, cheeks, hair, scrotum, ears—the wounds that ulcerated in unseen cavities. Our necks belted, and our legs latched in congruity until the crippling fear of touching fell asunder. The boy passed his scriptures into my mouth with his tongue and a bitter thrush swelled behind my teeth. I sucked on the absinthian spume, strangling to prevent it from flushing down my throat. I hated him then, for who he was and what he did. My nails dug into his forearm, drawing blood, hoping he'd vanish—but he remained, a certain kind of sorry in his eyes. He was in every way, unhealed. Convinced of what he thought he understood. Mistaken. A windstorm of sickness assailing through his body, and in our stronghold, it passed on to me. A virus latched on to the cells that comprise me—duplicated itself. Then we were no different. Two bodies so tightly joined, it seemed as if we were one body. The disciples gathered around us and applauded the battle. They pulled him from my side, held him down, Nahum portending above us. *Kill him! Destroy what the boy believes.*

I sliced a square of his flesh, maiming the purity of the boy, gored his throat, muting his screams. I fisted my hand into a dense ore and raced it through history, pummeled the child stretched out before me. Forged a hole wide enough to walk through—and I did. Curtain of flesh, gate of bone. That carcass, furnished with heart and lung, fainted onto me as I passed through to the other side. A second skin. He was just a boy. I was just a man, the city was just a building, with secrets, dying for years and years and years . . . without parade.

What was old came crashing through what was new, and what was new destroyed all that had been mine; a liberty of songs sung years before I walked this earth . . . all of it . . . in my breathing.

RACINE, YOU KNOW IF YOU PUT AN OLD PIECE OF POTTERY UP TO your ear, you can make a phone call to a thousand years ago. Like seashells, playing you conversations from creatures long dead.

I couldn't walk the distance from here to there. You walked a line. I just watched you walk.

We both walked, Racine. Both of us, Racine . . . we both walked a line and we were both bound to veer off into familiar territory, for the first time . . . again.

. . .

A man stood in the middle of a city, compelled to go inside a building, to listen to the sounds trapped in its mortar. A boy walked a line.

I was coming from, you were walking toward. You were walking up a long road, toward something. Walking up that yellow line . . . I couldn't walk as straight as that. Never could balance myself on that—

But it don't matter.

It don't matter. It happened. It already happened.

I was just trying to wake you up.

I'm trying to do the same thing for you.

Yeah.

Yeah . . .

I b i d

Since they cut out my tongue, another
tongue, it seems,
has been constantly wagging somewhere in
my skull,
something has been talking, or someone, that
suddenly falls silent
and then it all begins again . . .
I hear too many things I never utter.

—ALBERT CAMUS,
The Renegade from *Exile and the Kingdom*

I WAS WALKING TOWARD SOMETHING, HAVING ARRIVED AT NOTHING. He was crossing the avenue. The remains of a man crossing pernicious pavement channels. Moving. I stood still, watching him move. I wanted to leap into the swirl around him, not resolve myself to indifference. I wanted to call out to him but I wasn't sure what sound my voice would make, *if* it would make sound at all. Would it shriek? Could it holler? Was there still somewhere in me where the unleashed sound of involuntary yelps provokes seizures, summons the Holy Ghost, takes me back to places I've never been, in order to show me the place where I am? Could my voice even be heard?

Comin' in?

Behind him, on the opposite side of the street, a vacant lot trespassing memory. A vast empty space of dirt guarded by a cast-iron gate with horse heads.

The chariots honked their horns, a million musicians playing over his head. He ignored what bucked up from the bedlam of traffic crossing language as the headlights stormed around him, rushing back and forth in straight lines, flaming torches darting about like lightning, racing down, pulling up. He dodged through them with a toreador's grace, swaying his hips in, laughing out, propelling himself toward me until he was felled by one that came with a sonorous chorus of rubber grating against ground. He fell at first forceful blow of steel and flesh and bone. Collapse of head bending back, knees bent, ankles turning away from the natural progression of the heel, then a boy's yell. An alarm suspended between the great distance from standing to collapsing.

When his body hit the hard black pavement, you could hear a splash but there was no water. He lay crumpled beneath steel and chrome, reposed, and I rushed toward him, my boots planting firmly in certain grooves, accelerating, lunging. I gripped my hands beneath his armpits. They fit. Lifted him to his feet as the caravan of pilgrims maintained their stance at the curb. His body was in front of me, fourteen-year-old body of a boy disrupted. Soaking wet, waxy lips, smiling. The crack in his skull, hidden behind caked layers of sepia clay, as it had been in the casket draped in sheer white muslin. Bereft, haggard, dead. Reclining body of a boy with a half-cocked smile, closing his ears to songs about Jesus, tambourines, and Hammond organ. I wanted to run my fingers along the split edges of his gash, put my hand inside his head, feel around. Get a fistful of his voice again.

He turned a corner. I stepped out into a street. A street in a city that wasn't a city. I stepped out into a vacuous space . . . undefined. An empty space, waiting. I stepped out into lights, wove myself among cars, the sun raining down onto my shoulders, dripping through the elevation of train tracks that cut across buildings, old and dying on the land of their birth. The asphalt, dark . . . fresh . . . sticky, suctioned my steps. A world beneath the surface spoke up. That world hasn't forgotten. Those voices connected to my voice, and my voice made sounds and sounds made words—I'd watched my brother's body begin its journey, moving out of my grip, with nothing to save him from the cycle of tragedy or save me from the oracles of God. Nothing but our will to continue walking. He walked. I watched him walk . . . on either side of us, no headlights or speeding glass or steel. No artillery or decaying buildings. No sanctified armor. A bridge extends itself, stretches across a body of water and connects to land. A yellow line crawls up a black terrain, and vanishes where earth meets air.

Once, I stood still, between walls of green brush, fields of cornstalks in densely wooded areas, watched him column up a yellow line streaked through paved black road, a fourteen-year-old boy not afraid to walk out of something and into something . . . and once, I followed him up to the high point he had arrived at, and pushed him into a pit . . . But his walking continued, a yellow line vanished beneath his steps and the tundra of black melted into a landscape of air drinking two tiny dots of motion; a boy with a cracked skull still walking —a man on a Brooklyn street . . . remembering, for the first time, *how* to walk.

It is possible to remember what you never knew. It *is* possible.

Grateful acknowledgments to
Patrick Synmoie, Victoria Sanders, Imani Wilson, Malaika Adero,
Rosemary Ahern, Linda Roberts, Barbara Greenberg,
La Marr J. Bruce, friends and family, et al.

ABOUT THE AUTHOR

CARL HANCOCK RUX is an award-winning writer, poet, playwright, performance and recording artist. He is the author of the Village Voice Literary Prize–winning collection of poetry and prose *Pagan Operetta,* and the Obie award-winning play *Talk.* His fiction, poetry, essays, articles, and plays have been widely anthologized in the United States and abroad. Mr. Rux is also a New York City Foster Care alumnus and now lives in Brooklyn.

Printed in the United States
By Bookmasters